Sister Psychopath

Maggie James

Print ISBN 978-1-912175-64-2

Praise for Guilty Innocence

'This is a pretty pacey book, very tense and very descriptive. The plot is outstanding, highly recommended for suspense, action and thrilling entertainment.'

Susan Hampson - Books From Dusk Till Dawn

'There are twists and turns and unexpected events that build on the intrigue and suspense to such a level that you just keep turning page after page.'

Jill Burkinshaw - Books n All

'I thought it was a genuine page turner and the kind of book that is right up my street – I loved it!!!'

Donna Maguire - Donnas Book Blog

Praise for The Second Captive

'This is the first book I've read by Maggie James and it won't be the last. She has a way of writing that draws you right into the world she's created.'

Claire Knight - Crimebookjunkie

'Fast paced and binge reading worthy; I finished this novel in a single afternoon.'

Samantha Ellen - Clues And Reviews

'This is another heart rending and thought provoking book from Maggie that will have the reader turning page after page.'

Jill Burkinshaw - Books n All

This novel is dedicated to my two brothers, who may perhaps find the title amusing…

1

Suspicion

I jolted awake, fierce resentment welling inside me at the intrusion of the alarm clock. As I rubbed sleep from my eyes, I glanced around my shabby bedsit. On my desk sat the pile of proofreading I needed to tackle if I wanted to earn any money; the morning's work stretched before me in an endless stream of corrections. For a second, one glorious second, it was a day like any other. Then reality swept in, and with it the agony of what happened ten years earlier, on the same day. A wave of devastation hit me; salty tears stung my eyes, ran down my cheeks. The anguish was as raw, as brutal, as ever. I mourned, and hard too, plunging into the gut-wrenching sorrow I thought I'd locked firmly in the past. Buried under layers of denial, a pain so deep I feared I'd end up as unstable as my mother should I ever revisit it.

Today though, I chose to do so, unable to resist the lure that was Alicia. My fingers reached out to turn off the alarm clock. I pulled the duvet over my head, then curled into a foetal ball, allowing myself the luxury of remembrance.

***

One hour could have passed, or it might have been three. I had no idea how long it took before I cried myself dry.

At last I hauled myself, reluctantly, out of bed and padded into the bathroom. Impossible to tackle the pile of proofreading, not today. Instead, I decided, I'd head over to see Mum, knowing she'd also be remembering the horror of that day. Besides, I wanted to check her mood, which had been relatively stable in recent months.

Over breakfast, I prayed Chloe wouldn't be home. No way could I mention Alicia to her without provoking some hurtful jibe. Few people would ever call my sister a nice person, although the men she suckered would probably declare her a sex-soaked gift from heaven. Initially, anyway, until they realised she'd only been after their money. As for Mum, she'd blinded herself to her younger daughter's less desirable traits.

Chloe, my opposite in so many ways. How we looked, for example. Over the years, I'd grown accustomed to fading into the background once people spotted my sister. Something about her hooked people's attention, hoodwinking them into seeing her as an exotic orchid rather than the Venus flytrap she really was. Beside her, I rated as a daisy at best.

Because Chloe was beautiful. Petite, a mere five feet two, curved like an archer's bow. She came across as all soft chocolaty-brown, with her long dark hair and cocoa-rich eyes shooting out I'm-so-vulnerable vibes. Not to mention the pale cappuccino hue of her skin, a legacy from her father.

At least Chloe had always known who he was. Her genes came from Mum's fling with the Spanish teacher at the college where she worked back then. He'd left England before Mum had a chance to tell him she was carrying his baby. She'd never hidden the truth from Chloe though. If only she'd been as forthcoming with me about my father. Whenever I'd asked about him, Mum had always changed the subject. I had no idea who had given me my height, all five feet ten of it, along with my pale skin, blue eyes and mid-brown hair, such a contrast to Chloe's dark beauty. Father unknown, my birth certificate said. One thing was for sure, Mum hadn't given me the tall gene. Her height was somewhere in between Chloe's and mine. Same with her skin tone. As for her hair, she'd been a blonde before it had faded to grey.

Father unknown. It hurt. Rankled even.

I thrust all thoughts of my parentage out of my head. It wasn't the right time to scratch off that ancient scab. My breakfast finished, I placed my plate and mug in the sink, then grabbed my jacket and keys. I had no idea that later that day my emotions towards my half-sister would coalesce into hatred, after years of dislike and mistrust.

* * *

Within ten minutes, I was letting myself into my childhood home in the St George area of Bristol.

Not hearing any sounds, I called up the stairs. 'Mum? It's me, Megan.'

Her bedroom door opened, the creak reassuring me. My mother appeared at the top of the stairs. I exhaled a nugget of tension when I saw her. She'd made the effort to get dressed – always a good sign – and her black trousers and cerise top looked good, classy even. Her hair was brushed, her skin less pale than normal. She was having a good day then.

'I thought you might come over,' she said as she made her way downstairs.

Our eyes locked, hers filled with awareness of the date. No words were needed, not then. Instead, my mother walked into the kitchen, filled the kettle and busied herself with mugs and spoons, her back towards me. I ached for a hug, the press of her arms around me, despite experience telling me it was unlikely. Oh, she loved me, in a muted kind of way. It had never been enough though.

'I'm sorry, Megan,' she said. 'I realise you'll be hurting, today of all days.'

I choked back a sob.

'I miss my beautiful granddaughter,' Mum continued. 'I think of her every day.'

A tear escaped my eye and slid down my cheek. I was transported ten years into the past, my child's pale, lifeless body an unspeakable horror. In contrast, I recalled when she was alive, the soft grasp of tiny fingers against my own. Her wisps of dark hair, scented with baby shampoo and curling around ears as delicate as petals. Her precious body, cradled in my arms. Back then, I'd smile to myself, allowing my mind to roam through various scenarios: my daughter as a toddler, a teenager, a young woman. Would she take after me: awkward around strangers, gawky and lacking in confidence? Or would she be like Chloe: all sass, brass and sarcasm?

Perhaps Alicia would have resembled her father. He'd never known about his daughter's birth.

Or her death, nine weeks later.

Back then, I didn't think I'd ever recover from my loss. Ten years later, I knew I never had. Or would.

From what my mother had said afterwards, she'd also feared for me. For once, Tilly Copeland, in a break between episodes of depression, had been the stronger one mentally. Alicia had been born when Mum had been more stable, and she'd adored my baby instantly. God knows I needed all the support my mother had to give, what with being nineteen and a single parent. Mum rose to the challenge, attending antenatal classes with me, being there at the birth and doing everything possible to help afterwards. She'd even managed to stay silent about Alicia on the rare occasions when she'd seen my child's father.

'It should never have happened,' I whispered.

My mother turned to face me. 'Alicia's death was a tragic accident.'

'Do you think that makes it any better? It doesn't.' Mum must realise that. But what was she supposed to say to someone who had birthed and lost a child within nine weeks? Nothing would ever heal my wounds, the wonder being that I hadn't buckled under the strain, gone the way of my mother.

'I know these things happen,' I continued. 'To other people though. Not to me.' I wiped another stray tear away. 'I've always felt bad about Pepper. It wasn't her fault, poor old thing.'

Mum handed me my mug of coffee, then sat down opposite me. 'You must have hated me at the time.'

'No. I couldn't think of anything other than…' A strangled sob. 'Alicia's death.'

'That was why I did it. You were beside yourself with grief. I decided you didn't need any reminders.'

I sipped my coffee. 'I understand. It's just… you know how much I loved Pepper. But you're right. I'd have found it unbearable to have her around afterwards.'

Pepper. My cat, adored by me, loathed by Chloe, and tolerated by Mum. Brought home from a rescue centre after much pleading on my part. An animal which one day, while I'd gone shopping and Mum was supposed to be minding Alicia, had climbed into my baby's cot, seeking warmth. Her fur proved thick enough to smother the tiny child on whom my cat went to sleep. A sleep not disturbed until I, rushing upstairs on my return to check my baby, screamed my throat raw with the horror of what I'd found. A rare occurrence, they said at the inquest, but not one without precedence. The following day, Mum surreptitiously took Pepper to the local vet, telling him, without needing to lie, that the animal was eighteen years old. Then she added, not so truthfully, how it appeared in pain.

I, however, was the one in pain. So much so that I'd needed to defer my English degree at Bristol University. For weeks, I'd not ventured out of bed, sleeping most of the time, hardly eating. When I did get up, I spent hours slumped on the sofa, staring into space. My skin, always acne-prone, deteriorated into a lunar landscape of angry eruptions and my hair went unwashed for days. My progress back to being able to function again took months. Amy Hamilton, my only friend from school still around, tried to shake me from my depression but failed. My soul was too raw, too bruised.

One day I announced I couldn't live at home anymore, saying the house held too many memories and how the time had come to move out. I'd rented a tiny bedsit and got myself a temporary job at Waitrose until I felt strong enough to resume my degree. Mum had protested, Chloe not at all.

Back in the present moment, I sniffed. 'I should have put a net over the cot. Or shut my bedroom door to keep Pepper out.'

'You can't blame yourself. Either Chloe or I should have realised what might happen, made sure your door was shut.'

Mum's comment went unnoticed at first. Then my mental light bulb lit up, my mind clicking into place. What she'd said made no sense.

'Chloe? What do you mean, Chloe could have shut the door? She wasn't even there.'

Mum's face looked stricken. When she didn't answer, I continued. 'She wasn't, was she? Both of you said Chloe had been out all morning. She certainly wasn't there when I found...' My voice trailed off.

'You're right. Not when you found Pepper asleep on Alicia...'

'I'm talking about before. Was Chloe here with you that morning?'

Mum didn't reply, but my answer came from her evident disquiet, the way her eyes refused to hold mine. My unease, the sense that something was way off-kilter here, increased tenfold.

I leaned across the kitchen table, grasped her arm, my fingers pincer-like. 'Be honest with me. Was Chloe in the house when Alicia died?'

Tension coiled around us while I waited for her reply. Mum chewed her bottom lip, her gaze fixed on her coffee mug. When she answered, her voice was barely audible. 'Chloe was, yes. I wasn't.'

My mind did a mental somersault. 'You weren't with Alicia? What the hell do you mean?'

'Oh, Megan, you mustn't get all worked up about this.'

I stared at my mother, tears threatening to fall all the while. 'Worked up? My baby died, Mum. Don't you think I have a right to know what happened?'

Dismay stole over her face, and I sensed her withdrawal. I was pushing her too hard, I knew, but pressed on regardless. 'Tell me. Where were you that morning, if not with Alicia?'

Mum shrank back, clearly stung by my vehemence. 'I spent a lot of that morning in the garden, talking with Mrs Lucas next door. I was around, just not in the house.'

'And Chloe? What about her? When I left to go shopping, she'd already gone out.'

'You're right. She went out just before you did. But she came home not long afterwards. That's why I went into the garden, because Chloe was in the house with Alicia.'

'Yeah, sure. Like she ever bothered to lift a finger for my baby.' Bitter hurt, laced with resentment, washed over me.

'She spent most of the morning in her bedroom. Then, right before you got back and found Alicia dead, I asked her to go buy some milk, which she did. We didn't realise anything was wrong then, of course.'

'So why did both of you say Chloe was out of the house all morning when Pepper smothered my baby?' Anger at having been lied to surged through me. I'd been treated like a child instead of a grieving mother.

'It seemed best.' Mum's voice rose high, her tone agitated. Normally I'd be treading carefully, mindful not to upset her, but not this time. I needed to know why she'd lied.

'Why, exactly?'

'Chloe's so sensitive at times. So caring too, even though you don't give her credit for it. She came home with the milk, found you hysterical, the ambulance crew here, me in shock. She talked to me later, pleaded with me to say she'd been out all morning. She was only fifteen, and scared.'

'Of what, exactly? Why lie? Why pretend she wasn't there, if she was? That's the bit I don't get.'

'Because she was worried you'd believe – if you knew she'd been at home and I was occupied elsewhere – that she'd somehow been responsible. Even though she wasn't. You've always thought the worst of her. You've got to admit that.'

'Responsible? For what? It was an accident, they said at the inquest. Nobody to blame.'

'Of course not. But Chloe was scared you'd somehow accuse her. She saw you falling to pieces and didn't want you having a go at her. I must say it did seem the right thing to do at the time. A tiny white lie, to save everybody more grief.'

'To save herself, more like.'

Mum spread her hands in what I assumed was a request for forgiveness. 'I meant well. So did Chloe.'

'Yeah, right. When does she ever?'

Anger burned fiercely in my heart. Impossible to stay any longer, not with shock still pounding through me. A few minutes later saw me saying goodbye to my mother.

***

Later, back at my flat, fury at her raged in my mind, until I considered Mum's motive for telling such a full-blown lie. Understanding bloomed in me then. Her agreeing to protect Chloe, while making me out to be the unreasonable older sister, was Mum doing what she'd always done. She'd been hooked on Chloe since the day she was born, not once acknowledging her behaviour as anything worse than thoughtlessness and high spirits.

I seemed to be the only one who saw Chloe's faults, who didn't make excuses for her. Once I had loved her; I'd been delighted when Mum told me I would have a baby brother or sister, too young at four to see the weariness hidden behind her eyes at the thought of bringing up two children on her own. She'd been fine after the birth though, from what she'd told me. No post-natal depression, something she'd feared, having been laid low for months after I was born. Perhaps that explained why she'd never loved me the way she did Chloe, why she rarely gave me a hug; she'd simply never bonded with me.

I hadn't cared how absorbed Mum became in her new daughter, besotted as I was myself. When allowed, I helped bathe and change the baby, my small fingers quicker and more accurate than Mum's, singing to Chloe when she wouldn't sleep. I told myself we'd play together when she was old enough, share a bedroom as teenagers, be best friends.

Oh, the poignancy of spoiled dreams. When did my sibling love turn sour? Did it start with hearing Mum excuse my sister's behaviour towards other children yet again? Saying Chloe couldn't have hit little Tommy, Mandy, whomever. She wasn't like that, she was such a sweet girl, honestly she was. Despite the fact I witnessed the way she bullied the other kids. Or was it when I came across Chloe shovelling earth into a hastily dug hole, later connecting the dots when the neighbours reported one of their rabbits had gone missing?

Whatever had caused it, the damage seemed permanent. I distrusted my half-sister with the same intensity I'd once loved her. I feared her a little too. I didn't like to think about what the missing rabbit said about Chloe. Or about my baby's death.

In hindsight, I realised I'd always harboured doubts about that day. Maybe, on some gut level, I'd recognised I was being lied to, but been unable to acknowledge it due to the intensity of my grief.

I made a decision; somehow I'd uncover the truth about what happened ten years earlier. Because Mum's revelation wasn't the whole story, of that I was sure. A suspicion, vile beyond words, had seized hold of my mind, wouldn't let go. The thought pounded through my brain: had Chloe killed Alicia?

The more I considered the possibility, the more likely it seemed.

**

2

Confirmation

That night, unable to sleep, my brain a mess, I attempted to process what Mum had told me.

Chloe had been at our house the morning Pepper had suffocated my baby. Both she and my mother had lied about the fact. Their reason seemed logical enough at first glance. I had a long history of blaming Chloe whenever things went pear-shaped for me. Usually I wasn't wrong.

Alicia had been suffocated though. Something far worse than Chloe borrowing my toiletries without asking or eating the last of my yoghurt. My child had died, smothered by my own cat, the sight of Pepper's thick fur piled on my baby's face forever branded on my brain.

I couldn't stop thinking about Chloe having been around my daughter that day. Alicia had been despised by her even more than Pepper. What Chloe wanted, she inevitably got. Would it be too much to suspect the two might be connected?

My sister had hated her niece, of that I was sure. Chloe, first a sulky fourteen-year-old, fifteen by the time I'd given birth, hadn't taken much notice of me during my pregnancy. No, she reserved most of her spite for after the birth. Flooded with love for my daughter, I revelled in Alicia, but also in my mother's support. Desperate as I'd always been for her love, I delighted in our newfound togetherness.

Which meant Chloe's nose got pushed firmly out of joint.

Suddenly, she wasn't the focus of Mum's attention anymore. With hindsight, I should have taken heed, been on my guard; if

I'd been less absorbed in motherhood I'd have realised how, for someone as egotistic as Chloe, being ignored might prove intolerable.

Suspicion, vile and terrible, raged through my brain. All my prior knowledge of Chloe, her cruelty, her selfishness, suggested my sister may have killed my baby, simply because she couldn't bear the competition. She'd have needed to shove aside her loathing of Pepper sufficiently to carry her into my bedroom and deposit her on my baby's face. An act paying double dividends for her when my mother took Pepper the next day to be put to sleep.

The horror that engulfed me on finding my baby dead overwhelmed me once more, its force a tidal wave. Huge, hysterical sobs broke from my throat as I pounded my pillow, releasing a deluge of despair. The passing of the years had made no difference to the intensity of my emotions. The pain was as raw as it had ever been.

* * *

When I eventually stopped sobbing, my thoughts remained dark, still centred on Chloe. The urge to uncover more about her presence in the house that day gnawed at me. Should I pay my sister a visit, attempt to talk with her? The idea had its pros and cons. I remembered the love I'd felt when she was tiny, before her true nature became apparent. Regret stirred in me, temporarily ousting my anger. Doubt edged in as well. I didn't want to believe my sister guilty of something so terrible. Shouldn't I at least give her a chance to tell me her version of events? If she still denied she'd been in the house, then I'd be more convinced she'd engineered my baby's death. Not that I'd ever be able to prove anything; no breadcrumbs existed on the trail to lead back to Chloe. She was too smart for that.

The idea tortured me, wouldn't let go. I mulled it over for a few days, before I gave in. One way or another, I needed answers.

* * *

After I made my decision, I drove over to St George early one evening, safe in the knowledge that Mum would be at her bipolar support group. Chloe's expensive hatchback was parked outside the house. She had to be home, then. I'd chosen not to call ahead, too afraid she'd manufacture an excuse not to see me. So far, so good. I rang the bell, preferring on this occasion not to use my key.

The door opened, causing nervous energy to spark in my belly. Chloe looked me up and down, probably taking note of my charity shop coat. A frown rendered her pretty features ugly; she was obviously taken by surprise by my sudden appearance on her doorstep. Not pleased to see me, but then I'd never expected a warm welcome. For a second, I drank in her olive skin, the gloss of her hair, mourning the love I'd once had for her. Then I remembered Alicia.

I kept my tone civil when I spoke. It wasn't a good idea to provoke my sister, not if I wanted the truth. 'Can I come in? There's something I want to ask you.' I saw curiosity warring with her desire to get shot of me.

Curiosity won the day. 'You can come in. But make it quick.'

I followed her into the kitchen. She didn't ask if I wanted coffee or anything. Instead, she took an apple from the fruit bowl, along with a knife and plate, and sat at the kitchen table.

I pulled out a chair opposite. 'I came to visit Mum a few days ago.'

'Bully for you. You want a medal or something?' She sliced the knife through the apple, bisecting it neatly, the line of her mouth tight.

Such rudeness didn't deserve a response. 'How's your job-hunting going? Any luck?' I was pretty sure Chloe wasn't making any effort to find work, but I wanted to soften her mood a little.

She shrugged. As I'd expected. 'Why are you here, Megan? What do you want?' She continued to cut into the apple, her movements rapid, the blade slicing off thin segments.

'To talk. That's all.' One last chance, I reminded myself. If she carried on lying, my suspicion would become certainty. 'Like I said, I've been to see Mum. I have to ask you something. About Alicia.'

Wariness crept over her face. I took her silence as permission to continue. 'Were you there when she died? In the house, I mean.'

'No. You know I wasn't. I'd gone out shopping.' She shifted restlessly. 'Why are you harping on about it?'

I tried again. 'Yes, I know you went out. What time did you come back?'

Her hands paused mid-slice, her mouth twisted in an ugly frown. 'For God's sake, it was ten years ago. I was a kid back then. How am I supposed to remember?'

'Try.'

She huffed out a breath. 'God, you're a pain. I got back after you found her dead, all right? I saw the ambulance parked outside as I turned into the road. I'd been out all morning.'

My suspicions of her involvement in Alicia's death doubled, tripled. I'd asked her outright, and she'd lied. She was protecting herself, which indicated she knew more than she was letting on. Fury rose within me.

'Liar.' I spat the word at her, my anger fierce and hot. 'You were there. You lied at the time and you're lying now.'

More deceit in response. 'I'm not, I swear. I was out shopping. God knows I needed a break from the constant baby talk and stink of nappies. You've no idea how boring you and Mum were, banging on as though that ugly creature you produced occupied the centre of the universe.'

She'd pay for that remark one day, I decided. I wasn't prepared to let Alicia's death drop. 'Mum told me. How you persuaded her to lie for you.'

Chloe huffed out a breath. 'All right, you win. Yeah, I was there. For most of the morning, anyway. I went to get some milk shortly before you got back. You can't condemn me for lying though. You blamed me for everything back then. Still do. Like it was my responsibility to keep an eye on that flea-ridden cat of yours.' She stabbed at a segment of apple with the knife, the movement filled with suppressed fury.

'You lied, Chloe.'

'Yeah. Now I'm being reminded why. Honestly, you're so up yourself at times. A little white lie. What the hell difference does it make? It doesn't change anything.'

Oh, but it does, I decided. *It changes everything.*

'Anyway, it all turned out for the best. You were too young to have a baby, what with being fresh out of school and all that. What happened was a good thing. For everyone.'

For you, you mean, I thought. I drove my nails hard into my palms with the effort not to crack my hand across her face. Hitting her wouldn't get me anywhere, not at this stage. Later, I reminded myself. One day I'd have the satisfaction of staining her cheeks red.

Chloe snorted, her derision plain. 'Not as if the brat's father was anywhere to be seen.'

I didn't reply. She knew so well how to push my buttons.

'Toby Turner.' She clearly enjoyed every moment of tormenting me. 'You never told him you ended up pregnant, did you? Not a lot of talking between the two of you, is there?' She laughed, the sound ugly in my ears. 'He screwed you once and he's never wanted a repeat performance. That's what really bugs you.'

'We're friends. Good mates, nothing else.' The words sounded hollow even as I said them.

'Yeah, right. Like you wouldn't jump into bed with him in a heartbeat.' Another laugh. 'He only slept with you because he couldn't have me. Later, when he did, he couldn't get enough.'

I'd provoked her, and she intended to make me pay. I steeled myself for what would follow.

'He still wants me, I can tell. It would be easy enough to get him back whenever I wanted. I'd simply click my fingers and he'd come running.'

Her cruelty zipped my mouth shut. I couldn't reply even if I wanted to.

'I think I will. That'd be fun.' She grinned, her eyes narrowed and predatory. 'You wouldn't like that much, would you? The thought of lover boy shagging me again. I wouldn't keep him long. Just so I get to piss you off. Then I'd dump him.'

Chloe aimed one last jibe at me. 'Remember, I always get what I want. No matter what it takes. Watch your step, Megan.'

I stood up. Breathing the same air as my sister was unbearable. 'I'm going.'

**

Back in my car, her parting smirk imprinted on my brain, I clenched my hands on the wheel, fighting to get control of myself. A cocktail of emotions – anguish, fury, bewilderment – battled for dominance inside me.

I said the thoughts in my head aloud, examining them for how likely they sounded. 'My sister killed my baby.'

Yes. The words rang true. If my suspicions were right, Chloe had smothered Alicia by placing Pepper on top of her, and I'd never be able to prove a thing. My half-sister was, I decided, possibly a psychopath. She might not be at the serial killer end of the spectrum, but for a teenage girl to plan and execute her own niece's death, she had to be pretty far down the line.

The shock of the realisation, the horror of what she'd done, rendered me almost catatonic.

I sat behind the wheel of my car for the next hour, immobile, my mind looping through our conversation.

I needed to talk to someone, right then, before the thoughts squirrelling through my head drove me mad. My best friend Amy Hamilton was away in London until the next day. The only possible person was Toby. Fantasies flashed through my head; I saw myself telling him about Alicia, sharing the agony of her death with the man who'd fathered her, spilling out my concerns over Chloe. His arms would wrap around me, he'd say the right words, and the ball of tension lodged in my gut might ease a little. Even if I didn't share my suspicions about Chloe, I could at least pour forth the emotions that had churned through me since the anniversary of my baby's death. I pulled out my mobile.

He answered straight away. The words tumbled out of me, but to my relief my voice remained steady. 'Toby? I know it's been a while, but can I come over? There's something I have to tell you.'

His voice, warm and hypnotic as ever, sounded in my ear. 'Megan? Good to hear from you. What's up?'

'I can't go into it on the phone. But I need to talk to you.'

'Okay, sure. Can't manage tonight though.' A pause. 'Hey, I have an idea. Fancy a trip to O'Malley's wine bar tomorrow evening? We can talk then.'

I hesitated. A busy wine bar didn't seem the right place to spill what was on my mind. It had been too long since I'd seen Toby, however, and the old craving stole over me. Why not meet up, have a few drinks, enjoy his company? At the end of the evening, we could arrange to talk in private later. 'Sounds good. What time?'

'Eight o'clock.' His soft laugh sounded in my ear. 'It won't be just us. There'll be a few other people as well.'

Disappointment weighed like a stone in my stomach. I'd hoped to have him all to myself. I forced my voice to stay neutral. 'Fine.'

'And I'd like your opinion. On my new love interest, who'll also be there.'

My hopes where Toby was concerned withered, blighted by his words, his buoyant tone. I should have known better. Hadn't Toby always been a player?

All thoughts of telling him about Alicia vanished. In that moment, Toby and I were a million miles apart, despite having once made a child together. Perhaps I'd tell him one day, perhaps I wouldn't, but it wasn't the right time. Instead, I'd wait, and mull over my suspicions about Chloe some more.

***

3

Venus Flytrap

I glanced around, my eyes skimming over Chloe and Mum from my vantage point by the doorway of O'Malley's wine bar. What were they doing here? I didn't dare risk a sarcastic jibe from Chloe by admitting I had no idea. Toby was late, as usual, causing my palms to dampen with nerves. Places like O'Malley's, one of the flashier establishments at Bristol's Harbourside, made me uncomfortable with its wannabe trendy vibe, being full of business types, suited and booted, and gabbling management-speak into their iPhones. Eight ten, said my watch, although I'd arranged to meet Toby at eight. Not late at all by his standards.

A voice sounded behind me. 'Megan! How long has it been?'

Toby grinned as I spun around, and damn me if he wasn't the same six feet two of sex appeal he'd always been. I melted into his trademark rib-cracking hug, savouring the essence of the man. He smelt of Hugo Boss aftershave and I inhaled his scent deeply, returning his hug before pulling away to poke him in the stomach.

'Too long. Are you going to enlighten me about this?' I swept my arm in the direction of Mum and Chloe. 'How come I seem to have gate-crashed an evening out for my mother's workplace?' My swinging arm encompassed the tall man heading towards Mum's table, carrying a tray of drinks. 'You said your new love interest would be here tonight. I didn't expect all this.'

'The two events aren't mutually exclusive, you know.'

I stiffened. *He means Chloe*, was my first thought. I guessed she was here as Mum's means of transport, given the phobia our mother, who'd never learned to drive, harboured about buses. Hadn't Toby been burned enough the last time they got it on together? Maybe I was underestimating her. My sister had the ability to reel men in like a lizard catching flies on its tongue. Besides, hadn't she threatened to use him as a plaything? Perhaps she already was.

'Don't look so sour. I'm not planning a walk down Memory Lane with Chloe. Been there, done that. No repeat performance planned.'

I didn't share the same conviction. Despite my sister tossing him aside like a used rag once she'd finished with him, I'd never heard Toby say a bad word about her. The excuses got trotted out when her name was mentioned: she'd been too young, he'd rushed her, she hadn't meant to be cruel. One thing was clear: Chloe's relentless pursuit of what she'd set her mind on, despite the casualties. She was right; she had only to click her fingers to get him back.

I thrust the thought aside. 'So what are you doing here? How do you know the people at Mum's office?'

'James invited me.'

'James Matthews? Her boss?' I glanced over towards the tall guy I'd seen earlier, who was placing a lemonade and lime before my mother. A man with whom I was already familiar through my former friendship with his wife. I noticed how both Mum and my sister fixated their gazes on him. Not surprising. Not my type, but definitely attractive, well preserved for a man in his fifties. He sported a gym body, hard and muscular, demonstrated by his tight polo shirt and well-fitting jeans. The glow from the candles on the tables highlighted the grey creeping into his brown hair. His grin was as lopsided as Toby's, but on the opposite side. His eyes struck me every time I met him. Pale blue, they made an unusual combination with his dark hair. A looker all right.

'So which one of them do you reckon is my new love interest?'

I looked around at the women from James's firm. A couple of twenty-somethings, all spiky heels and fishnet stockings, talking too loudly in an effort to impress. Two older women, clearly ill at ease, staring into their wine glasses. My mother and my sister, the latter with her hand on James's arm, smiling, aiming her honeyed darts at him.

'I've no idea. You say it's not Chloe, thank God, and my mother's obviously off limits. One of them, I suppose.' My hand waved in the direction of the giggling fish-netted pair. Toby laughed.

'Give me a break. As if.'

'You've changed. Thought you'd shag anything female with a pulse.' Including me. Once. Such a long time ago.

'Yep. Okay, so my new love interest isn't my usual type, but my tastes have altered since we last ran into each other.' He winked at me.

'You going for tall, dark and intellectual these days?' The words, 'so do I stand a chance with you after all?' never made it out of my mouth. I'd fancied Toby like crazy at school, for one mad summer, knowing he was way out of my league. All the girls were wild about him. He could take his pick, and he did. One night, during our final school term, he chose me; why, I was never sure. On my down days, I told myself he'd been working his way through the girls in our year and sex with me had been necessary to complete the set. We never spoke of it. To my surprise, he'd remembered me when we'd bumped into each other five years later.

'I've left London. Back in Bristol,' he'd said. 'Working here as a graphic designer.'

We went for a drink that night to catch up and had stayed friends ever since, sharing a curry or a bottle of wine on a regular basis. Before tonight though, we'd not run into each other for a good six months or so.

He laughed in answer to my question. 'Yeah, I suppose. Definitely tall and intellectual. As for the dark... mostly, but there's a bit of grey creeping in.' What was he talking about? I looked back at the two older women on the table beside Mum.

Both of them had pewter-toned hair sculpted into middle-aged waves. I didn't attempt to picture Toby getting down and dirty with either of them; the idea was absurd. Toby had never gone for cougars, preferring to be the predator, not the prey.

He saw my puzzled look and laughed again. 'You haven't a clue what I'm talking about, have you?'

'No. Enlighten me. Have you found yourself a sugar mummy? Am I treading on their toes by being here? If so, why ask me along tonight?'

'Two reasons. I've not seen you for ages; I reckoned we should catch up. As well as having someone to talk to, if things get a bit weird here. It's all been flirting and innuendo so far. Nothing's happened with…' He shrugged. 'Not even got to first base yet.'

'It's not like you to be slow off the mark. Is she married?'

'Yep.'

Surprise hit me. Toby had never gone for married women before. Too many complications, he'd always said. As well as all the single females needing his attention.

Messy, I thought.

Toby wasn't looking at me anymore. His gaze rested over my shoulder. I turned and saw James Matthews making conversation with Chloe. I glanced back at Toby, confused.

Then I twigged. He'd not been joking when he said his tastes had altered.

I decided to play it cool. Despite the fact that what I'd discovered bothered me. Badly. I'd found his numerous flings with other women hurtful enough. Now he liked guys as well?

No way would he discover how I felt though. When I replied, my tone was light, breezy. 'Get you! I never would have pegged you as swinging both ways.'

He laughed. 'It's an age thing. Quite common, apparently, for people to believe they're straight, then in their late twenties they get curious about the alternative. I've been testing the waters that way for a while.'

'The fact he's married doesn't bother you?'

Toby flushed. 'If I'm honest, yes.'

'It gets worse, Toby. His wife's a friend of mine.'

'Seriously?'

'Yeah, although I've not seen Charlotte for ages. We did art classes together. Right up until the time when she lost the use of her legs.'

Toby drew in a breath. 'She's disabled? I didn't realise.'

'She's been in a wheelchair for the last five years. Car accident.'

Silence from Toby. I decided to steer the conversation away from Charlotte Matthews. 'How did you meet James?'

'Through work. My firm booked James to give a presentation on pensions. Anyway, there I was, prepared to be bored witless and in walked James. The guy has something about him.'

'Yeah, he's easy on the eye, all right. Since when have you targeted mature and sophisticated though? Whether it's male or female.'

Toby grinned. 'Maybe the rules change when you switch teams. The other men have been older too. Yeah, go on. Tell me I've got a father fixation.'

The words 'other men' pained me, but I ignored them. 'Armchair psychology's not my style,' I replied. Ironic, considering my recent suspicions about Chloe.

He shook his head. 'Who cares anyway? Does anyone know what attracts one person to another? I'm telling you, he got to me, right from the start. I've seen him a few times since, always for professional reasons. That is, until now. He invited me, out of the blue, to come along tonight. Some leaving do for one of the secretaries, he said. Probably the one over there in the skirt doubling as a belt.' He grinned again. 'I've flirted with him. Subtly, of course.'

I laughed, despite my disquiet. Subtlety had never figured in Toby's game plans for getting laid.

'Although I'm not sure whether I'm having much success. He has all the hallmarks of being straight: the wedding ring, the occasional mention of his wife. Despite the warning signs, I still reckon he's interested. Call it a gut feeling. And then he asked me here tonight.'

'Doesn't have to mean he's set his sights on you. Perhaps he's being friendly, nothing more.' I hoped so, for Charlotte's sake.

Mine too. I squashed that particular thought.

'He's interested, I'm sure. I've no idea what the set-up is, what with him being married, but it isn't a one-sided thing.'

'That doesn't mean he'll want to take it further.'

'Time will tell. Let's go join them.'

Shit. That meant risking Chloe's sour tongue. My mother – I'd long ago resigned myself to her lack of interest in me. Acceptance of Chloe and her barbed comments didn't come so easily.

Her eyes scratched over me as we approached, her hand dropping from James's arm. I braced myself. Whatever she said, it wouldn't be pretty.

My mother spoke first though. 'I didn't expect you to be here tonight, Megan. Oh, you're with Toby. Nice to see you again, young man.'

'You too.' Toby returned Mum's greeting, but his gaze stayed fixed on her boss.

James smiled briefly at me, but it didn't reach his eyes.

'This is a pleasant surprise.' His tone was polite, but his expression seemed wary. Although I wasn't in any sense competition, I felt this man viewed me as such. Definitely not as straight as he made out, then. In possession of a jealous streak too.

'You're one of Toby's friends?'

'We were at school together.'

'Megan and I go way back,' Toby said. 'She's a good mate.' The emphasis increased ever so slightly on the final word. The smile I got from James then seemed more genuine.

'I thought I'd ask her along for moral support,' Toby said with a laugh. 'Call her backup. Or my wingman.'

Chloe edged nearer, angling her mouth close to my ear so that only I could hear her words. 'I always thought you'd make a good man, Megan.' Her voice, laced with equal amounts of cruelty and amusement, warned me what was coming. 'That flat chest of yours could double as an ironing board.'

I'd heard that particular jibe from my sister so often it barely registered. Besides, it seemed I wasn't worth any more of Chloe's attention. My sister had turned her gaze to James, replacing her hand on his arm, her smile all sweetness and sugar. 'So, James, tell me more about your dog. What did you say his name was… Sienna?' Her smile grew wider, more faked. 'I've always adored dogs. Especially German Shepherds.'

Liar, I thought. Chloe wouldn't have known a German Shepherd from a Chihuahua and if she ever mentioned dogs, it was to comment on how disgusting and smelly they were.

'Senna, not Sienna. Named after a famous racing driver.' Irritation threaded its way through James's tone. His eyes had already slithered away from Chloe; her hand fell off his arm as he turned towards Toby. 'Glad you could make it. Can I get you a drink?'

'Pint of Doom Bar'll do me. I'll come with you.'

Amusement stirred in me, along with a smidgen of satisfaction. Score a first for James Matthews, I thought; at last, a man who was unimpressed by Chloe's charms. He was probably too old to fall for her wiles.

I noticed my mother's gaze follow James as he headed for the bar. *She has a thing for him*, I thought, noting the puppy-like devotion written across her face. My heart ached for her; such a clichéd situation, a middle-aged woman fancying her boss. Not that she stood a chance. Too old, too grey in both hair and character, beaten down by years of pills and psychiatric wards. As for him, he was too married, too out of her league, to notice her as anything other than an employee, if he noticed her at all.

Too bisexual as well, it seemed.

And Chloe also wanted to sink her carefully manicured nails into Mum's boss. Through me she already knew he had a wife who'd never walk again. Meaning Chloe would view her as less competition. My sister was clearly targeting James's wealth, figuring all she had to do was bat her eyelashes to get her hands on it. She'd know about his financial consultancy business from my mother, the fact he was pretty well heeled. Money was Chloe's driving force, always had been. She'd never been worried about working for it either. My sister seemed incapable of holding down a job. Either she ended up sacked or else she walked out, claiming she deserved something better.

The only thing she'd like more, I thought, would be if I fancied James too. She'd love it if she could find a way to hurt me as well.

I shrugged. Toby seemed to stand more chance with James than Chloe or Mum did.

***

The rest of the evening passed quickly. Toby, as always, proved good company, and I was curious about this new thing he had about men. I kept tabs on him and James, noticing the way he frequently touched Toby's arm, making it seem merely casual. Along with the fact that Toby didn't pull away.

I wondered how things would pan out. James probably wanted a little fun on the side, and with Toby's reputation as a player, I couldn't see that being a problem. They'd have a brief fling and then go their separate ways. None of my business, I told myself.

***

'I definitely got the vibe from him tonight.' Toby's voice cut across my thoughts towards the end of the evening. James had just left, brushing Chloe aside as she tried to engage him in conversation, my mother's eyes stapled to his back as he moved through the bar.

'Just a vibe? Nothing more concrete?'

'Not sure what his game is, to be honest. You might be right. Perhaps he doesn't want to take things further.' Toby sipped his beer. 'Hey, I almost forgot. What was it you wanted to tell me?'

It was impossible to talk about Alicia in this crowded wine bar, my sister a few feet away. Much as I'd loved catching up with Toby, I needed space to sort out my head. 'Nothing. It can wait.'

* * *

Later, once I was in bed, I'd almost fallen asleep when fear jolted me awake, a terrifying thought pounding through my brain. Chloe had clearly set her sights on James, which meant that Toby might be at risk from her. Physically, not just emotionally, and not as paranoid a notion as it sounded. A memory drifted back to me: one of Chloe's ex-boyfriends, whom she'd pursued with disturbing tenacity, despite his fiancée. They eventually got together a year after his girlfriend was discovered stabbed to death; her killer was never found. Chloe had dumped the poor guy two months later. With my doubts about Alicia's death fresh in my mind, a sliver of suspicion pulsed through me. Had my sister been behind the girl's death?

Toby wasn't the only one in danger. What about Charlotte Matthews? Didn't James's wife pose a greater threat to Chloe's plans than Toby? Could my friend be at risk from her machinations?

My eyes gritty from lack of sleep, I lay in the dark, terrified for Charlotte. For Toby.

* * *

4

Half Makes A Difference

The visit to O'Malley's had made me yearn to visit my mother again; we hadn't had a chance to talk at the wine bar. My love for her, along with my concern over her mental health, made me call the next morning and arrange to go to the house in St George. Mum had taken a few days off work, hence her being at home on a weekday. Before we ended the call, I'd already established that Chloe wouldn't be there. Thank God.

My mother was in the kitchen as I walked in. I hugged her, noting her newly done hair, the touch of mascara on her eyelashes, her lipstick. A faint trace of perfume, something she didn't usually bother with, hit my nostrils.

'You look lovely,' I said, and meant it.

Mum smiled. 'Thought it was time I made more effort with my appearance.'

My heart rose, dizzy with hope. Her words boded well for the future.

'It's not too late. For me to meet someone, I mean.'

She was right, but disquiet stirred in me, sinking my fledgling hopes. The way she'd stared at her boss crept into my head.

'Do you have someone in mind?' I kept my tone light but my senses were on alert.

She flushed, her gaze sliding away from mine. 'Not really.' She'd always been a piss-poor liar.

My suspicions grew when she turned the conversation to James Matthews within a minute. Inwardly, I winced. My mother fancied herself in love with her married boss, and that couldn't end well. Not if I'd correctly interpreted the tension between James and Toby the previous night.

I let her talk, happy to see her so animated, despite my misgivings.

After an hour or so, I glanced at the clock on the wall. Twelve thirty, and I'd arranged to meet Amy for lunch at the Watershed. I needed to get going.

'I'll call you,' I promised Mum. 'Soon.'

***

As I drove down the A420 towards Bristol's city centre, I mulled over whether to discuss my angst over Chloe with Amy. Besides my mother and sister, she was the only person who knew how badly I'd suffered after Alicia's death. And she was fully aware of my antipathy towards Chloe, although, like Toby, she'd always made excuses for my sister. Would she believe me? What proof could I offer, other than my gut feelings and the fact I'd been lied to?

I decided I'd play it by ear. If the timing seemed right, I'd go for it. By then I was desperate for someone to confide in.

***

Amy was waiting for me when I arrived. We hugged, ordered our food and got glasses of wine from the bar. Around us the atmosphere pulsed with chit-chat and laughter, the twin smells of garlic and fried onions heavy in the air.

Once seated at our table, we chatted for a while, my brain alert for an opportunity to guide the conversation to what was on my mind. When Amy made some comment about her regrets over being an only child, I seized my chance.

'I tell you, Amy, having a sibling's not all it's cracked up to be. Especially when you have the sister from hell, like I do.' I smiled to take the sting out of my words.

Amy leaned back in her chair. 'I'll get another glass of red if this is going to turn into a rant about Chloe. I can't be back at work any later than two. You self-employed people don't realise how easy you have it.'

'You only children don't appreciate your luck, more like.'

'Yeah, whatever. You joining me in another glass of wine?'

'Go on. Like you say, I don't have to be home by any particular time.' Except for the pile of manuscripts needing to be proofread, all with a deadline of the following week. Some things could wait; I needed to vent. Seeing Chloe always had that effect.

Waiting for Amy to return with our drinks, I gazed out over the Bristol waterfront at the boats that bobbed up and down in the breeze. *Calypso*. The *Ella Louise*. *Sea Siren*, a boat perfect for Chloe, although nautical locations didn't figure in my sister's tendency to lure men onto the rocks.

Amy placed a glass of wine in front of me. 'There you go. Try a shot of – let me pronounce this right – Sangiovese Poggio. Get that down you and let it wash away your Chloe blues.'

I gulped back a large mouthful. 'The thing was, she didn't behave as badly as usual when I saw her last night. I got invited to a works outing, you see, and Chloe was there to chauffeur Mum. Apart from the odd barbed comment, she pretty much ignored me.'

'So what's the problem? Because when you walked in here, you had your Chloe face on, the one you get when she's upset you. I've never understood why you always take the bait. Sure, she's spiteful at times, even cruel, but she doesn't mean it. She just does it to get a rise out of you.'

I chose to ignore Amy's excuses for my sister's behaviour. Only I knew how much Chloe meant every slight, every taunt. 'She's set her sights on a married man. A well-heeled one, of course. Aren't they always? Except this one comes with baggage.'

'Don't all men?'

'How about a wife in a wheelchair?'

Amy's eyes widened. 'Your friend Charlotte's husband?'

'Yup. But that's not the only problem. He's also my mother's boss.'

'Does that matter? I can understand you being pissed off if Chloe's after your friend's husband, but so what if he employs your mum? Are you worried Chloe's antics will end up getting her in trouble at work?'

'It's not that. Mum was… kind of weird last night.' I gulped down more wine. 'It seemed obvious to me, from how she was looking at James, getting all flustered if he spoke to her, that she has a thing for him.'

Amy laughed. 'A last gasp at seeking love before middle age sinks in its teeth. Fair play to her, I say. Even if he is married.' Her face straightened as she saw the hurt work its way over my own. 'Sorry, babe. I didn't mean to be disrespectful to your mother. I know she's suffered some serious issues over the years.'

I shook my head. 'This isn't going to end well. From what Charlotte's said in the past, when we were more in contact, she's had her problems being married to James. But she's never mentioned anything about him and other women.'

'Let's hope your mum doesn't get too cut up over not being able to score with her boss. I take it he's fallen for Chloe's busty bait instead? I've always thought she must hide man magnets in her bra.'

'That's the odd thing. You should have seen her. She was giving him her all, what with the flattery and the "I'm vulnerable, please take care of me" looks. He barely glanced at her, let alone gave any sign of being interested.'

'Wow. That must be a first for Chloe.'

'I'll say.'

'So what's the problem? Aren't you pleased there's a male on the planet immune to your sister's charms?'

'The problem is, if I'm reading things right, James would indeed like to play the unfaithful husband. Just not with my mother or sister.'

Amy whistled, loud and long. 'Whoa, girl! You're telling me this guy's after you? His wife's friend?'

'No. Not me.'

'Who then? Spit it out.'

'It seems he'd prefer to get down and dirty with Toby Turner.'

'Toby from school?'

'The very same.'

'He was there last night? How come?'

'Like I said, it was a works night out for James's firm. Apparently Toby's been taking financial advice from him, and got invited along as well. He also told me he'd been getting come-on vibes from James even though there's an age gap, James is married, and so on.'

'He's out of luck with Toby. The guy has always flown straight as an arrow. Not a gay gene anywhere to be seen.'

'Apparently not these days.'

Amy nearly spat out her red wine. 'Toby? The boy who had all the girls in our year running after him? You're telling me he's now batting for the other team?'

'So he says. Batting for both teams, and he's keen for something to happen with James. If James were to offer. Which I doubt he would. He seems so... so married, Amy. Even if not happily.'

'A law should be passed against such things. I call it a crime against womankind to take Toby Turner out of circulation.'

'It won't happen, Amy. Yes, from what I saw last night, they're interested in each other but I could be reading things all wrong. Hard to tell. James isn't a man who's exactly upfront with his emotions.'

'You mean you're hoping nothing will happen.'

Silence from my side of the table.

'It's been quite a while since you've been able to fool me. So you still have a thing for Toby.' My friend shook her head. 'You know it's hopeless, right? I realise you and he got together one time, but he was merely adding you to his collection, babe. Nothing more. Sorry if that sounds harsh.'

Amy had touched a nerve and I'd only just realised how raw it was. I quashed the hurt her words engendered. 'He's just a friend. We meet up every now and then for drinks, curry, whatever. I listen to his exploits with women and I tell him about work, what evening classes I'm doing, what books I'm reading. We chat, we have fun, and then we go home. Separately.'

'So long as you don't get your hopes up. You need to get out more. Meet someone available, a man who'll take your mind off

Toby. You should ditch the baggy tops and combat trousers, get yourself some pulling clothes. You'd be pretty if you put some effort into it. Your hair's lovely, what with being so thick and glossy. Not to mention your skin's a lot clearer these days.'

Amy. Always direct, often uncomfortably so.

'It's improved a lot since the doctor prescribed the pill for me,' I said. 'Seems it helps women with adult acne.'

'Then what are you waiting for? At least you won't get pregnant.'

A tense silence. 'Shit. I'm so sorry. I didn't think... I didn't mean to...'

Tears pricked my eyes, and my face flushed hot and red. Amy hadn't meant to be insensitive, of course she hadn't. She'd scraped against another raw nerve, and a barrier slammed down in my mind. No way could I discuss Alicia's death, and my suspicions about it, with her, not now.

I drained the last of my wine. 'Isn't it time you were getting back to work?'

Amy shot a glance at her watch. 'Yes. Babe, don't mind me, what with my clumsy mouth. Let's not leave things so long next time.'

'Definitely.' I struggled to inject conviction into my voice. 'I'll be in touch.'

We hugged goodbye.

I thrust Amy's words out of my head as I drove back to my scruffy rented bedsit, situated in an equally rundown area of Bristol. A metaphor for my life, I decided.

***

Once there, the pile of unread manuscripts fired arrows of guilt at me. I didn't even glance at them, too wired to nit-pick over typos and grammar. Instead, I headed into the kitchenette and slopped a large measure of red wine into a glass, despite the fact I'd drunk too much already. I needed another alcoholic hit. Chloe, or any discussion about her, had that effect on me.

My half-sister had always been able to needle me, crawl under my skin. Loved doing so as well. Ah, yes. My skin. When mine started the teenage spot phase, it soon became apparent it wasn't going to limit itself to a few pimples. Chloe had revelled in every eruption, every blackhead. 'Look at that one, Mum! If it grows much bigger, it'll turn into a mountain. Yuk, it's growing a pus head…'

Our mother's failure to curb Chloe's schadenfreude had hurt me, scarred me every bit as much as the spots. 'She's still so young, Megan. You need to make allowances for her, stop being so sensitive. She doesn't mean to upset you.' Whatever Chloe said or did, she could do no wrong in our mother's eyes.

I'd persuaded myself the spots would go once I hit eighteen and got shot of puberty. They didn't. They'd persisted, although not so badly, but the damage to my confidence had been done. I might have been considered pretty without the angry eruptions and the pits denting my cheeks. I had the height my mother and sister lacked, and with it went slimness. As Amy had pointed out, I had thick, glossy hair, along with decent eyes, blue and soft. Chloe tended to ignore my good points, finding plenty to focus on elsewhere.

I heard a sigh and realised it came from me.

I needed to get on with the proofreading, and fast. Time spent worrying about my sister's intentions was time wasted. From what I could see, Chloe had set her sights on James Matthews. I knew her too well. She wouldn't hang around before launching her attack.

The suspicion I'd harboured over the death of Chloe's ex's former girlfriend pulsed again in my head, as did my fears about how Pepper ended up asleep on top of Alicia. No matter how hard I tried, I couldn't shake my fear that Charlotte, Toby, or more probably both, would get hurt in Chloe's crossfire. In addition, I still had no idea how to uncover the truth about Alicia.

***

32

5

High Heels And Wheelchairs

James grimaced, having spotted Chloe Copeland sitting in her car, waiting for him as he left work. No surprise; he'd been expecting her. She'd been there every day for the past two weeks.

Her pursuit of him had started on the Monday following the evening at O'Malley's. He'd barely noticed her that night after her mother introduced her. Parent and daughter were nothing alike. He'd hardly said two words to Tilly Copeland since offering her a part-time job as an admin assistant; she was the sort of woman who faded into the background and nobody ever cared. Sometimes he'd catch her staring at him, as though she were sucking him inside her soul with her eyes. On the rare occasions when he did notice her, she always looked away, as though his presence burned her, her replies to his questions so quiet he barely heard them.

The daughter – Chloe – she seemed something else entirely. He watched her as she swung her legs, bare and shod in high heels, onto the pavement. The rest of her, clad in a sleeveless peach-coloured dress, followed. The material hugged her curves, flowing up and over her waist to cup her breasts. A classy mix of style and sensuality, what with her dark hair pulled into a French pleat, the absence of jewellery giving her look an understated simplicity. At the same time, Chloe exuded something overtly sexual, missing the mark where he was concerned. He'd never been into breasts or legs. A nicely firmed butt did it for James. A particularly fine specimen had been on his mind way too much the last couple of months, and it didn't belong to Chloe Copeland.

He decided not to waste time with niceties. From what he'd seen of the girl, hints were wasted on her, their subtlety unable to pierce her overwhelming self-belief. He'd tried being polite, disinterested, and it hadn't worked. If anything, she'd viewed it as a challenge. Best to get straight to the point. As she opened her mouth to speak, he got in first.

'You have to stop this nonsense, Chloe. All this weird waiting for me after work. Look.' He held up his left hand, complete with its wedding ring. 'I'm married. I have a wife. Who I love.'

Chloe laughed her dismissal of his words. James found himself noticing her perfect teeth, white and straight, framed by her peach lip-gloss, a shiny reflection of her dress. She didn't need war paint, he thought, not with features as regular as hers, along with those soft brown eyes and olive skin. There was no denying she was pretty, if he'd been in the market for what she was offering.

'Yes, you are, and no, you don't.' Her bluntness repulsed him. She'd hit the target with the second part, but only by chance; her mother must have told her about the accident. Charlotte's situation was common knowledge at work, although he rarely discussed his wife with his employees. Occasionally one would ask, in deliberately empathetic tones, how she was doing; he'd brush them off with some glib response, keen to change the subject. If he allowed himself to think about his wife's accident, and her subsequent depression, the guilt would crush him.

He became aware Chloe was talking again. With an effort, he forced his attention back to her, inching away as she edged closer. Not that she seemed to notice.

'I can give you what she can't, you know.' Her crassness, her insensitivity, infuriated him. She'd pushed too far with that remark. She was wrong anyway; since the accident, he'd realised people often believed victims of spinal injuries lost sexual function along with the use of their legs. Not always true. And definitely not the case with Charlotte, but Chloe's words tripped every one of his guilt mechanisms where his wife was concerned. Disgust welled up in him, thick and cloying, and he swung away from her towards his car.

To his annoyance, Chloe followed him. Seemed the girl had a skin thicker than tarpaulin.

'Chloe,' he said, injecting more force into his tone. 'Leave me alone. I'm married. I employ your mother. What would she say about you behaving like this? Find someone your own age. I'm fifty, for God's sake. Old enough to be your father.'

Chloe flashed him a dismissive look. Had she even registered what he'd said?

'But I like older men. Always have.' She inched closer again. 'I've never gone after boys my age. I prefer a man who's lived a bit. Put it down to some sort of daddy complex, if you want, seeing as I've never known my real father.' She smiled at him. 'You're a very attractive man, James.'

A cold finger of concern traced itself down his spine. Under her glossy veneer, he sensed something unpleasant, hard, even cruel, in this woman's psyche, and he couldn't wait to put distance between the two of them.

'I mean it. Leave me alone.' Ignoring whatever she prattled in response, James got in the BMW and started the engine, hearing it purr quietly into life. He forced himself not to glance in the rear view mirror as he drove off.

***

Five minutes from home, he swung into the car park of the Rose and Crown, his local pub. Alcohol was in order; he'd let whatever guest ale they had wash Chloe Copeland out of his head. Beer would nudge his mind towards the point where he'd be able to face his wife. He'd stick to one, mindful of driving, but he'd make every drop count.

It worked. Mostly. He managed to forget about Chloe by about halfway down his pint, but then Toby Turner thrust himself into his mind and refused to leave. Damn the man. He'd got under his skin the minute they'd met in a way no woman ever had, or could. Women were too soft, too fleshy, their squidgy breasts abhorrent to him. Not that he was loud and proud about his sexuality, never had been. As a young man, he'd been steeped in denial. Raised in a strict Catholic household, he'd escaped into marriage with his first wife, Emma, and his preference for men got shelved for a few years. Then Emma had divorced him, an act that incited his deeply religious father's wrath. When Charlotte came along, James had seized on the solution she'd offered. Except that from time to time he strayed from the marital path. His past dealings with men had been furtive one-offs, casual pick-ups made in gay bars on infrequent occasions. He'd hung on as best he could, spinning out the time between men as long as possible.

Pull yourself together, an angry voice in James's head demanded. He was a married man, for God's sake. He might not love his wife the way she wanted, but damn it, he cared about her, always had. His failure as a husband wasn't her fault, and he owed her, in every way possible. If only Toby's face would get out of his head, along with the mental picture of his long fingers and what they could do to him. The tempting idea ensured his trousers grew snug, and he threw the rest of the beer down his throat, slamming the glass on the table. Time to go home.

***

Charlotte was in the living room, as always, when he walked into their flat. He saw the eagerness in her eyes, the neediness. He gave her his usual kiss on her cheek, her skin dry against his lips, aware she'd smell the beer on his breath but not comment on it. Part of him almost wished she'd get angry because he'd not come straight home after work, but he knew she wouldn't. The accident had killed more than her spinal cord; some spark of life that should have been there, wasn't, even though it had once existed. A very long time ago, when they'd first dated, she'd been all fire and feistiness. Not anymore.

'I was worried,' she said. Her eyes were still full of need.

'I'm here now, Charlotte. Have you eaten?'

'I've been waiting for you. There's ham in the fridge. We can have that with pickles and crusty bread. There's something I have to tell you...'

Despite his best intentions, he found his mind wandering, wishing himself back at the Rose and Crown, minus the BMW, getting hammered. What the hell had happened to him since Toby Turner had muscled into his life?

'What do you think?'

He forced his attention to Charlotte, noting the way her fingers twisted around themselves in her lap. She was anxious about most things these days, he thought.

'About what?'

'The weird phone call, James. I've been telling you. Calls, actually. I got one last night too. I didn't say anything to you because I thought it must be a wrong number. But when it happened again tonight...'

'What, exactly?'

'Whoever it was didn't speak. I assumed yesterday it must be someone embarrassed at misdialling, perhaps someone elderly. Tonight though... it was exactly the same. The caller didn't speak, but it went on for longer. No deep breathing or any weird stuff, thank God. I kept asking who was there but they didn't say a word. I put the phone down eventually.'

So that was it. A wrong number, probably. He bent down to kiss her cheek again, guilt reproaching him at how her expression turned happy in an instant. She seemed so desperate for any scrap of attention he threw her way.

He reached down to squeeze her hand, a reassuring smile on his face. 'Probably a child, playing with the phone. Pressing numbers at random. Nothing to worry about. I'll fix us something to eat.'

He was pulling the packet of ham from the fridge when his mobile rang. He did a double take when he saw the caller ID on the screen.

Toby. Calling him in the evening. Probably not business related, then.

He'd only seen Toby once since the night at O'Malley's. A meeting at his office about his finances, and not enough, not even close. James had wanted to call, arrange something out of work, just the two of them, but he'd been unable to come up with a suitable pretext. He shouldn't be thinking along those lines anyway. He was too old, too married; Toby too young, probably too straight.

'Toby.' He kept his voice even, neutral, pushing away his mental picture of Toby's arse. 'What can I do for you?'

'James, hi. Megan called me earlier. Seems her sister – you remember Chloe, don't you, from the night at the wine bar? – wants to go to that wildlife photography exhibition, the one they hold every year at the museum. Her mum told her you're into taking photos. Chloe phoned Megan, suggested the four of us go together. Thought I'd ask you, see if you're up for it.'

Damn Chloe Copeland. The only wildlife she'd ever be after would be prey she hunted in nightclubs. Yet another ploy to get her hooks into him, and no way would he play ball.

Except if he said no, Toby would get the message he wasn't interested.

James considered his options. Perhaps it was a chance to do something for Charlotte, spend time with her, get her out of the house. Not to mention the fact she'd be a shield against Chloe and the temptations Toby's nicely shaped rear end offered.

Besides, he'd been intending to check out the exhibition anyway; he might as well do so with Charlotte. Why not? And he'd always liked Megan, despite not having seen much of her in recent years.

'James? You still there?' Toby's voice sounded tight, the words running into one another. Like he was nervous about asking. Surely there'd be only one reason for that?

Don't go there, James warned himself. *He's too young, and you're married.*

'Still here. Can I call you back, once I've had a chance to check something? Say in ten minutes?'

They wrapped up the call. James finished fixing his wife's meal, smiling as he placed the plate in front of her. 'Love, how do you fancy an afternoon out this weekend?'

Surprise flitted across her face, sparking his guilt again. Had it been that long since he last suggested they do something together?

Charlotte gave him a tentative smile. 'What did you have in mind?'

He told her about the exhibition, noting the joy that crept into her expression. She leaned forward, touching his arm. 'I'd love to. We've not done something like that for ages, just you and me. We could go for a meal afterwards. Maybe at Greens.' Too late, he realised what he'd omitted to say, guilt hammering in his brain. He watched the animation drain from her face as he mentioned Toby and Chloe.

'Megan will be there too,' he said. 'Wouldn't you like to catch up with her again? You've not seen her for ages.'

Charlotte shook her head. 'I'd hoped...' She sounded so tired, so defeated. 'Never mind. I'm sorry, James. I don't know this Toby, or Megan's sister. I'm not up to meeting strangers. You know that.'

He did. Why hadn't he thought this through? 'I'm sorry,' he said, as he leaned over to kiss her. 'I meant well.'

***

Later, James retreated to the kitchen to fix them coffee. He took out his mobile, locating Toby's number. He answered on the first ring. No need to mention to Toby he'd asked Charlotte to accompany them.

'This photography exhibition. Yeah, I'd be up for that.'

'This weekend?' Obvious pleasure in Toby's voice.

'Okay. Sunday afternoon suits me best.'

'That ties in with what Megan suggested. I'll call her back, then text you what time to meet.' His voice sounded more assured. 'I'll be in touch. And James?'

'Yeah?'

'It'll be good to catch up.'

James agreed. Even if it meant seeing Chloe Copeland again.

He didn't give the weird phone calls Charlotte had been receiving another thought.

***

6

Pictures And Platters

'You wouldn't look so round shouldered if you didn't slouch. Okay, so you're tall and men prefer smaller girls, like me. Doesn't mean you have to behave like a hunchback. Not to mention those clothes; even Oxfam would reject them. Honest to God, I'm embarrassed to be seen with you sometimes, Megan.'

Typical of Chloe to fire off more of her poisoned arrows as we stood outside the Wildlife Photographer of the Year Exhibition, waiting for James and Toby. A flush of shame heated my cheeks as I glanced down at my baggy trousers, my charity shop coat, all I could afford on my meagre income. I didn't respond, refusing to let her needle me. The air was chilly, a hint of rain in the breeze, and I hugged my jacket around me, praying the others would arrive soon. I turned my back on Chloe, pretending to study a poster for the exhibition, my mind on Toby and James. I was curious; I'd get to observe how things stood between those two. Besides, time spent with Toby was always a bonus.

Talk of the devil. I caught sight of his long legs striding up the steps to the museum. He flashed me his trademark grin before turning a muted version towards Chloe. Before I could hug Toby, James also arrived, his eyes searching the museum entrance hall. I saw how he spotted Toby first, the way his mouth pulled upwards into a wide smile. The one he gave me seemed more reserved, yet still warm, friendly. Then he noticed Chloe, and his expression turned glacial. My inner self smiled with satisfaction.

I glanced at her as she pretended to study the same poster about the exhibition, no doubt to persuade James of her serious side. She looked stunning as usual, her flawless skin mocking my pitted complexion. Tight jeans hugged her bottom; the V-neck of her soft green top led the eye down to her generous cleavage. She'd gone heavy with the perfume too, a rich odour of musk strong in my nostrils. My sister was in full-on man-hunting mode, from what I could see.

James pulled open the door, waved us inside. 'Let's get going before it gets too busy.'

The exhibition was small, the walls of the venue white plasterboard, the silver pipes of the overhead ducts a stark contrast to the photos on display. Around us, people milled, their conversations echoing in my ears. A riot of colour depicting wildlife from every corner of land and sea hung from the plasterboard. I wondered to what extent Chloe, who hated animals even more than she despised her fellow humans, would feign an interest in both the photographs and their subjects.

'Look at the colours in that one! Amazing depth of field too.' I shot Chloe a look. I'd been right; she'd clearly been reading up about photography. I noticed James didn't comment or even glance in her direction, despite her remark being aimed his way. Instead, he moved closer to Toby, murmuring something I couldn't catch. Toby leaned in slightly, the distance between them less than one might expect from two people little more than acquaintances. I steered Chloe towards the special awards section, leaving the two men scrutinising the winners' wall.

'How's Mum?' Since I'd left home, monitoring her wellbeing had been difficult, to say the least. Not that I could rely on Chloe for an accurate update; she wouldn't notice, or care, how our mother was faring unless the money supply dried up. She'd always used her, along with the men she dated, as a convenient cash cow.

Chloe's mouth twisted. 'She never stops talking about James. I have to suffer her banging on about it all the time. As if he'd ever notice her. It's embarrassing, at her age.'

Typical Chloe. I tried again.

'Is she taking her medication properly? You know she forgets sometimes, and that's when she doesn't do so well.' Did my sister really need reminding?

All I got was another shrug. 'How should I know? It's up to her, not me.'

My hand itched to slap her. I clenched it fiercely.

Chloe moved off in the direction of James and Toby, down the far end of the exhibition hall. I grabbed her arm, hoping to keep her away from them, but she shook me off with a gesture of irritation and strode towards them, with me following.

Toby and James were standing, still closer than the norm, by the Young Photographers awards, pointing at the outstretched wings of a red kite silhouetted against the sky. Judging by James's expression, my previous suspicion was confirmed. This was a two-way thing.

'I'm starving. Let's go eat. We can go next door, to Greens.' Chloe's hand rested on James's arm, her eyes fawn-like and pleading. She didn't seem to care we'd not had time to see the whole exhibition. An opportunity to take control, even if just once, I decided.

'I've not seen these yet.' I gestured towards the outstretched wings. 'You two aren't ready to leave, are you?'

'I'd like a bit more time,' James said.

'Me too.' Toby's gaze rested on Chloe's hand, still glued to James's arm. His expression was blank. Did he realise that Chloe, who had tossed him aside so many years earlier, was homing in on the man he was after? From what I'd seen so far, if it came to a competition, Chloe would lose for the first time in her twenty-five years.

I watched as James pulled away, Chloe's hand falling off his sleeve, his own reaching up to touch Toby's jacket as he gestured towards a photo of emperor penguins. I admired it with one eye while keeping the other on Chloe's sulky face, chalking up a small and undoubtedly hollow victory to myself.

***

We'd finished seeing everything ten minutes later. I hoped James and Toby wouldn't want to go to Greens afterwards. I'd never been there but had glanced at the menu when passing; the prices, typical of a restaurant close to upmarket Clifton, scared me. Besides, enduring an hour of Chloe had shredded my patience. I was ready to go home.

It seemed that wasn't an option.

'So who's up for Greens?' Chloe kept her gaze fixed on James as she spoke. It didn't waver when James and Toby turned to look at each other. An unspoken question seemed to hover between them.

'I'll give it a go,' said Toby.

James's expression was unreadable. 'Me too.'

* * *

A couple of minutes later, we arrived at the restaurant. The terrace was already full but we managed to secure a table by the huge cathedral-like windows. I watched as Chloe slid into the seat opposite James, feeling relief when Toby took the seat next to him. I sat facing Toby, and picked up a menu.

'I'm going for the fillet of beef steak,' Chloe announced.

Of course you are, I thought, what with it being the most expensive item on the menu. My stomach clenched with longing for a plate of juicy beef, done rare, the sort of dish my freelance journalist and proofreader income wouldn't stretch to. Chloe hadn't worked in months, as far as I knew; she must have bled some money out of Mum before coming out. Or did she plan on James paying for her? I didn't know which possibility I disliked most.

'Roast breast of duck for me,' James said.

'Fish and chips for me,' said Toby. 'What about you, Megan?'

Thank God for Toby. He obviously noticed my hesitation, my inability to find anything on the menu in my limited price range. Toby had known me long enough to be aware of the precarious state of my finances, and came to my rescue.

'Scrub the fish and chips. Let's share a couple of the platters, Megan, one meat, one vegetable, with a side salad. What do you say? My treat. I reckon I owe you from the last time we went out.' He didn't, but I was grateful for the lie.

'Sounds good to me. Thank you.' *You're the best*, I mouthed across the table to Toby, seeing the others had their heads stuck in the drinks menu.

Too right, he mouthed back, with a grin.

'Let's get some wine. Red would be good. Say a couple of bottles of this Syrah. French Shiraz.' Chloe stabbed a finger at the first item on the list, its price exorbitant in my view.

Time to take control again. I smiled at her. 'Sparkling mineral water for me.'

'I'll grab a Coke,' Toby said.

Chloe's mouth pursed into a pout. 'What about you, James?' She injected honey into her voice. 'Can I persuade you to try something more exciting?'

'Mine's a Becks,' James said, not looking at my sister.

The rest of the meal went better than I'd anticipated. The food was superb, the lamb from the meat platter succulent in my mouth, and I felt myself unwind a little. James talked mostly to Toby about motorsport; Chloe interjected a few questions about James's car, then his dog, again pretending an interest in both. His answers were brief before he turned back to Toby. James and I chatted when Toby went to the toilet, agreeing how I must visit Charlotte soon, perhaps persuade her to do more art classes with me. Behind the talk, I sensed his dual purpose of flashing a neon sign in Chloe's face: *I am married, so forget it.*

The sulky vibes poured off Chloe thick and fast; I took pleasure in her obvious irritation. She seemed oblivious to the attraction between James and Toby, probably attributing their mutual absorption to the stereotypical thing of men and their cars. I doubted she believed a man indifferent to her charms could exist.

After the main course, we were discussing whether to squeeze in a dessert when Chloe seized her chance.

'All this talk of cars….' At first, neither man paid her any attention. Then she pounced. 'Yours is beautiful, James. But is it running okay? You've had it every day I've seen you this week, except for Friday, when you drove some big silver car.'

I zeroed in on what she'd said. She'd seen him every day this week?

I could tell by the way Toby turned an enquiring look on James he was also curious. So I'd been right; Chloe hadn't wasted time in launching her attack on Mum's boss. As for Toby, he harboured no illusions about my sister. If he'd not sussed before that she'd fixed her attentions on James, he would now, and the knowledge ought to be flashing warning signs in his head.

'I took the BMW in for a service. The Audi was a courtesy car.' James's tone was curt, the words clipped. He returned Toby's gaze. 'Chloe has been coming to the office to give her mother a lift home each evening.'

Toby nodded, the matter apparently settled for him. I wasn't so gullible. Chloe's appearance outside James's offices owed nothing to daughterly assistance and everything to her intention to milk his wallet.

The conversation drifted back on course as we all declined desserts and ordered coffees. Chloe stayed quiet, thank God, while we drank them and then she headed off towards the toilets.

'I've no idea where our waitress has gone. I'll nip over to the bar and request the bill,' I said.

Afterwards, as I made my way back to the table, I managed to catch the last part of James and Toby's conversation.

'Eight o'clock will be fine. See you in there. Not been in the Cornucopia before. It's in Regent Street, right?'

'You got it.' James looked up as I sat down. 'The bill on its way, Megan?'

'Coming right up.'

'Remember I'm treating you,' Toby said.

I didn't reply, too preoccupied with what I'd overheard.

So James and Toby had arranged to meet for a drink. I didn't kid myself for a minute it was business related. Things were moving fast between them. I quashed the rush of jealousy that threatened to swamp me.

Chloe returned from the toilet; the waitress brought our bill shortly afterwards. James put down enough cash to cover the cost of his meal, Toby taking care of his own and mine, leaving Chloe to stump up for her share. As she should, I thought, savouring her sour look as she slapped her credit card on the table.

She seized her moment as the two men were putting on their jackets, absorbed in another conversation about cars. My sister leaned towards me, her voice low, so only I could hear.

'James seems too pally by far with your ex,' she said. Her grin turned vicious. 'Toby needs to watch his step. I always get what I want, remember.'

***

7

Man Date

James sat at the bar, watching the door of the Cornucopia pub, nerves forcing his fingers to caress his pint glass. Quarter past eight. Would Toby even show up? A slight sweat, born from nerves, cooled the skin on his neck. What was he doing? He should be at home, with Charlotte, where he belonged. This was insane.

His hormones had been raging the other day at Greens when he'd suggested to Toby getting together for a drink. He'd made the excuse of needing to finalise some details on his pension, but James had not brought any paperwork with him. It could all be sorted via email anyway. He hadn't been able to fool himself about the real reason for being here, and he didn't think Toby had been deceived either. They'd gravitated towards each other like horny magnets since the first time they'd met.

Don't go there, James warned himself. *This can't happen.* They were just two guys going for a drink. No big deal.

Then Toby strode through the door. Relief washed through James.

'Hey.' Toby, a grin on his face, wearing tight jeans and T-shirt, walked up to him, and the sight went straight to James's groin. He clamped down hard on his reaction. They were here to talk business, nothing else.

He stood up. 'What can I get you to drink?'

'Make mine a pint of Doom Bar.' Toby gestured towards an empty table at the back of the pub. 'I'll grab us some seats.'

James ordered their drinks, then took their beers back to the table where Toby was sitting. As he passed his pint to him, his fingers brushed against Toby's, the touch electric. James was certain, from the flush on Toby's face, that he had felt it too.

If so, he wasn't letting on. 'Cheers.' Toby raised his glass, clinked it against James's. 'Good idea of yours, coming here. Glad you suggested it.'

They sipped their beer, made small talk, before Toby's tone turned serious. 'Can I ask you something? I've been curious about it since the afternoon at Greens.'

'Ask away.'

'Chloe Copeland.' Toby took a gulp of beer. 'She said she'd seen you several times over the past week. Is she really waiting for her mother, like you said?'

So his explanation hadn't rung true. What lay behind the question was another matter.

'No.'

'She was waiting for you.'

'Yes.' Did that bother Toby? 'She's been sticking to me like glue ever since that night I first met her, at O'Malley's.' James sipped his beer. 'I've no idea what it'll take to shake her off, but so far the blunt approach hasn't worked.' He eyed Toby to gauge his reaction. What was his interest in Chloe Copeland?

'It doesn't surprise me. She can be very determined.'

'You know her well?' Stupid question. Toby and Megan were friends; odds were he'd met her half-sister too.

'I dated her for a while.' Toby's expression was unreadable. 'Didn't last long.'

'When?' Toby and Chloe, together. The thought made James's stomach clench.

'Years ago. One summer, after I returned to Bristol after graduating. I'd lost touch with Megan by then; we didn't re-establish contact until later. Chloe was seventeen, I was twenty-one. I'd always known her as Megan's little sister, cute but just a kid. Then one day I bumped into her in town, and was knocked out by how gorgeous she'd become.'

'What happened?'

'We started going out. I fancied myself in love, couldn't get enough of her, although she was high maintenance. It felt like I was treading on eggshells at times, skirting around what to say in case she flared up, which happened quite a lot. I told myself I'd found a girl with a bit of fire, not some deadbeat. Convinced myself it was exciting. Except it wasn't. More like bloody draining.'

Not surprising, thought James. Anyone thinking with their brain and not their dick would realise the girl was trouble.

'Not just emotionally,' Toby continued. 'I racked up several hundred pounds on my credit card on expensive meals out, presents, and so on, before she dumped me.' He laughed. 'Megan says I got what I deserved. She doesn't have a high opinion of her sister.'

'Megan's a smart girl. I don't know her well, but from what I've seen, she seems sound.'

'She is. Maybe I should ask her for advice on my love life.' Another laugh.

Jealousy struck again. When James spoke though, he kept his tone light. 'Need a lot of advice on that, do you?'

Toby shrugged. 'I've played the field in my time, sure. Hardly unusual. Doesn't do any harm to experiment.'

He seemed to be steering the conversation down a different track. Was he hinting he'd tried sex with other men?

'If you get what I mean.'

Discomfort flooded James's brain, forcing his gaze away from Toby. He didn't have the wherewithal to talk about this. His father's voice – *You one of them queers, boy?* – boomed through his head.

Toby's voice cut through his introspection. 'Do I have to do all the work here?'

James's unease grew. 'What do you mean?'

'See, I'm not that familiar with how this works. Women – no problem. I can chat them up until the cows come home. Men, on the other hand – they're a whole new ball game for me.'

James winced at Toby's directness. What would Philip Matthews, long dead, make of another man coming on to his son? Even though he was fifty, the memory of his father's heated homophobia still scarred him. 'You've been sleeping with men recently?'

'Don't sound so shocked. Yes, I've been with guys. Not many. It came as a surprise to me too when I found myself interested in batting for the other team, but, hey, I decided to play along.'

'And?'

Toby grinned. 'Not sure why I hadn't given it a go before, except that up until then it hadn't occurred to me that I might be anything other than one hundred per cent straight.' He shrugged again. 'Guess that's how it goes for some people. You?'

'Me?' A desperate play for time on James's part.

Toby gave a little laugh. 'Yes. You were the one who asked me here tonight. You didn't expect me to buy your excuse about discussing my finances, did you? I bet a pub isn't your usual place to do business.'

The guy was right, of course. James had used work as a cover, but they'd both known that was a sham.

Toby was speaking again. 'I've told you my side of things. Now I'm asking about you. Ever done much with other guys?'

'None of your damn business.'

Anger flared in Toby's face. 'Can't you at least be honest about what's going on here?'

James met his gaze. 'I'm married.'

'You're seriously telling me you've always played a straight hand? Because that's not the impression I'm getting.'

He'd not banked on Toby being so forthright. No harm in being honest though. Toby deserved no less.

'A few guys now and again. Not many, and not often.' James took a gulp of beer. 'You satisfied?'

Toby gave a slight smile. 'At least you're being more truthful.'

'Thing is, I'm married. All that's behind me.'

'You're straight?' Toby spat out the words. 'I'm sick of you trying to deny what's going on. You've been putting out all the signals and don't insult me by making out I've got that one wrong.'

James almost got up to walk away, nearly told Toby he wasn't queer, damn it; no way was he interested in guys. But he didn't. He found himself compelled to ride this out, hear what the man had to say.

It seemed like he had plenty.

'I don't know what the deal is with your wife, but she's not the reason you're holding out on me. Don't get me wrong...' Toby swigged his beer and James watched, fascinated, as Toby's Adam's apple rose and fell. 'I don't like the fact you're married. I don't normally go for anyone with a wedding ring. It gets too messy. You though... something's been simmering between us since the day we met. I'm sick of tiptoeing around the issue. If it's not your wife, then the reason must be because you're stuck in the closet.' Toby drained his glass and set it down hard.

James found himself unable to bear Toby's gaze, skewering him as it did with the truth of his words. He pulled his eyes away, down into the dark depths of his beer glass. How the hell should he reply? Impossible to say yes, he did want him, this man with the craggy features and lop-sided grin, the guy who had occupied most of his thoughts since the day they'd met.

'I'm not gay,' he found himself mumbling.

Toby snorted. 'You sure as hell aren't one hundred per cent straight. I don't care if you're gay, bisexual, or whatever label you prefer. The point is you want me. I want you. Can't you at least admit this is a two-way thing?'

James got up, shoving the table as he did so, slopping his unfinished beer. 'I can't listen to any more of this.' He grabbed his jacket. 'I have to go. As you rightly point out, I have a wife. At home, waiting for me. It's best if we don't meet again.'

'Coward.' Toby's undisguised contempt shot through James's gut.

The scornful word echoed in his head later, making sleep impossible. Damn the man.

***

The next morning, James scanned his emails. Shit. One from Toby.

The message asked him to meet up, saying they needed to talk. James cursed and jabbed at the 'delete' icon on his computer. He wouldn't be doing that anytime soon. An early lunch beckoned. Maybe beer and food would sort his head.

He stretched his meal out over a couple of hours, the lasagne tasteless in his mouth as his thoughts tormented him. The email from Toby, his marriage to Charlotte, the whole goddamn mess that passed for his life, churned through his head. He'd told Toby they shouldn't meet again. Which meant his focus ought to be on Charlotte, on whether they should continue their marriage. Impossible to ignore her feelings for him, despite his inability to love her back. Wasn't it bad enough she suffered from depression, without crushing her hopes for their relationship? Her accident, the fact she needed a wheelchair was his fault, his alone, and shouldn't he pay the price?

She'd always wanted more than he could give though. His mind slid back to the evening of the car crash. Charlotte had been unhappy, in a mood to complain.

'I never see you. You're always at work.'

'I have a business to run, Charlotte.'

'You're married to me, not the bloody business.'

'What exactly do you expect from me?' He'd run his hand through his hair in frustration. 'Don't I give you everything you want?' Hell, the new Smart sports car had been delivered for her birthday only the week before. She'd seemed pleased enough at the time.

Charlotte moved closer, got right into his personal space. Determination flowed off her in waves. 'I want,' she said, her mouth inches away from his face, 'more of you. We're married, for God's sake. I'd like us to go out for meals, have weekends away, spend evenings in together. Is expecting you to act like a husband, rather than an expense account, too much to hope for?'

The row had rumbled on and on, and had only ended when Charlotte, her face red and tear-stained, grabbed her car keys and ran from their flat, saying she couldn't bear to be near him. How she had to think. Relief had hit him as she drove away.

***

That emotion morphed into guilt when, two hours later, he found himself at the hospital, with Charlotte fighting for her life in intensive care. Too upset to think straight, she'd been driving fast and furiously, a combination guaranteed to end badly. She'd ploughed through the central reservation on the M4, straight into an articulated lorry, crushing her legs and severing her spinal cord amongst a host of other injuries.

After her discharge from hospital, they'd resumed some semblance of married life, but Charlotte refused to leave the flat, sliding into depression, cutting herself off from friends. Their marriage struggled on, James too guilty about his part in the accident to mention divorce.

And there he was, five years later, uncertain as to how much longer the situation could continue.

Lost in his thoughts, James started when his mobile vibrated in his pocket. Pulling it out, he saw Toby's name flash up on the screen. A text. He threw the phone on the table, cursing again.

***

Less than a minute later, he picked it up and clicked on the message. Two words only. 'Call me.'

Not going to happen, he told himself. Toby had better get used to that fact.

He downed his beer and headed back to the office. Not that it offered him any respite; Chloe Copeland was leaning against his car as he walked onto the office forecourt. Damn.

She didn't give him time to speak.

'You're late. Doesn't matter.' She moved closer, forcing him to take a step back. He didn't want any of his staff, and definitely not

Tilly, looking out of the office windows and spotting him with Chloe. He grabbed her arm and pulled her around the corner.

'What on earth are you doing? Your mother might see us.'

Chloe laughed. 'Do you realise she has a thing for you? Bangs on about you all the time. As if you'd ever notice someone like her. Especially when I'm here.'

'You're forgetting I have a wife.' James knew he sounded rude, but he didn't care. The sooner she got the message the better.

'Charlotte. Right.' He heard the amused contempt in her voice. 'Still pretending to be the happily married man, are you?'

He ignored the jibe. 'I need to get back to work.'

She edged closer. 'She must know she can't hang on to you for much longer. She'll be happier once you've left her and she can move on.'

'Left her?' He heard the incredulity in his voice but couldn't believe what she'd just said. She had to have been joking, except that he got the impression Chloe Copeland didn't joke around.

'You have to listen to me.' He grabbed her arm again, too forcefully, but he didn't care. 'Nothing can ever happen between us. For God's sake, haven't I told you enough times?'

She didn't answer at first, but something dark and angry snaked into her eyes. He stared at her, at her face that would have most men tenting their trousers but which left him unmoved. In that moment he understood how, at her core, she harboured an element of ruthlessness, cruelty. Something fundamentally flawed.

'You don't mean that.' She looked at him, smiling, reaching out to touch his arm, but he pulled back. 'You're confused. I understand you're clinging on to some misplaced loyalty towards your wife, but that'll pass. You'll be better off without each other.'

'No.' He made to leave, but she grabbed his arm again, and he was reluctant to shake her off in case she caused a scene. 'I'm married, Chloe. I intend to stay with my wife. We're not right for each other, you and me.'

'But you're exactly what I like in a man.'

'I'm too old for you.' He decided to try flattery. 'You're a beautiful girl. You could have any man you choose.'

'I want you.' Iron determination threaded through her voice, and he sensed again the dark anger coiled inside her. Probably furious because she couldn't get what she wanted: his money. Hadn't Toby warned him about how Chloe had drained his bank account? Owner of a successful financial consultancy, James had the Georgian flat in upmarket Clifton, the flashy sports car, the expensive suits, all demonstrating his wealth. Chloe Copeland had sniffed him out, making him her prey. She'd found one man who wouldn't fall into her honey trap. He simply needed to hold his resolve. He doubted she'd pursue him for too long; too many other wealthy men looking for a little action on the side existed for her to waste time with him.

He shook her hand off his arm. 'I have to go. Don't contact me again. No more hanging around at the office. I mean it.'

She took a step backwards. For a moment, he was afraid she'd persist, keep singing the same song, but he sensed a shift in her mood. He wasn't prepared for what she said next though.

'It's okay, James. I understand. I'm sorry to have been a nuisance. I won't bother you again.' Her voice shook and he felt a pang of guilt. Had he misjudged her? Then he remembered: she was a gold-digger and a mighty fine actress. Crocodile tears went with the territory.

She gave him a half-smile. 'It's because you're a good man. I admire your loyalty to your wife, I really do. She's a lucky woman. If you ever change your mind...'

'I won't.'

'I'll be waiting for you.' With that, she walked away, and relief soaked through him. It was finished; he'd be able to get back to normality. Concentrate on running the business and try, he didn't know how, to be a better husband to Charlotte.

Along with forgetting he'd ever met a man called Toby Turner.

***

8
Blowing Hot And Cold

'Honestly, Megan, I can't work out what's going on in the guy's head. Talk about blowing hot and cold.'

Toby looked tired. Faint dark circles were painted under his eyes and he'd not shaved. Not that I minded; the rumpled look suited him. Flickers of desire stirred in me; I squashed them firmly back down.

We'd decided to meet for a curry at Spice of India, our favourite restaurant. The waiter had given us the menus and was hovering for our order but Toby seemed too distracted. His hand ran repeated furrows through his floppy blond hair, irritation oozing from him. Whatever he needed to vent about, it obviously wasn't good. I'd not mentioned overhearing the arrangements for his get-together with James at the Cornucopia. I'd not needed to; Toby had begun sounding off as soon as we sat down.

'We should order.' I figured I was in for a long evening. Fine by me. At least I could lend a friendly ear on a full stomach.

'I suppose so.' Toby didn't seem that bothered though.

I signalled the waiter.

'Lamb bhuna for me, with pilau rice and a side of tarka dhal,' I said. 'And a Kingfisher.'

'Make that two of everything.' Toby plainly wasn't interested in food; James Matthews appeared to be rattling his cage pretty well. I'd not seen this side of him before. Toby, the casual love-them-and-leave-them type, the man who hadn't loved me but had still left, who seemed incapable of a stable relationship. A flicker of jealousy joined the embers of desire I'd felt earlier. Toby was unattainable, and not just because he preferred something more masculine these days. I simply didn't hold any appeal for him, not since that night in his car when he'd flicked the recliner lever on my seat and pressed me towards the floor. We'd ended up having sex, the steam on the windows concealing the loss of my virginity, and afterwards Toby had simply moved on.

I pushed the thought aside. 'So you went for a drink with him?'

Toby sipped his Kingfisher. 'Yes. He asked me to meet him at the Cornucopia, said some paperwork needed sorting. How we might as well do it over a pint. The way he said it, I didn't anticipate a business meeting.'

'You weren't reading something into the situation that wasn't there?' I didn't believe my own question. Having observed the two men at O'Malley's and at Greens, I'd become convinced their attraction was a two-way thing.

'No. I know you're sceptical, seeing how his wife's a friend of yours. That's the excuse he's hiding behind, how he's a married man, wears a wedding ring, blah, blah. I don't buy it. He didn't bring any paperwork along to the pub.'

'So what happened? Did you get to discuss any of this?'

'Eventually. Honestly, it was like pulling teeth. I figured, bearing in mind he'd asked me there, he'd make the first move. Didn't happen. We talked about Chloe, of all people. Remind me to tell you about her later. Anyway, I decided to leap in and get things moving, seeing as James seemed reluctant to take the initiative.'

Our food arrived. I dished out rice, lamb and lentils, wondering why my sister had featured in their conversation and intending to find out why. The stink of her rotten behaviour permeated almost everything, I reflected sourly. Meanwhile, Toby expounded on what had gone on between himself and James at their last meeting. Hurt flashed behind his eyes when he told me James had said they shouldn't meet again.

'It's total bullshit, Megan. The guy's not as straight as he makes out – he told me as much – but for some reason he's retreating into the closet. Thing is, there's no way he's a happily married man, whatever he says.'

I couldn't disagree. The bit about James being bisexual surprised me though; I'd assumed Toby must be a one-off for him. 'He's been with other men?'

'A few, apparently. So it's not as if I came on to some ramrod-straight hetero who'd rather cut his dick off than have another man touch it.' He raked his fingers nervously through his hair again. 'I tell you, I can't work the guy out. I'm beginning to think I'm wasting my time.'

'You might have to let this one go, Toby.' The suggestion held definite appeal for me, although Toby getting shot of James would hardly bring him running to my side. Still, at least we'd be back on familiar territory if he were playing the field once more. And it would seem a lot less weird if he weren't pursuing my friend's husband. A man old enough to be his father.

Toby nodded. 'I should, after the way he behaved the other night. I told him he was a coward and I meant it.'

'But you don't intend to let it go, do you?'

'Not yet. Thing is, he's a prick, but a sexy one. I'll give him another chance. See how things pan out. I'll email or text him again in a couple of days. Hell, it's not as if I came on strong or anything. Nothing to make his queer side run for the hills. I wasn't doing a Chloe on him.'

Back to my sister again. 'Has she been causing trouble?'

Toby slid his fork on his plate, his lamb bhuna demolished. 'Seems like she's latched on to James. Developed a thing for him. She's being a bit of a nuisance, from what he said.'

'The picking Mum up after work thing?'

'Yeah. He said Chloe had been sticking to him like a leech. How she seemed pretty determined.' Toby laughed. 'You're probably well aware of that side of her nature.'

Indeed. I was very familiar with Chloe's persistence. 'I can't imagine she'll handle rejection well.'

'You saw the way he acted at Greens when she kept trying to get his attention. He bordered on rudeness towards her.'

'Because he preferred to talk cars with you.'

'Yeah. I can't work him out. What's he like?'

'I don't know him much better than you. I've mostly only ever seen him at the flat when I've visited Charlotte. I haven't been there for ages though.'

'How come? You two fall out?'

'No.' I'd been good friends with Charlotte, despite the twelve-year age gap, our love of art the glue holding two very different personalities together. Sadness pricked me when I thought of her. I'd wanted us to stay friends, but the car crash had driven a wedge between us. She'd retreated into some dark world where I couldn't reach her. Gradually we'd drifted apart.

'Her accident,' I said. 'She changed overnight from the lively extrovert she once was. At first I visited, in an effort to cheer her up. It didn't work.'

'She suffers from depression?'

I nodded. 'She stopped going out, seeing her friends, withdrew from everyone except James. I'd text and email, suggesting we get together. She never replied. Eventually I gave up.'

'She didn't withdraw from James?' Toby looked pensive. 'Perhaps they're closer than he makes out.'

'No.' I didn't want to lie. 'Charlotte's always adored him. She's told me things though. How she always felt she had to work so hard to get him to notice her, show any affection, how she sometimes wondered if he loved her at all.'

'A cold fish, then.'

I shook my head. 'I don't think so. Something about him seems closed off. As if he has emotions but never allows them to surface.'

Toby grimaced. 'Repressed and in the closet. I can definitely pick them.'

'Must be the lapsed Catholic in him.'

'He's Catholic?'

'Yes, although he doesn't practise. Might be why he takes fright at the idea of a man hell bent on dragging him off to bed.'

I drained my Kingfisher and ordered another. 'But whatever the reason he's not getting it on with you, whether because of his marriage or his upbringing, the result is the same. He turned you down. You need to accept that. Otherwise, you'll end up doing a Chloe on him.'

Defeat crept into Toby's face. 'You've got a point. I don't want to bother the guy if he's genuinely not interested. The thing is, I still reckon I've read this right. He simply can't or won't follow through for some reason.'

Anger sparked in me then. 'Probably because he's married. However much you pretend she's not a factor, James has a wife. A disabled one, who suffers from depression. She deserves better than to have someone sniffing around her husband, whatever the state of her marriage.'

Toby reached across the table and took my hands, his skin sliding over mine, the sensation throwing fuel on the flickering lust inside me. 'I don't want to fall out with you over this. I get you think I should lay off, find someone available. And you're probably right. But he's got under my skin.'

Toby wasn't giving up without a fight, it seemed. At the sight of his lop-sided grin, my anger melted away.

'Tell you what,' he continued. 'If he doesn't respond to my texts or emails, I promise I'll let the whole thing slide. Anyway, enough about me; I've not asked about you. Everything going okay?'

'Yeah. Work's patchy but then it always is. Chloe's her usual self where I'm concerned. One of these days I'm going to slap her so hard they'll hear it in Australia.'

'Not a tad over sensitive about Chloe, are you, Megan?' My hackles shot skyward. 'She's immature, I'll give you that. Cruel and thoughtless too. But you're always so quick to condemn her.'

'You don't know her the way I do.' *He'll never believe my suspicions about Alicia*, I thought bitterly.

'Okay, so you two don't get on. And yes, she likes to tease. Thing is, you bite every time. No wonder she keeps dangling the bait.'

Shades of what Amy had said. I didn't trust myself to reply. We might not fall out over Toby's pursuit of my friend's husband but we definitely would if he carried on defending my sister. 'Can we get the bill, please?' My voice dripped ice. Toby knew me too well where Chloe was concerned. Well enough to know he should have reined in any comment about me being over sensitive.

He must have realised he'd overstepped the mark. 'Don't mind me. I guess I'm a bit wound up over James, that's all.'

The apology poured balm on the wound he'd inflicted. I relaxed, smiling at him before slapping down my last twenty pounds for my share of the bill, mindful of Toby treating me at Greens. *You're too honest, too scrupulous, Megan*, I thought. *Doesn't get you anywhere. Nice people finish last.* I only had to look at Chloe to understand that. Being nice hadn't netted me Toby. Whereas Chloe could have hooked him for life if she'd chosen to. The jerk didn't even realise how hard I had to fight to shove down those flickers of desire every time I saw him.

No frigging justice in this world. I stood up. 'Come on. Let's get out of here.'

***

9

As Sticky As A Spider's Web

'Who the hell is this? What do you want?'

Charlotte's rudeness shocked me. Swallowing my confusion, I replied, 'Charlie? It's Megan Copeland.'

Silence, firing up every one of my insecurities. Then, 'This is a nice surprise.'

'I'm outside your flat,' I said into my mobile. 'I happened to be passing and thought we might catch up. If you're not busy?'

I hadn't been passing. I'd come by deliberately. It really had been too long since I'd last caught up with Charlotte – three years, at least – a fact I felt guilty about. Perhaps I'd let our friendship slide too easily. Too ready to accept Charlotte's failure to return any of my texts or emails, her depression over being told she'd never walk again. Why hadn't I pressed harder to keep our friendship alive?

Time to soothe away some of my guilt.

I realised Charlotte hadn't responded. 'Charlie? Are you still there?'

A pause. Then: 'Still here. I'd been taking a nap, that's all. Sorry if I was rude. Yes, let's catch up. It's been way too long.' The connection went dead.

A light came on in the hallway as I made my way towards the front door, which opened before I got a chance to ring the bell. Charlotte's wheelchair appeared through the gap, and I had to work hard to suppress my reaction when I saw her face.

She looked rough. Her hair obviously hadn't been near a brush recently. Her skin, the colour of cooked porridge without any of the warmth, reflected the fact she no longer got any sun or fresh air. Thin lines of weepy red framed her bloodshot eyes.

Her body shocked me too. I'd always envied her gentle curves, so unlike my own flatness and Chloe's overdone ripeness. They were long gone, her figure almost gaunt, frail in my arms as I bent to hug her. Charlotte clearly wasn't a comfort eater.

'I'll go. This isn't a good time…'

Charlotte's hand grabbed my arm. 'Don't leave.' Tears prickled in her voice. 'I'm not accustomed to visitors. But now you're here… I could use a friend.' She wheeled herself back through the communal hallway into their ground floor flat, not giving me a chance to say no.

Once in the lounge, I sat opposite her, awkward, tense, not sure what she wanted to share. It would involve James. What else did Charlotte have in her life, besides the depression? As far as I was aware, she didn't even paint any longer. My eyes went to the portrait of James on the wall, done when we took art classes together.

Charlotte motioned towards an open bottle of red wine. 'Join me. The glasses are in that cupboard.' She had a half-empty one in front of her. The bottle was close to three-quarters gone.

'Make mine a small one. I'm driving.' I tried to make a joke of it as I fetched myself a glass. 'Looks like you started without me.'

'Yeah, well, my husband's not here, is he? As per usual.'

So I'd been right. James was the root cause of the reddened eyes, the bag-lady hair.

'He's still at work. Staying later and later these days.'

I sipped my wine, welcoming the alcoholic warmth. 'Business is going well for him?'

Charlotte snorted. 'Either that, or else he's got someone at the office.'

I wasn't sure how to respond. Surely she couldn't suspect Mum?

'I'm not serious, Megan. Most of the women at James's office are either happily married or like your mother, not bothered with men any longer.' *You're wrong there*, I thought. 'Besides…' Her mouth twisted bitterly. 'It's not as if sex is a great motivator for my husband.'

Embarrassment flooded through me. 'Charlotte…'

'Too much information?' She drained her wineglass, poured herself another. 'It's the truth.'

'I'm not sure James would want you to…'

'I don't care.' I braced myself, ready for whatever she needed to vent, dreading the intimacies her rancour might reveal.

She gulped down more wine. 'We never make love anymore. He always says he's tired, how he's got a lot going on at work. But I know he's simply making excuses.' Barely suppressed tears hovered in her eyes.

'It's me, I'm sure. He's repulsed by me.' The tears weren't being held back any longer. I moved towards her, awkward, unsure, putting my hand on her shoulder as comfort.

'I know I've let myself go. Can't even be bothered to get dressed some days. I'm not the woman he married, Megan.'

No, I agreed silently. *You're not.* Sadness for my friend filled me.

'Thing is, he promised me. When we got married. In sickness and in health, he swore.' She drained her wine, refilled her glass. 'I may be crippled, I may have to spend my days in a wheelchair, but I'm still a woman, I still want James. Sex with him, I mean.' She reached into her sleeve and grabbed a tissue, blowing her reddened nose. 'It's been months. I may not be able to do what I once could, but I can still function.'

'Perhaps he really is tired. Hassled by building the business, probably. Stuff he keeps to himself because he doesn't want to bother you. Don't make it more than it is.' *Liar*, a voice in my head said, but Charlotte's pain was driving me to platitudes.

'We have to sort it, me and James. We can't go on like this.'

I fumbled for the right words. 'Do you think you'll stay together? Find some way to fix things?'

She shook her head. 'Emotionally he's moving further away all the time. Especially recently. I can't help wondering if he's met someone else. Someone who's not at the office, I mean.'

He has, I thought. *It's simply a question of whether he acts on it.*

Her next statement floored me. 'I want a baby with him. It's not impossible. Or too late. I'm only forty-one, for God's sake. But he refuses to discuss having children.'

Christ. How was I supposed to respond? This wasn't news to me. When we'd talked in the past, Charlotte had never made any secret of the fact she wanted kids with James. After her accident, what with her being so depressed and with the two of us hardly seeing each other, I'd allowed it to slip from my mind. I'd assumed, obviously wrongly, that Charlotte had given up on her dream of motherhood. Had I been blinkered in assuming it was impossible because she was in a wheelchair?

'Thing is, Megan…' She blew her nose again. 'What I said before. About the sex. It's never been good between us…'

Oh, shit. She seemed determined to get into specifics. If I'd been out of my comfort zone before, I'd moved light years away from it after her revelation.

'Charlie, James wouldn't want you to tell me–'

'Fuck him.' Stunned, I shut up. The Charlotte I'd known never swore. The fury in her face kept me silent.

'It's always been me initiating things between us, right from the start, and even before we were married sex had tapered off. Now I wonder if another issue is at work here. He's never opened up to me about why his first marriage ended.'

'You think he had someone else?'

She snorted again. 'No. And I don't really think he does, no matter what I just said.' She gulped, and the tears flowed again. 'It's like he's got no interest in sex. Because he never did, not even when we first got together. So, you see, it's more than the fact I'm confined to this wheelchair.'

What could I say? Besides, she needed me to listen, not talk.

'He just doesn't want to make love to me. So I've precious little chance of ever becoming a mother.' Her laugh held desperation. 'Why, in God's name, did he marry me?'

'I'm sure he loves you, Charlotte.' Did I sound patronising? At least I'd found something – anything – to say.

'Like he loved his first wife?' Another laugh that held no mirth. 'He's never talked about what happened, simply how they married too young. He didn't go into details and I didn't press him. When he told me, we hadn't been dating long. I was so certain everything would work out between us.' Her words were starting to slur a little. 'Even then, he didn't seem keen on sex. He'd often make excuses about being tired through work, how he needed an early night. And when we did make love…'

'Charlotte, please…'

She ignored me. 'It was like he was there in body only, like his mind was elsewhere. He'd take ages to come too. I've wondered if perhaps he's gay. Deep in the closet because of the Catholic guilt thing.'

'Have you talked to him about marriage counselling?'

Charlotte's smile held bitterness. 'Can you really picture James in front of a counsellor, discussing our problems? Talking about messy things like emotions doesn't come naturally to him. He acts as if nothing's wrong. That is, when I get to see him, talk to him. Which isn't often.'

'Would you consider going for counselling yourself?'

'What for? Because my husband can't bear to make love to me? Or to help me deal with the fact I'm a cripple?' The venom in her words stung me, as she'd clearly intended. Silenced, I stared into my wineglass.

'Or because,' Charlotte continued, 'I'm so pathetic nobody else will listen to me? Which is it, Megan?'

When I didn't respond – no words seemed equal to her pain – she drained her wine. 'Sometimes I wish I were dead.' Her eyes were glassy from the alcohol.

Again I couldn't speak.

The silence stretched between us, as sticky as a spider's web, causing my palms to grow clammy around my glass. I yearned for my scruffy home, for Toby, for Mum. Anywhere other than this flat, overflowing with its myriad of suppressed conflicts.

'I'm sorry.' She touched my hand for a second, a gesture of apology. 'You didn't deserve that. You came here as a friend, after all. Right now I could use one.' Her fingers twisted restlessly in her lap. 'I've been getting these strange phone calls, you see.'

'What sort of calls?'

'Silent ones, several times. They're getting more frequent too. The last one was yesterday evening. Whoever it is never speaks, but it's scary as hell. That's why I was so rude when you phoned. I thought it was another malicious call.'

'Have you told James?'

'Yes. He dismisses it all, says it's kids playing a joke. But it isn't.'

'How do you know?'

'Because whoever's behind these calls, they never phone when he's here. They know his working hours and when he takes Senna for a walk. That's what frightens me.'

As well it might. 'Do you have any idea who it might be?'

She shook her head. 'No.'

I did though. Not that I could voice my suspicions.

* * *

10
Time To Tell Him

O n the way home from Charlotte's, I decided to stop off at Mum's, check on how she was doing. As well as to enquire as to Chloe's whereabouts the night before. Okay, so she could have made a malicious phone call from anywhere, but I'd have more reason to suspect she was the culprit if I knew she'd been at home the previous evening between seven and eight. I'd already ascertained from Charlotte that was when James took Senna for his evening walk.

Mum's appearance both cheered and disturbed me when I walked into the kitchen, where she was sitting, a mug of herbal tea between her hands. With her hair neat and brushed, her clothes ironed, she looked well. What bothered me was whether this transformation was in the hopes of bagging herself James Matthews.

Footsteps sounded on the stairs. Chloe appeared in the doorway, barely acknowledging my presence. She crossed to the coffee maker, busied herself with fixing a drink. She didn't offer me one.

'Thought I saw you last night while I was driving home, Chloe,' I lied to her turned back. 'On Church Road.'

'Wasn't me. I didn't go out yesterday evening.'

So I had an answer, of sorts. A frustratingly intangible one. Short of stealing her phone, checking the call logs for Charlotte's number, I couldn't be sure Chloe was behind the prank calls. My gut told me she was though.

I chatted with Mum for a few minutes, Chloe flicking through a fashion magazine all the while.

'You'll come over for lunch this weekend, won't you, Megan?' Mum's voice was animated, excited. 'I'll cook us all a lamb roast.'

'Any particular occasion?' I queried. Something was going on with her, and I intended find out what.

Mum smiled. "I have some news to share. I think you'll both be pleased."

I watched interest and curiosity flit over Chloe's face. As for me, I was also intrigued. Maybe she'd received a promotion at work. No doubt Chloe was thinking the same thing, probably already making plans to spend the extra money.

'You're not going to tell us?' I asked.

Mum shook her head. 'You'll just have to wait. Can you get here by twelve thirty?'

***

As I walked through the door the following Sunday, the smell of roasting lamb tantalised my nostrils. I made my way to the kitchen, where Mum stood basting the meat, her expression harassed. The tiny kitchen was steamy, causing beads of perspiration to stand out on her forehead. No sign of Chloe.

'Can I help?' The last thing I wanted was for Mum to get stressed, and cooking wasn't her forte. 'Let me see to the vegetables and get the gravy going.'

She looked relieved, and I knew I'd said the right thing. 'Would you mind? I can't cope with so much at once.'

I laid my hand on her arm, my love for her hot and strong. 'You should have done a salad or sandwiches. Honestly, Mum, I wouldn't have minded. Neither would Chloe.' The latter part I knew to be untrue. Chloe would have bitched about the lack of a hot meal all afternoon.

She shook her head. 'I wanted to cook something special for my girls. Remember what I told you the last time you were here? Got something to share with you both.'

I set about making the gravy, and draining the carrots and peas. Above us, I could hear Chloe moving around in her bedroom. Too much to ask that she should come and help.

***

The meal went well. For once, Mum hadn't undercooked the meat, and the vegetables weren't overdone. Chloe, to my relief, occupied herself with her food, not saying much. Neither did Mum.

Once we'd all finished eating, I shot Chloe a barbed look. 'I'll make us all some coffee. Can you stack the dirty plates in the dishwasher, Chloe?' My sister's face turned sulky, but she made no comment, getting up to do as I'd requested.

After I'd made the coffee, I took our mugs through into the living room, choosing one of the armchairs near the window. Chloe plonked herself on the other one, with Mum opposite us on the sofa. Both of us looked at her expectantly. She sipped her coffee, then glanced at us, a smile on her face.

'You must be wondering what I have to tell you,' she said. 'I got a phone call on Friday. The solicitor has finally completed wrapping up Grandma's estate. I collected a cheque from his office that afternoon.'

So that was her special news. I'd almost forgotten about the difficulties involved in sorting our grandmother's affairs, so long had the whole thing been dragging on. Mum's mother had died intestate, leaving one hell of a mess for her solicitor to untangle: investment properties, several bank accounts, and a healthy portfolio of stocks and shares. At the time, I'd been worried about Mum, but she'd never been close to our grandmother, and the emotional collapse I'd dreaded didn't happen.

Thanks, Gran, I thought. Despite being a remote, almost unknown figure, she'd always ensured Mum had money when her mental health issues rendered her incapable of work. For that, I'd long been grateful.

My gaze flitted to Chloe, sitting erect in an armchair. She reminded me of a bloodhound sniffing out a fresh trail, and I could almost smell her barely repressed excitement. Odds were she was making plans for our mother's money. Might it be too much to hope she might quit her pursuit of James's wealth?

Mum smiled fondly at her. 'Now for another surprise. Wait here.' She set down her coffee and went upstairs.

When she came downstairs a couple of minutes later, she held two envelopes, offering one to each of us. Chloe couldn't tear into hers fast enough.

'Go on,' Mum urged me, noting my hesitation. 'A little present for you.'

By the time I'd eased the envelope open, Chloe already held the contents of hers in her hands. I leaned closer, enabling me to discern it was a cheque. Mum was old school; computer illiterate, unable to deal with online banking.

I pulled out my own cheque. To my astonishment, it was for a seriously large sum of money.

'Thank you,' I said to Mum, my throat closing over with emotion. I was stunned and delighted by her gift. My finances, always precarious, were in desperate need of this money. Maybe I'd be able to afford something other than charity shop clothes for once.

I noticed Chloe hadn't bothered to say thank you. Instead, she held the cheque in her hands as though it were the Holy Grail. I wondered how long it would take her to burn through it.

'So,' my sister remarked, flashing a Judas smile at Mum. 'Spill the beans, then. How much did Grandma leave?'

'Chloe!' I was incensed. 'That's none of your business.'

'For God's sake, don't be so stuffy. Mum doesn't mind me asking, do you?'

She did, I could tell. Our mother's old-school principles extended to a reluctance to talk specifics about money. Nevertheless, she offered no rebuke to Chloe. Of course she didn't. Her golden daughter could do no wrong in her eyes.

'Let's just say that your grandma has left me very well off.' She smiled. 'And I wanted to pass some of that onto my girls.'

I went over to hug Mum, her body stiffening as I placed my arms around her. Her reaction pained me, but it was what I'd come to expect. 'Thank you,' I told her again, no hint of hurt in my voice. 'You've no idea how grateful I am.'

Even though I kept my voice low, Chloe must have heard what I said. As I returned to my armchair, a sarcastic grin curled the corners of her mouth.

'Not hard to see what you should spend some of that money on, Megan,' she remarked. 'Look at the state of you. Those clothes have 'charity shop rejects' written all over them.'

I held my tongue. What had Toby and Amy said about me rising to the bait too readily? Perhaps Chloe would back off if I ignored her.

She didn't, of course. Instead she pressed on, a nasty snicker escaping her. 'Who knows, if you didn't look like a refugee from a jumble sale, perhaps you'd stand a chance with Toby at last. Not still pretending your feelings towards him are just friendly, are you?'

I turned away so that she wouldn't see the hurt that must have stolen across my face. Instead, I blew on my coffee, pretending it needed cooling. I doubted Chloe was fooled; her next comment proved me right.

'Although I keep forgetting,' she continued, smug delight permeating her voice. 'He's already taken his turn with you, hasn't he? And not gone back for seconds. I suspect it will take more than a designer dress and a decent haircut to switch Toby's attention your way. Let's face it, you blew your chances a long time ago where he's concerned.'

'Chloe, my love,' Mum said, nervousness in her voice. Was she going to stand up for me at last?

'Oh, come on, Mum, for goodness sake. I'm only telling the truth, aren't I?'

'You shouldn't tease your sister that way. I know you don't mean what you're saying, but Megan's sensitive.'

'Besides, she didn't even have the sense to—' Chloe stopped, probably realising she was about to take a step too far. I didn't doubt that the words 'stop herself getting pregnant' would have completed that sentence. She smirked. 'I wonder what he'd say if he knew he'd once been a father.'

At that, I'd had enough. I drained my coffee in a couple of large swigs, then got up from my armchair, smiling at Mum. 'That was a lovely lunch. Thank you. Sorry to leave so soon, but I've got work to crack on with.' A lie, but our mother would never know otherwise. Out of the corner of my eye, I saw Chloe smirk again.

***

Back in my flat, my fingers travelled over the cheque, making plans for it. The amount was enough to pay off all my debts and leave a tidy sum over to put into savings. I'd deposit it at the bank at the first available opportunity.

Meanwhile, my thoughts roamed over Chloe's remarks about Toby. It wasn't the first time she'd needled me about our one-night stand, and I was sick of it. What scared me most was the veiled threat to tell Toby about Alicia. My stomach churned; it was unthinkable for him to find out from Chloe. I needed to get my act together and tell him. Decision made. I'd go round to his flat, and be honest about the baby we'd made together. It was the only way to defuse the lingering menace Chloe represented.

I glanced at my watch. Four thirty. Delay wasn't an option; I'd visit him that evening, before I lost my courage.

I stood up, heading into my bedroom. From the top drawer in my bedside cabinet, I took out a leather-bound photo album. In it were precious memories of Alicia, from the first minutes of her life right up to just before she died. I seldom looked at it. On the rare occasions when I did, my grief threatened to engulf me with its intensity.

I owed Toby a photo of his daughter though. That much, at least, I could give him. As I opened the album, tears stung the backs of my eyes, sliding unchecked down my cheeks to drop onto the plastic covering the photos. There in front of my eyes was my baby girl, the child I had loved so much, and still did. I traced my fingers over each picture, marvelling at her tiny smile, her little fingers, her sweet toes. Time ceased to exist as I swam back into the past, remembering how it had felt to hold her in my arms, to feed her, to bathe her. My mind became dark, twisted, hysterical.

By the time I was all cried out, I realised evening had already come.

I shut the album with a snap, replacing it in my bedside cabinet. Despite my intentions, no way could I take one of those photos to show Toby. Later perhaps.

Did I say I was all cried out? As I drove towards Toby's flat, I could barely see the road ahead, my eyes were so full of tears.

***

11

The Truth Will Out

I'd bottled up my emotions for too long. By the time I got to Toby's flat, the sobs hadn't let up for the entire length of the journey, meaning Toby found a tear-soaked mess outside his door when he answered my knock.

He'd never seen me cry before, and I think it shocked him. To Toby, I'd always been Megan Copeland, ever composed, not the type for easy tears. He took one look, pulled me inside his flat, and shoved me onto the sofa while he poured a glass of wine and opened a can of beer for himself. Then he wrapped his arms around my shoulders, squeezing tightly, before handing me the wine and sitting beside me. I downed it in two, my need for an alcoholic hit desperate by then. My head pillowed on his shoulder, I didn't speak, not at first, too content in relishing his body against mine. The silence stretched between us, until at last he spoke.

'Talk to me. What's up?' The concern in his voice tore into me.

I'd never been good at preamble; better to dive straight in with the news. 'I've got something to tell you. It's not going to be easy.'

'I'm listening.'

Crunch time. I drew in a deep breath. 'Remember the time, the one time, when we... you know. When we had sex.'

He pulled back, studying my face, his expression wary. 'Yeah, sure. Why bring it up now?'

'I had your baby.' Too blunt by far. Stunned confusion washed over his features, every one of which I'd kissed that night so long ago. When he didn't respond, I added, 'We didn't use anything. I'd hoped my safe period would be enough, but obviously not.'

He didn't say anything for a while, a long moment that opened up a gulf of tension between us. Then he swallowed hard. 'Why have you never said anything before?'

'You'd gone to London. I didn't have a clue how to get hold of you.'

'Did you try?'

'No. I was one of many for you back then. You'd forgotten all about me by the time you left for university.'

'And afterwards? When I came back to Bristol?'

I wiped tears from my face. 'I'd buried it deep inside.'

'I don't know what to say.' I noticed how pale he'd gone. Then came the crunch question. 'What happened to the baby?'

The words wouldn't come out, not yet. I had to work up to revealing the painful truth. Maybe I did have a knack for preamble after all. I chose to ignore his question.

'I suppose I could have tracked you down somehow, but it came as such a shock, discovering I was pregnant. I didn't know what to do, whether you'd be interested. Besides, I didn't find out until I was quite far along.'

'I'd have been interested. I may have played the field back then, long and hard, but I'm not a total bastard.' Did he resent me not telling him? With hindsight, I didn't blame him. Back then, my dread of his possible rejection had played a large part in my silence.

'You didn't answer my question. What happened to the baby, Megan?'

'Can I tell you this my own way?' I poured myself more wine. 'I'm not ready to get to that bit yet.'

'Go on.'

'I found out I was pregnant that autumn and had the baby the following February.'

'How did your mother react?'

I smiled, remembering. 'She was shocked, even angry at first; she thought her bookish daughter must still be a virgin. Lectured me about being, careless, as if I didn't already realise that.

But then...' I savoured the memory, recalling how Mum's concern had soothed me. 'Once she'd got over the shock, she hugged me, told me everything would be all right. It was the best feeling in the world, knowing she'd be there for me.'

'You were worried she wouldn't be?'

'Yes. What with her being so wrapped up in Chloe, and not having taken much notice of me for years. And Mum had her mental health issues, don't forget. Remember when you came round after school one day and she was so weird and flaky? At the time I got pregnant, though, she was in one of her stable periods.'

I took another gulp of wine. 'The fact Mum's always loved babies helped. Once she got over the shock of finding out she'd be a grandmother, she warmed to the idea. We discussed names, went shopping for baby clothes together; we were building the closeness I'd always craved.'

'How did Chloe react? Not well, I imagine.'

'She didn't like it one bit.' I told him about her jealousy, the spiteful comments. We were approaching the hard part. I steeled myself to get through it.

'Alicia was born and she was so beautiful, such a doll; I intended to be the best mother ever.'

'You'd make a great mum.' Toby's words poured balm on my bruised soul. He smiled, which lightened the tension in the room. 'And thank goodness Alicia didn't resemble me. Can you imagine a baby with something this gross?' He tapped his hooked nose, and I laughed.

'Mum was over the moon as well,' I continued. 'She held Alicia at the hospital, saying she looked just like me when I was a baby. I realised my mother did love me after all. She might prefer Chloe but she cared about me too.' My voice cracked at the mention of my sister. 'I should have realised. I already knew what Chloe was capable of.'

Toby's expression turned puzzled. 'What do you mean?'

'Remember Pepper, my big fluffy tortoiseshell cat?'

He looked surprised. 'Vaguely, yes, but I don't see...'

'I came home one day and went upstairs to check on Alicia.' The emotions flooded through me, leaving me sobbing again. I edged closer, a silent plea for him to hold me again, and he didn't disappoint. My head on his chest, I inhaled his scent deeply. If I could, I'd have stayed there forever.

'What happened?' His voice against my hair was gentle.

I gulped back tears. 'Pepper had gone to sleep on Alicia's face. Her fur suffocated my baby.'

'Jesus, Megan. I'm so sorry.' Toby's arms wound round me again. 'How old was she when she died?'

'Nine weeks.'

'Christ. I've heard of cats sleeping on top of babies; never knew if it was just an urban myth. But what does Chloe have to do with this?'

'She lied about her whereabouts that morning and got Mum to back her up. I only found out recently. That's why I'm telling you all this.'

'But why? Why would she lie?'

I drew in a deep breath. 'Because she deliberately put Pepper into Alicia's cot.'

Shock flew into his face. 'Megan, that's quite an accusation. Okay, so the two of you don't get on, but even so… to accuse her of killing your child? She must have been, what, fourteen… fifteen at the time?'

I'd never kidded myself he would accept the truth straight away. 'Fifteen. I wouldn't have said anything if I wasn't certain. Mum finally told me about the lies. You've got to believe me.'

He frowned. 'It's not like you to make wild allegations.'

'I have no proof. None. All I have are my gut instincts.'

'I've never really got to the bottom of why you hate Chloe so much. You say finding out she lied about her whereabouts all those years ago is a recent thing. You've always had a downer on her though. Why?'

I told him how, as a child, Chloe had bullied other kids. 'She never had any friends and if she did bring someone home, they never came back. Not hard to see why. A couple of times I'd caught her doing stuff to them. Bad stuff, I mean. One time she had another child backed up against our garden shed, and she was hitting her. The kid looked terrified. What's more, the expression on Chloe's face – it scared me, Toby. As if she was in her element, unable to get enough of hurting the other girl.'

Another frown. 'Isn't such behaviour quite common? Kids bullying other kids? Doesn't make them grow up into murderers or psychopaths. I don't see where you're going with this.'

Please believe me, I prayed silently. 'Like I said, it wasn't a one-off. She could be cruel to animals too. She killed the neighbours' rabbit, I'm sure of it.' I decided not to mention my suspicions over the murder of her ex's former girlfriend. Too easily dismissed as coincidental, especially given Toby's scepticism. Instead, I continued my rant. 'And she always seemed so cold, never wanting affection, pushing me and Mum away if we tried to hug her. Like even the smallest amount of human contact was repulsive to her.'

'Yeah, I remember her as one cold fish. Although she could put on an Oscar-winning act when she wanted to.'

He meant sex. My mind shied away from the idea of them in bed together. 'That's how Chloe operates, don't you see? She's sly. Always makes sure nothing can ever be traced back to her, along with being brilliant at acting, all big eyes and innocent looks. She has a real dark side, but people can't believe she's capable of doing anything wrong.'

'You sure this isn't just a bad case of sibling rivalry, Megan?'

Christ. His scepticism hurt.

'I still don't buy her being behind your baby's death. I can't help wondering whether grief has led you to twist the whole thing way out of shape.'

His words sliced through me. *Your baby*, not *our baby*. They hurt, as did my failure to convince him. Why was I the only one to recognise how twisted my sister was? Not that persuading Toby of Chloe's guilt would achieve anything; I'd never be able to prove any of this. All I could hope for would be to stay one step ahead of her scheming.

I stood up, in need of time alone after the emotional roller coaster I'd been on. 'Time I got going.'

Toby also stood up, reaching out his arms for a hug. He gave me a sheepish smile. 'I need to get going too. I'm meeting some friends in half an hour. We should go for a curry again sometime.' His voice lacked warmth however.

I nodded. 'I'd like that. I'm sorry if what I said came as a shock. Maybe I should have told you before.'

'Yes, you should have.' His face looked pensive. 'Can't wrap my head around it.'

'I get that.' I smiled, despite how I felt inside. 'See you soon.'

Outside, the night wind whipped cold and fierce against my face. In need of fresh air and thinking time, I didn't drive home, not at first. Instead, I walked, not caring where, replaying Toby's reaction to having been a father in my head, his refusal to understand how warped Chloe was. Everything spiralled round and round in my brain, and I wondered whether I'd done the right thing in telling him about Alicia. On the plus side, I no longer had to fear Chloe's threats on that score. Besides, it was too late to seal the worms I'd released back in the can.

At last, I returned to my car and drove home.

***

Later, I was preparing for bed when my mobile rang. I glanced at my alarm clock; it was eleven pm and I couldn't think who'd be calling at that time. When I picked it up, Toby's name was on the screen. Once I answered, his voice, high and agitated, sounded in my ear. A torrent of words followed, forcing me to interrupt.

'Hold on a minute. Slow down, Toby. Your flat's been burgled?'

The sound of a deep intake of breath reached me. 'Yes. Found out when I got home after seeing my mates. Nothing's been taken, as far as I can tell. The place is a mess though. Whoever did this – it was personal.'

'What do you mean?'

'They trashed every room. Smashed crockery, ripped pictures off the wall, the works.'

'What have the police said?'

'They're sending someone round in the morning. Seems it doesn't qualify for their attention any sooner.' He gave a bitter laugh. 'I'll need to get my door fixed. Whoever it was, they broke the latch. Not surprising; it was old and flimsy. Been meaning to get a new one for ages.'

'God, Toby. I'm sorry. Any idea who could have done this?'

'No. But whoever it was, they're pretty screwed up.'

Should I risk saying what was on my mind? *Go for it*, I told myself.

'You don't think…' I hesitated, remembering his earlier defence of my sister. 'That Chloe might be responsible? Wait a minute,' I said, as I heard the denials issue in my ear. 'Please, just hear me out. I know you think I'm too hard on her. But you don't know my sister the way I do. She's twigged that James is interested in you. That won't sit well with Chloe, believe me.'

'What are you saying? That she trashed my flat out of jealousy? As a warning?'

'Yes. I doubt she thought it through, just acted out of sheer spite. I'm betting she's mad because James isn't succumbing to her charms, and she sees you as part of the reason. In Chloe's world, you're standing between her and what she wants. And Chloe can't bear that.'

'God. You're serious.' I heard the shock in his voice. 'You really think she's behind this.'

'Think about it. Who else would have done something like that, if you're right and it's personal? I realise you don't want to think badly of her. But it makes sense.' Silence from the other end of my mobile. 'Don't you agree?'

He huffed out a breath. 'You might be right, although Chloe's probably more interested in James's money than the man himself. This though? To wreck my flat? I find that hard to believe.'

'I don't.' My tone was firm, decisive, leaving Toby in no doubt about my opinion. 'Remember what I said about Chloe having a dark side? Your flat getting trashed fits in perfectly with the kind of person she is.' Concern edged into my tone. 'You need to be careful she doesn't take things further. That she doesn't hurt you far worse.'

***

12
The Comfort He Offered

James took in the view over Bristol's Downs from his flat, Toby Turner hammering through his head. *I'm here if you change your mind*, his latest text had said, the accusatory tone of their last meeting gone.

God, he yearned to call Toby, wrap himself up in the comfort he offered and let him wash away the pent-up guilt and shame. Could Toby work such high-level miracles? Too much to expect, possibly. Should he be considering dumping all his angst on some man whose agenda might only include casual sex?

The answer was yes. His life threatened to overwhelm him. Chloe and her goddamn persistent pursuit, his suffocating marriage to Charlotte; it was all too much. He'd lost his bearings and only one person held the power to find them for him.

No more bullshit. He needed Toby. Even if they only went for a drink, his presence would take the edge off his angst. And if the opportunity for more arose, maybe he'd go with it this time.

He reached for his mobile. He'd call Toby and arrange to get together, before he had time to persuade himself otherwise.

To James's relief, Toby agreed readily enough to meet, although he sounded somewhat guarded. Was it his imagination or did Toby's tone become less cautious as the phone call progressed?

Minutes later, he'd finished the conversation, only then noticing how his heart was hammering. They'd be meeting, for better or for worse, at eight the following evening at the Cambridge Arms in Redland.

***

The next day crawled by, every minute laden with expectation, hope, anxiety. That evening James arrived at the Cambridge Arms at five to eight. Toby strode in a minute afterwards. One lop-sided grin from the man and James felt certainty hit him. He'd done the right thing.

An awkward moment flashed between them before James gestured towards the bar. 'What'll you have?'

'Pint of Theakston's please… for a change. Thanks.'

Once they got seats at the back of the pub, Toby took a sip of his beer, before leaning in closer. 'It's good to see you.' He looked away, seemingly unsure how to go on. 'After the last time, I didn't think we'd ever meet up again. You were pretty angry. Mind you, so was I.'

Discomfort prickled under James's skin, despite the anticipation of earlier. Would he be able to handle things if Toby came on to him a second time? He realised Toby was waiting for an answer. 'Yeah, I was angry. Thrown off balance, more like. What did you expect? I'm not used to men giving me the vibe. This isn't easy for me.'

A small grin tugged at Toby's mouth. 'So you've decided to stop pretending. At last.'

'What happens now?'

'We take things slowly. Find out where this leads us. That good with you?'

'Fine.'

'Talking of where this leads… how about drinks at my flat?' Toby grinned. 'Don't give me that deer in the headlights look. I said drinks and that's what I meant. We're taking things slowly, remember?'

James drained his beer. 'Let's get out of here.'

Toby's flat was close by. Silence settled between the two men as they walked, James wondering why it had taken him until his fifties to get to the point where something other than a one-night stand was on the cards. Why he'd waited so long, denied himself so often. Damn his Catholic guilt.

***

Back at Toby's flat, James pushed him up against the wall as soon as they got through the door, his hands cupping Toby's face. As their lips met, something out of kilter in his life finally clicked into place. No more doubts, not with this man. Toby's mouth against his own felt right. His body, pressed against James's, promised something equally good.

Eventually he pulled back. Toby stared at him, bemused. 'Wow. Whatever happened to going slow?'

James cocked an eyebrow. 'You really want that?'

'Hell, no,' grinned Toby. 'Screw going slow – fast is good!'

Somehow, he couldn't remember how, they made it into the bedroom, ending in a contest as to who could strip their clothes off the fastest. Then they were on the bed, Toby's erection pressed against his own. The delicious touch of skin against skin at last, as a question gathered force in James's mind. He'd need to lay his pride on the line to ask it. They had all night though. Talking could wait.

***

Much later, the question got asked. Answered too.

'No way is this a casual fling, at least not for me,' Toby said, his head on James's chest. 'I know a good thing when I find it. Recognised you as such the first time I met you, but you were too busy denying what was happening… I found it damned frustrating. I couldn't get my head around it.'

'Around what?'

'That you might mean more to me than just a quick roll in the hay. I'd been quite the player before we met, you see. With both men and women.'

Dark jealousy stirred in James. He suppressed the emotion, not wanting to unleash his inner control freak.

'But not anymore. I don't know how this will play out, but I'm putting all that behind me. I'm not going to fuck around anymore.'

'You'd damn well better not.' Harsh words, belied by the grin on James's face.

'No regrets? No wishing yourself back in Straightville?'

'None. I'm making up for too many years of self deprivation.'

'Hmm. Sounds as if you've quite a backlog of sexual frustration to work through.'

'Want to help me with that?'

'Definitely. You won't wear me out anytime soon.'

'I'll take that as a challenge.'

'You'd better. So why the self deprivation? You've already said you've always known you preferred men. What were you trying to prove?' Toby shot him a knowing glance. 'More to the point, to whom?'

'My father.' Why had he spent so long trying to please a bigoted bully? None of it made sense. He'd been right when he said to Toby he was making up for his past deprivation. The man beside him represented a well in the desert and he intended to drink long and hard.

Toby nodded. 'Thought it might be.'

'How'd you figure that?'

'Couple of things you said when we chatted at Greens. I added them together and came up with a father who wasn't exactly liberal in his views.'

'You can say that again. When he was alive, he scared me shitless, even after I reached adulthood. It wasn't until after his death I bedded my first guy.'

'He was a bully, then?'

'With a capital B, as well as a complete dickhead. I wish to God I'd realised that sooner. But I didn't.'

'Did he hit you?'

'Just the one time, when he found out I'd kissed another boy. He beat the shit out of me. To him, having a gay son was an abomination, a travesty that reflected badly on him.' James remembered his father's hand cracking against his skull, the man's face reddened with rage, the harsh words he'd shouted. *Poof, pansy, queer.* Regret at having allowed the bastard so much sway over him flooded through his brain. Such a waste, and for what? Two failed marriages and only the occasional man to water his sexual wasteland.

'What about your mother? How did she react?'

'She agreed with his views. So when he went berserk at me for being with another boy, she supported him.'

'Even when he hit you?'

'Even then. She watched him punch the hell out of me without any attempt to intervene. She told me I deserved it, said my behaviour was unnatural, perverted. Maybe you get now why I tried so hard to convince everyone, including myself, I was straight.'

'Yeah, I do.'

'It's a shame I ever got married. I wish I'd discovered all this at a younger age. I regret both my marriages. Emma and Charlotte are two decent women who deserved better.'

'You do too. Better than a father who punched you because dogma mattered more than his son, or a weak, ineffectual mother. If the abuse you suffered made you put up barriers to survive, most people would understand that.'

'No more barriers. I need this.' He leaned in closer. 'There's Charlotte to consider. The last thing I want is to hurt her, although I've no idea how to avoid doing that. Make no mistake, Toby. I want you.'

'Me too. You get that, don't you? Okay, so I'm a lot younger than you are. I don't care. And I've fooled around in the past. Not anymore.'

Ah, yes. Their age difference. Him being fifty when Toby hadn't yet reached his thirties. Did it matter? They seemed in tune in so many ways.

James shrugged. 'So I'm older than you. What the hell. Doesn't matter to me, either. As for the fooling around – yes, that would bother me. A lot. Are you sure you want this? Me, a relationship, the works?'

Toby didn't respond immediately; James was oddly grateful as Toby weighed up his response. It meant his words held more substance when he did reply.

'Yes. You're what I want. I'm willing to find out where this ride takes us. If you are.'

***

13
Nil Carborundum Illegitimi

A my was late for the lunchtime drinks we'd arranged at the Watershed. I sipped my Coke and stared out of the window as I waited. With any luck, I'd racked up some good karma when I'd lent Charlotte a shoulder to cry on, because I needed to cash in those karmic chips with Amy when she did arrive. This time I was the one in need of a friendly ear.

A glass of red wine landed in front of me.

'Thought you could use some of the hard stuff. Saw you when I came in, nursing that Coke, looking like you'd found a pubic hair floating on top.'

Amy sat down opposite me. 'Before you ask, the wine's Italian. Sicily's finest, apparently, according to the barman. Nero D'Avola.'

'Thanks. I'd rather be in Italy, believe me.'

'So who's wormed their way under your skin this time? Chloe again?'

I nodded. 'She's fighting for top spot, along with a few others.'

Amy laughed. 'Isn't she always? You sounded pretty fed up when you called. Least I can do is listen if you want to bounce some crap off me. Get rid of whatever's bugging you.' She held her glass up for a toast. 'Nil carborundum illegitimi, as they say. Don't let the bastards grind you down.'

'I'll drink to that.' I clinked my glass against hers in a toast, the wine mellow and fruity as I swallowed.

'So what's Chloe done to piss you off?'

'No more than usual, I guess. Remember when I told you she's fixed her sights on my friend Charlotte's husband?'

'Yeah, I remember. Has she wangled her way into his bed yet?'

'I doubt it. She seems to have met her match in James.'

'Is that because Toby's now batting for both teams? You reckon they're an item, him and James?' Amy laughed. 'Now that'll annoy your sister, all right.'

'No, I don't think they're together. At least they weren't when I last caught up with Toby.'

'So what's holding them back? I'm guessing James is the one hesitating.'

'Toby said as much.'

'What about your mother? Has she still got a thing for this guy? God, he must be one foxy fifty-year-old.'

James's face strode into my mind, his blue-eyed charm teamed with a smile hot enough to melt steel. 'Yes. He's good looking, all right. As for Mum, when we've spoken on the phone, she always seems to slip in something or other about him. How hard he works, what a good boss he is. Thing is, Amy, at first it seemed like a silly crush, nothing to worry about.'

'And now?'

I shook my head. How best to describe the way Mum sounded? 'She's had her issues over the years, as you're aware. Bipolar disorder, mild schizophrenia. For a long time though, she's been relatively stable. But she seems to be slipping back. Little things, like she's talking more, speaking faster, isn't her usual self. She's wearing makeup, does her hair nicely, wears perfume.'

'Isn't that good? I mean, if she's suffered depression in the past?'

I braced myself. Explaining Mum's mood swings to someone like Amy, perennially on an even keel, wasn't easy. 'This is how she gets when she's nearing one of her manic phases. Most of the time, she's not bothered about her clothes or hair. When she's heading towards hyper, she slips into a higher gear, speeds up, lives life in overdrive.' Amy's expression told me she wasn't getting it. 'The thing is, if she's still mooning over James, and her mood is veering off course, she'll never cope if he finds out how she feels and turns her down. She'll swing the other way, into one of her lows.'

'Then do something about it. You can't rely on Chloe to help, so sort it out yourself. Talk with your mother, check if she's taking her tablets.'

'I've tried. I went round there last night, asked Mum about her medication. She swore I needn't worry.'

'Something tells me you don't believe her.'

'I didn't, no. Something felt off, but I couldn't put my finger on what. Maybe I imagined it, but she seemed to be talking more rapidly than usual. Almost babbling at times.'

Amy frowned. 'All you can do is keep an eye on her. Drag her to the doctor if need be.'

'You're right. I will.' Her words held truth. I'd visit Mum as soon as possible, either that day or the next, I promised myself. With any luck, Chloe would be out. Mum and I would talk, I'd get her to open up to me, see if she was keeping up with her medication. I'd do my best to persuade her a visit to the doctor might be in order, if necessary. I'd skirted around the issue for too long. Time to take control.

'I'll get another round in.' Trust Amy to drag me out of my self-pitying funk. I'd buy her a large glass of Sicily's finest in return.

As I waited at the bar, I mentally scrolled down my list of worries. Top was Mum, of course. Next came Chloe, and the malicious phone calls to Charlotte. Toby was third on the list.

My mind remained glued on him as I carried the wine back to our table. Toby's man-crush seemed pretty full on, leaving no room for even the slightest hope something might happen between us.

'Next.'

Amy's comment dragged me from my self absorption. 'What?'

'Don't tell me your mother and Chloe are the only things giving you a face like a smacked arse. I'm guessing Toby's still bugging you.'

I was stunned. 'Are you psychic or something?'

Amy laughed. 'I've known you a long time. You might think you're the strong, silent type, but you're not. You get this wistful look when your mind's running on Toby. Every time you get your hopes up. I've not seen it for a while, but it's back full-force.'

'I'm that obvious, huh?'

She laughed again. 'Clear as brand-new crystal.'

I sucked in a deep breath. 'I've told him. About Alicia.'

Surprise registered in Amy's face. 'What brought that on?'

I shrugged. 'I thought it was time he knew.' I didn't elaborate.

'Must have come as a shock.'

'It did. He says he needs time to get his head around the whole thing.'

'I'm guessing this torch he carries for James hasn't gone down too well with you.'

'It's stirred up a boatload of memories. The thing is, he doesn't appear to have even a smidgen of interest in me. If he ever did.'

'Oh, Megan.' Amy's voice held a wealth of pity.

'Would it really be so impossible? For Toby and me to get together at last?'

She reached over, took my hand, her skin cool against mine. 'Yes. If Toby's into guys right now, I mean.'

'What if he's just scratching an itch? You said it yourself; when we were at school, he chased every girl he saw.'

Amy remained silent. She wasn't convinced, I could tell. I tried again. 'Will you help me?'

Her expression turned puzzled. 'How?'

'This thing with Toby and men. I think it's just a passing phase. When he realises he prefers women, I want to be ready.'

'Meaning?'

'I need a new image. Make myself prettier, try a different look.' I'd struck the right note, I knew. Amy had been making subtle remarks about my appearance for years: the occasional offer of a makeover, shopping trips to choose new clothes. What better time to avail myself of her help?

'Don't do it for him. Do it for yourself.' Amy's eyes sparkled with purpose. 'We can do this, Megan. Reinvent you, I mean. I'll sort out your hair. I'm thinking a French pleat would look good on you. We'll get you something more flattering to wear than baggy trousers and oversized tops all the time. I'd kill to be as slim as you – why hide your figure? Perhaps you're right. Maybe you could hook Toby with a little effort.'

'He's not a fish, Amy.' She didn't flinch from my glare. 'I'll leave the man hunting to Chloe. She does it much better than I ever could.'

'I'm not suggesting you take dating tips from Chloe. All I'm saying is, if you want Toby, give it your best shot. And if he's not interested, then someone else will snap you up. Guaranteed. You're prettier than you think, especially now your skin's so much clearer.'

'So what are you suggesting?'

'We'll go shopping. Don't panic; we can get everything from charity shops. No need to splash the cash to look good. The rest is up to you.'

'Which is?'

'Spend more time with the guy, damn it. Sit opposite him in your new clothes, with your spruced-up hair. Listen to him when he bangs on about the wonderful James. Be there when he tells you he's moving on. With any luck, it'll be in your direction. If not...' She shrugged. 'Like I said, he's a fish. Plenty of them around.'

Amy's strategy appealed to the coward in me. It meant I didn't have to lay my soul on the line by asking him out.

'One thing, babe.' Concern in her tone. 'Don't get your hopes too high. I'd hate to see you get hurt.'

'Message received.' I decided to ignore Amy's words, however. In my head, I made plans. I'd call Toby tonight, check if he was free later in the week.

I'd worked my way to the last concern on my mental list. 'Charlotte, James' wife,' I said. 'I went to see her the other day. First time in ages.'

'How was she? Still struggling with depression?'

I decided not to mention the malicious phone calls. Or my suspicion Chloe was responsible. 'She's changed beyond all recognition. She used to be so strong, so vibrant. Now...' I spread my hands in a gesture of futility. 'I'm worried about her. She said she wished she were dead.'

'Shit, Megan. She needs help.'

'I suggested counselling. She practically bit my head off, chewed it up and spat it out again. I'm not sure what else I can do. Don't tell me it's none of my business. Someone wanting to kill themselves is everyone's business.'

'I agree. Any chance of talking to her husband, mentioning Charlotte's a bit down, without giving too much away? Prick his conscience into paying his wife some attention?'

I considered what Amy had said. Part of me loathed the idea of broaching Charlotte's depression with a man as emotionally constipated as James. And yet it had its merits. If James were a better husband, my friend might be saved from the black dog's bite. Moreover, the more time James spent with Charlotte, the less he had available for Toby. A win all round.

'I'll think about it.' But I was pretty sure I'd contact James, suggest lunch together. Try to shove the message through his repressed skull that his wife needed him.

Amy and I would hit the charity shops at the weekend, ready for another meal out with Toby. Italian perhaps, something hinting at a tad more romance than our trademark curries. Meanwhile, I'd visit Mum, get her on her own, suss out what was happening with her medication.

All systems go in sorting the worry list in my head. Nil carborundum illegitimi, indeed.

Or so I thought.

***

That evening, I got a call from Toby.

'Sorry I've not been in touch,' he said, after we'd dispensed with the usual greetings. 'Can I come over? If you're not busy, that is?'

I said yes, of course. Inside me, hope blossomed, all warm and delicious. It wasn't like Toby to call round; normally our get-togethers took place in the pub or at a curry house. Perhaps we were moving to something beyond being friends, sparked by my revelation about Alicia. Had he changed his mind about wanting to hook up with James? Despite my best efforts, I couldn't quell my rising anticipation.

Within half an hour, a buzz from my doorbell announced Toby's arrival. He stood before me, all rugged good looks and floppy blond hair, sporting the same ever-ready grin, and my heart melted. 'Come in,' I said, standing back to give him room to pass. 'I'll get the coffee going.'

Minutes later, I handed Toby a mug of Kenco, before sitting opposite him, trying to work out what had changed. Nothing about him outwardly appeared any different, yet a flicker of awkwardness sat in his expression, coupled with something akin to excitement. The former I put down to the bombshell I'd dropped about Alicia. Our dead child hovered in his eyes and in the nervous hitch to his voice. Neither of us mentioned her, however.

As for the excitement, it was as if someone had lit a flame in him. He seemed more alive somehow. My earlier hopes took a swift nosedive. Far more likely that Toby had hooked up with Mum's boss rather than experiencing a sudden desire to move our relationship into the romantic.

I was proved right.

After a while, Toby leaned against the back of the sofa, running one hand through his hair, his mouth quirked in his trademark lop-sided grin. 'I've got some news,' he announced, the excitement in his words barely suppressed.

'Hit me with it.' I steeled myself, fearing the worst.

'James Matthews. We're seeing each other.'

From somewhere, I dredged up my best happy-for-you smile. Before I could say anything, he continued. 'I wanted to tell you in person, Megan. After all, we've been friends for years, and I owe you that. I knew you'd be pleased for me.'

'Thank you,' I forced out. Time for a word of caution. 'But what about his wife?'

Toby's face sobered. 'From what he tells me, his marriage has struggled from day one. He's talking about moving out. A divorce.'

He must have noticed my pained expression. 'You're concerned about Charlotte.'

My poor friend. If James made good on his intention, I'd need to be there for her, offer her support. 'Will the two of you live together?'

'It's way too early for that. If James ends up telling Charlotte he wants a divorce, then he'll need to come to that decision on his own. I don't want to put pressure on him.'

I nodded. Impossible to shove aside my misgivings however.

He stood up. 'I should go. James is coming round to my place at nine.' He gave me a quick hug followed by a peck on the cheek. His trademark grin surfaced again. 'Make sure you let slip to Chloe that James and I are together, won't you? With any luck, that'll put paid to her relentless stalking.'

I shook my head. How little he knew her. 'It'll make her even more determined. You need to watch your back, Toby. Remember your trashed flat.'

* * *

14
Stalker

The next day, James took Senna, his German Shepherd, to the local park for their morning walk, as he always did. The air was fresh, cold, invigorating, as he sucked it deep into his lungs, willing its coolness to clear his head. Toby was on his mind – the touch, the taste, the feel of the man imprinted on his brain. All he wanted was to bask in him, in how right their fledgling relationship felt. Lost in his thoughts, he'd not walked far when he spotted Chloe Copeland. Cursing under his breath, he pulled Senna down a side path, pretending not to have seen her. Without success. From the corner of his eye, he saw her break into a run in his direction. He resigned himself to the inevitable.

'James! What a lovely surprise.' Her voice rang out, high and false, her breath coming harsh and fast with the exertion of running. She glanced at the dog with distaste, keeping her distance.

'What are you doing here, Chloe?'

'I've decided to take more exercise.' A flirtatious laugh. 'Thought I'd start with a daily walk.'

James eyed the height of her heels, but decided not to comment. 'This isn't close to where you live.'

She smiled, bright and utterly false. 'I'm going clothes shopping afterwards. Clifton has some lovely boutiques, don't you think?' As she prattled on, James wondered how she'd found him. He was damn sure he'd never mentioned to anyone in the office he walked Senna there every morning, meaning Chloe couldn't have heard about it from Tilly. Had she followed him, been tracking his routine? Apprehension stirred in his gut.

From somewhere he found his voice. 'You need to stop this, Chloe. No more turning up where I work or where I walk my dog. Get this through your head.' James angled his body closer, invading her space, the better to get his message across. 'Nothing can happen between us. Ever.'

'You don't mean that.' The false smile remained, but dark anger sparked in her eyes. 'We'd be good together. Don't you get that?'

James injected steel into his voice. 'I'm not interested in what you're offering. Stay away from me, you hear?'

He didn't catch the words she spat after him as he walked away, but the hostility in her tone was plain. Disquiet needled him, wouldn't let go. Had he been unwise to provoke her?

* * *

Once at his desk, he was aware of the foul mood that hung around him, and what had caused it.

Kerry Harris, his secretary, noticed it too. 'Something's crawled up your butt and died this morning,' she remarked.

James ran a frustrated hand through his hair. 'Chloe Copeland. If you're asking what's bugging me… it's her, Kerry. She's everywhere I turn. I've told her to back off, leave me alone, but she's too thick-skinned to get the message.'

Kerry laughed. 'It's perfect skin though. Along with the rest of her. Don't tell me you haven't noticed. You'd need to be blind or gay not to, neither of which applies in your case.'

'She's not my type. Even if I were single, which I'm not.'

'She's certainly very pretty. I've spotted her hanging around on several occasions.'

'Yeah. Like a bad smell.'

'But isn't she here each day to give her mother a lift home? Or is that just her cover story so she gets to hang out with you?'

'Put it this way. She never bothered with giving her mother lifts until she met me. Now I can't get rid of her. It's not just at work I see her, either.'

Kerry lifted an eyebrow. 'Meaning?'

'She follows me. I ran into her this morning in the park, for example. She was allegedly taking a walk. On a logical level, what she said sounded plausible enough. It didn't ring true though. She certainly hadn't dressed for exercise.'

Kerry laughed. 'I can imagine. I've noticed she favours skirts and heels, and pretty smart ones as well. No way does she shop in chain stores.'

'All funded by the latest sap she's managed to con, no doubt.'

'Aren't you being a bit harsh? The girl has a crush on you. She'll back off, given time, if you keep putting out the message you're not interested. The way she looks, she's bound to have guys flocking round her. She'll be chasing one of them soon, and you'll be ancient history.'

He didn't reply.

'You reckon there's more to it than that?'

'I'm not sure. Possibly.'

'Why? Has she said or done something?'

James sighed. 'Charlotte keeps getting these weird phone calls. Silent ones. The line's open, she knows someone's there, but they never say anything. It's spooking her out.' He paused, choosing his words. 'I did wonder if Chloe might be behind them.'

'But why? She'd have to be pretty messed up in the head to pull a stunt like that. And how would she get your home number if you've not given it to her?'

James shrugged. 'Probably through Megan, Chloe's half-sister. From her phone, I mean. Megan's friends with Charlotte, not exactly close, but they've known each other for years. I know,' he said, on seeing Kerry's look, 'I sound a bit paranoid, don't I? Chloe's starting to make me feel that way.'

'Probably just kids, playing pranks.'

'That's what I told Charlotte.'

'But you're not sure?'

'Not entirely, no. There's something about the girl. She seems so determined to get me. Like she's not used to not having exactly what she wants, when she wants it.'

Kerry laughed again. 'And you've reminded her you're married? Flashed your wedding ring at her?'

'She says she doesn't care.'

'Excuse me? I'm sorry to bother you.'

The timid voice at his office door broke up the conversation. Tilly Copeland stood there, looking at James as if he were a wolf and she a lost lamb. 'I've located that report you asked for.'

'Drop it on my desk, please.' He smiled at her. 'And thank you.' The fright in her expression relaxed somewhat.

Kerry spoke up. 'Your daughter seems very considerate, Tilly, giving you a lift home at night. Will she be doing that every day, or is it a temporary thing?'

Tilly beamed at his secretary's words. 'She's such a kind girl. It'll just be for the time being, until she finds a job. It's so hard to find work these days, even for Chloe, as talented as she is.'

Annoyance shot through James on hearing he could continue to expect the bare legs and high heels of Chloe Copeland outside his office every working day. Christ.

'That'll be all, Kerry, thank you. I'm going out. I won't be back today.' He didn't glance at either woman as he grabbed his jacket. Time for some air; too many damn females around.

***

Five minutes later, he was sitting in a local coffee shop, nursing an espresso, considering his options when it came to Chloe Copeland.

Was he being stalked? He'd heard about obsessed fans targeting Hollywood celebrities, convinced they were in love with them, but he was a greying fifty-year-old businessman, for Christ's sake. Stalking was an issue for other people, not him. Nobody would give the idea any credence anyway. The girl had a valid reason to be outside his place of work each day if she'd arranged to give her mother a lift home. He had no proof she was behind the silent phone calls to Charlotte. She'd never called him at work or on his mobile. There had been no letters. No threats. Meeting in the park one time hardly constituted stalking.

The espresso jolted through his veins, easing his tension a little. All the drama with Chloe, along with his messy marriage, was grinding him down. He needed to sort what to do about Charlotte, and soon, but without jeopardising his relationship with Toby. Too bad his boyfriend wasn't available tonight. An old school friend visiting from Germany, he'd said.

***

Once home, James made an effort with Charlotte, opening a bottle of wine, listening as she talked, suggesting they watch a play on television.

Later, in bed, she seemed happy, almost her old self; then, to his horror, her hands slipped into his pyjamas to stroke him. At first he froze, before gently pushing her away, the rejection softened with a kiss.

'I'm tired, Charlie. Let's get some sleep, okay?' She withdrew her hands as though they were burned, shame flaming her face red. Without a word, she closed her eyes, blanking him, her face shuttered.

James cursed silently. He'd hurt her, when that was the last thing he wanted.

***

After a while, Charlotte snored softly beside him. James felt his own eyelids growing heavy, until a plaintive whine reached his ears. *Senna*, he thought; damn, he'd forgotten to take the dog into the backyard to pee. Careful not to wake Charlotte, he swung his legs out of bed and pulled on his dressing gown, making his way into the hall.

Senna greeted him with another soft whine, moving into the kitchen at the back of the flat. James unlocked the door, the dog running past him to squat on the concrete outside.

As James stood watching, he became conscious of a soft rustle to his left, someone moving out of the shadows. Then Senna leapt into action, unleashing a furious volley of barks, his teeth bared in attack mode. A startled sound followed, halfway between a shriek and a curse, as a sharp pain, hot and fierce, stabbed James's left side. Gasps of shock ripped from his throat as he struggled to comprehend what was happening, his brain frozen in disbelief. As he slumped against the open door, grasping it for support, he became aware of someone running towards the back gate and disappearing through it.

With a groan, he reached out a hand, placing it over the source of the pain. His fingers encountered a rip in the fabric of his dressing gown, the edges of which were wet. When he withdrew his hand, the tips, glimpsed in the light coming from the kitchen, were stained red.

God. Dear God. He'd been stabbed. But by whom? And why?

As he attempted to stagger to his feet, get to a phone, the answer flashed into his mind. Prompted by the dark anger he'd glimpsed earlier in Chloe Copeland's eyes.

***

15
What Can I Do?

'Can you make lunch today?' Amy's phone call offered a welcome break from work. 'I've a two-for-one voucher for that French place in Cabot Circus. Want to give it a go?'

***

Later, when I entered the restaurant, I glanced at the plush decor, the fat leather menus stacked on the bar, the immaculately attired waiters, a sense of being out of my league overwhelming me. A few seconds of doubt passed before I remembered Mum's cheque. I could afford a splurge, especially if it came half-price.

'Hey, babe,' Amy said, shaking me from my thoughts with a hug. 'Let's go eat.'

Over steaming platefuls of beef bourguignon, thick with baby onions and button mushrooms, I filled her in with the news about James and Toby.

'So you were right about those two,' Amy said.

'I wish I weren't.'

'Charlotte will be devastated.' Amy picked at a chunk of meat. 'Mind you, Chloe won't be pleased either. I take it she knows?'

'Yes.' My sister knew, all right. The evening before, I'd called round to check on Mum. While there, I did as Toby had suggested, mentioning to Chloe about him and James. 'She didn't take it well,' I told Amy.

An understatement; I'd seen fire ignite behind my sister's eyes. The spite in her expression had scared me. As had her

102

words. 'He's a bastard,' she'd spat, fury in every word. 'He'll pay for preferring a man over me.' When I'd questioned her as to why her feelings had changed so rapidly, when James had spurned her all along, she'd told me to mind my own business and stormed upstairs.

'She frightened me, Amy. The hate in her eyes – it was petrifying. Chloe's not used to rejection.'

My friend reached over to squeeze my arm. 'She'll have to accept it, babe. What else can she do?'

The dead rabbit, along with the murdered girlfriend, intruded into my mind. As did Alicia. I pushed away my half-eaten plate of food, no longer hungry. 'I'm not sure. But I wouldn't put anything past her.'

***

Half an hour later, as we made to leave, my mobile vibrated in my pocket. When I took it out, Charlotte's name came up as the caller.

'Do you mind if I take this?' I asked Amy. She shook her head.

I kept my tone upbeat as I answered. 'Charlie? Hi, how are you doing?'

'Megan? I could use a friend right now.' Her voice sounded panicked.

I checked my watch. I needed to get back to work, but something in my friend's voice told me this couldn't wait. Hadn't I said I'd be there for her? Time to make good on my promise.

'What's wrong? Has something happened?'

A strangled gulp. 'James has been stabbed.'

'Oh, my God.' I grabbed my coat from the arm of the hovering waiter. 'I'll come right away. Will he be all right?' The words tumbled from my mouth.

'The doctors say so, yes. But I need you here, Megan. I can't deal with this on my own.'

Charlotte wrapped up the call, telling me which ward James was in at the Bristol Royal Infirmary. As I put on my coat, I gave

Amy a rundown of what had happened. 'I'll call you later,' I promised.

***

When I entered James's ward, I spotted him immediately, in the second bed on the right. Charlotte was to his left, her wheelchair as close as she could manage. As I came nearer, she raised her eyes to mine, exhaustion in her face, her cheeks stained with tears. *Poor Charlie*, I thought, compassion squeezing my heart. James lay against his pillows, his countenance pale but otherwise he looked okay. On hearing the scraping sound as I pulled up a chair, he opened his eyes.

'Good of you to come,' he said, his voice strong, confirming Charlotte's assertion he'd be fine. 'Charlie could use a friend right now.'

I leaned towards him, concern in my face. 'What happened? Do you know who did this?'

He shook his head. 'It was all so sudden. Besides, it was dark, and I was tired. I didn't see much.'

'What have the police said?'

Another shake of his head. 'Wasn't able to give a description. I doubt they'll catch whoever's responsible. Thank God it's just a flesh wound, nothing worse. Senna saved my life. Bless him, he's too soft to do more than bark and growl, but it worked. Whoever stabbed me disappeared fairly sharpish.'

'James thinks it was a woman,' Charlotte said.

I stared at her. 'Isn't it rare for women to do something like that? Commit knife crime, I mean?'

She shrugged. 'Unusual, yes, but not unheard of, from what the police have said.'

'I can't be sure,' James said. 'But whoever stabbed me made a noise as the knife struck home. An angry sound, full of hatred. And before that, when Senna went on the attack, a different sound, this one more startled. My impression was that they came from a female, not a man.'

'We should move out, James.' Charlotte's voice betrayed her fear. 'I don't feel safe living there anymore.'

I reached over, placed my hand on her arm. 'I can understand that.' What this meant for James and his plans to leave Charlotte, I couldn't be sure, but I prayed for her sake he wouldn't do anything hasty.

I turned my attention back to James. 'Do you think…' I hesitated, uncertain how to phrase such a loaded question. 'That whoever did this intended to kill you?'

He closed his eyes, his expression tired. 'There's no way of knowing. It's possible, yes. But why would anyone want to murder me?' His eyes met mine, and intuition told me he wasn't being truthful. He already had an idea whom his assailant was. I had no idea how to respond.

Charlotte looked all done in. 'Can I give you a lift home?' I asked her. Thank God she was in her lightweight, collapsible wheelchair.

She nodded. 'I got a taxi here. So yes, I'd appreciate that.'

After we'd said our goodbyes to James, we made our way to the hospital car park. As we got closer to my ancient Fiat, Toby's car caught my eye. He didn't see me, driving past us to park at the far end of the row of spaces. Thank God Charlotte had no idea who he was or what vehicle he drove. James must have called him, told him Charlotte was leaving, asked him to come.

'Let's get together soon,' I told Charlotte once I'd seen her inside her flat. 'I'll call you.'

***

Later, I phoned Amy, as promised. 'He's being kept in for observation, but will probably be discharged tomorrow. Charlie's a mess. Not surprising.'

'Was James able to give the police any clues?'

'Not really.' I hesitated. 'He thinks it was a woman though.'

'A woman?' Amy's voice held the same surprise mine had done earlier.

'I think Chloe's responsible, Amy.'

A sharp intake of breath sounded in my ear. 'Are you serious?'

'Deadly.'

'Why though?' Amy continued. 'Because she found out about James and Toby hooking up?'

'Yes. I wish to God I'd never told her.'

'You couldn't have known she'd do something like stab James.'

'I should have though. I grew up with Chloe. I know what she's capable of.' Her ex's murdered girlfriend intruded into my thoughts again; hadn't she also been stabbed? It wouldn't be the first time my sister had turned violent to get what she wanted. Or, in this case, because she hadn't.

'I reckon she was furious when James turned her down,' I said. 'Next she finds out it's because he prefers men. That won't have sat well with Chloe. She can't deal with rejection, with not getting what she wants.'

'So she stabbed him. In a fit of rage, I guess.'

Her anger of the night before sneaked into my brain. 'She's always had poor impulse control. Along with a tendency towards violence. Hell hath no fury, and all that.'

'Chloe must have felt scorned, all right.'

'He said his German Shepherd saved his life. She hates dogs.' A memory came back to me. 'A while back, the four of us met at Greens for a meal. While we were there, Chloe was trying it on with James, faking interest in his dog. James mentioned he always let Senna into the yard to pee last thing at night. He joked with us how Senna was a big softie, how he wouldn't offer much protection should someone attack him. Don't you see? She must have remembered that remark; used it to her advantage when it suited her. Chloe knew where James was guaranteed to be every night, when it would be dark, with few people around. The perfect opportunity to stab him. Except that both of them underestimated Senna.'

'You can't prove any of this, Megan.'

'You're right, but I called my mum this morning. While we were chatting, she mentioned Chloe went out last night after I left, how she came back late. The timeframe fitted with her being in Clifton when the attack took place. I don't have any proof, but it makes sense. James thinks the same, I'm sure of it.'

'Will you talk to the police?'

I shook my head, even though Amy couldn't see. 'It's all just conjecture. If the police can't prove anything, I'll get labelled the bad guy by Mum and Chloe. I don't give a damn about my sister, but Mum's a different matter.'

'What about James? Do you really think he suspects Chloe?'

I nodded. 'Yes. Whether he mentions anything to the police is another matter.'

Silence for a while. I was aware I'd pushed a lot onto Amy's shoulders, but I had nobody else to talk to. Toby was out of the question, following his comment about sibling rivalry.

'I'm worried,' I said at last. 'About Charlotte. Toby too.'

'You think she'll try to hurt one of them? Both even?'

'It's possible. Chloe doesn't work, and Charlotte's alone in that flat all day. When Chloe's had a chance to calm down, I'm betting she'll renew her campaign to get James. Or rather, his money. She can switch moods in an instant. Which means either of them could be her next target.' I remembered something else. 'Toby's flat was trashed recently.'

'You think she was behind that?'

'Who else would have a reason?'

'God. He needs to be careful. Chloe's more dangerous than I'd realised.'

'You're not wrong there.' My tone was flat. 'What can I do though? It's not as if I can warn Toby. He'll laugh in my face. And I can't warn Charlotte either, given how fragile she is.'

'Here's what you'll do.' Amy's voice was firm, decisive. 'You watch and wait. Keep an eye on Chloe, what she does, where she goes. If you're right, and she stabbed James, then she's rash, impulsive. Which means she'll slip up, make a mistake. Make sure you're there when she does.'

***

16
Secrets And Lies

The following evening, I went over to see Mum, keen to check on how stable – or not – she was. Despite what Amy had said about keeping an eye on Chloe, I'd prayed my sister wouldn't be there; I wasn't sure I could handle her machinations. My luck was out however. Mum even made a joke about it.

'Chloe seems keen to spend time with her daft old mum for once,' she said with a laugh. Behind her, as I hung up my coat, I spotted Chloe in the kitchen, opening a bottle of wine. Anger bubbled within me. Surely she knew Mum shouldn't drink alcohol, not with her medication?

I walked into the kitchen, drew out a chair, and sat down. An aroma of roasting chicken reached my nostrils; inside the oven I spotted a casserole dish. Mum bustled in, sitting beside Chloe, her face reddening as she clocked my gaze on the bottle of wine. As usual when embarrassed, she babbled.

'Chloe's treated us to some of that Merlot I like,' she said. 'Will you join us, Megan?'

Nice one, Chloe, I thought. I felt wrong footed. Any protest on my part would only come across as churlish. Nevertheless, concern for Mum compelled me to try.

'Should you be drinking? With those tablets you're on?'

Chloe snickered, a harsh unpleasant sound. 'Typical Megan. Not two minutes inside the door and already behaving like a party pooper.'

Mum took her side, of course. 'A small glass won't matter.' She shot me a pointed look. 'Chloe's right. You need to loosen up,

Megan. Have some fun once in a while.' She smiled, an obvious attempt to soften her words, but they still stung.

'You've heard what happened to James, I take it?' I asked her.

'Yes. His secretary, Kerry, told us the news.' Her face was pale, her expression concerned.

'I visited him in hospital yesterday. Charlotte was there too,' I added for emphasis. 'He's as well as can be expected.' I watched Chloe as I spoke.

'Thank God,' Mum said. 'I've been so worried about him–'

'Will he be discharged soon?' Chloe interrupted.

'What's it to you?' I countered.

Chloe's look hardened. 'Nothing. He was rude as hell to me when we last met.'

Mum reached into a cupboard for wine glasses. As her back was turned, I leaned towards Chloe so only she would hear. 'Nothing you didn't deserve, I'm sure.'

'Yeah, I was pretty damn mad at the time. Not anymore.' She smirked. 'I like a challenge. Especially when it comes in a rich package.'

Dumbstruck, I held my tongue. Once Mum had placed the glasses on the table, I seized the bottle of wine, pouring her a tiny measure, with more generous ones in the other two glasses. Small victories, I told myself, as I sat down. To my relief, Mum didn't say anything; her attention had already switched to my sister. Opposite me, Chloe prattled on, while I drew in some deep breaths, reminded myself to stay calm. Then something she said snagged my attention.

'Mum? Mum, you're not listening!' Chloe's voice was shrill, impatient.

'I'm sorry, darling. What were you saying?'

'I was asking you about James's wife.' So Chloe had meant what she'd said; she still had her sights set on him. Unease stirred within me as I recalled. Amy's comment: *Chloe's more dangerous than I'd realised.*

'He rarely talks about her. I've been so worried about him. We were all so shocked at work when we heard about the stabbing–'

'But what's his wife like? Focus, for God's sake! What is it with you today? I swear you're getting worse. How would you cope without me to look after you? I won't always be here, you know. One day I'll meet Mr Right and then what will you do?' She leaned in, spitefulness in her eyes. 'Maybe you'll have to live in a care home. With all the other crazy people.'

My sister's cruelty rendered me speechless. Hurt flashed across Mum's face. In her head, I knew she'd be making excuses for Chloe's behaviour.

'It's like I said. He rarely talks about her.'

'His wife being in a wheelchair must be hard on James,' Chloe remarked.

'Yes. But he's so good about everything. Never complains. He should be back at work soon–'

'She doesn't go out? Not ever?'

'Not from what I can make out. Kerry says Charlotte was quite the party girl before the accident. But now...'

'No life at all, then. She can't walk. She never goes out. I don't imagine they have sex anymore – don't look at me like that, you must have thought it too – so what's the point of her being alive?'

'God, Chloe.' Her spite had shocked me into speech at last. Even for her, that remark was insensitive, unwarranted.

My sister simply laughed. 'You're so easy to wind up.' She leaned closer towards our mother. 'What kind of life does the woman have? None. She's like an animal that needs to be put down, Mum.'

Shock hit me. Had Amy heard Chloe's remarks, she'd have been in no doubt who'd stabbed James. Or the danger she represented to Charlotte.

'Remember when Mum took that scruffy old cat Megan was so fond of to be put to sleep? After...' Chloe paused. 'You know.'

She'd crossed a line by referring to Alicia. I stood up, barely repressing my anger. 'I have to go.'

'Don't get all upset, Megan. Chloe didn't mean to hurt you, did you, darling? There's a chicken casserole in the oven. Why don't you eat with us?'

Should I? On the one hand, I'd had all I could take of Chloe's vindictiveness. On the other, I still wanted to gauge how Mum was. And if I stayed, I'd get a chance to discover how deep my sister's interest in James's wife ran. I sat down again.

Mum pulled plates from the cupboard, put them inside the oven to warm. 'We'll have a cosy supper at home, all three of us. Won't that be lovely?' Happiness rang out in her voice, and I was glad I'd not stormed out.

'Pour us more wine, would you, while I serve?' Her words were directed at Chloe. I eyed my sister as she tilted the bottle towards Mum's glass. 'Only a tiny amount,' I mouthed, too low for Mum to hear. A sarcastic grimace twisted Chloe's mouth, but she did as I asked, pouring an inch into Mum's glass before handing it to her.

It seemed my sister hadn't finished with James as a topic. 'I can't think why he doesn't get a divorce.'

'I don't imagine he'd want another one of those.'

Surprise registered in Chloe's face. 'He's been married before Charlotte? You never said!' She turned my way, her expression accusing. 'Neither did you.'

'Didn't I?' Mum spooned chicken in a thin sauce onto the plates. She'd most likely forgotten something from the recipe; the food didn't smell or look right and Chloe would be bound to comment.

Chloe speared a chunk of chicken. 'Spill the beans, Mum. How long was he married for? Who was she?' She pulled a face. 'I can't taste a bloody thing in this sauce.'

'I don't know a great deal. One of the girls at work told me. They gossip all the time about him. What with him being the boss and so handsome.'

'What did she say?'

'Only that he'd been married once before. They divorced, then later he met Charlotte. Of course, his first marriage came after...' Horror crossed Mum's face. I couldn't think what she meant, or why she'd stopped so abruptly.

'After what?'

'Nothing, Chloe.'

'Tell me. I'm curious. Did this girl tell you something else about him?' Chloe's voice was syrupy with manipulation.

'I shouldn't be gossiping about James.'

'What harm can it do? I won't tell anyone, I swear.'

'It's nothing. Really. More chicken?' Chloe's face turned sulky, but to my relief she didn't pursue the subject. I didn't doubt Chloe would prise it from Mum before too long, and when she did, I'd find out too. Maintaining secrets had never been Mum's forte, and I knew only too well how susceptible she could be to Chloe's persistence.

If she did know something she wasn't telling, I couldn't think what. Although I'd not seen much of Charlotte recently, we'd often talked about our lives during our evening classes. I couldn't recall anything she'd said about James before his first marriage. Whatever it was, it couldn't be that secret, not if it was the subject of office gossip, as it must be if Mum knew about it. So why was she holding back in telling Chloe?

We ate our meal, with me gauging Mum all the while. I didn't like what I saw. Her cheeks were flushed, and a light sweat glistened on her forehead. Was it a reaction between her medication and the wine, or because she was struggling to keep something hidden from Chloe? Her mood seemed more elevated than usual, her speech too quick, her laugh too ready. In the past, Mum's switch into manic behaviour had been marked, leaving no room for doubt. Tonight, I couldn't be sure, forcing me to realise that for most of the time, she operated in a chemically induced calm.

As she stacked our plates in the dishwasher, I edged her way, noting that Chloe was absorbed in studying her perfectly manicured nails. 'Mum,' I whispered, not wanting to attract my sister's attention. 'Is everything all right? With you, I mean? You're taking your medication okay?'

She remained stooped over the dishwasher, her eyes not meeting mine. 'You worry too much. I'm fine.'

'You're remembering your pills each day?'

'Of course.' Something in her tone told me she was lying. She'd never been any good at it. Worry clawed at me. The thing was, if she was veering off course with her tablets, how on earth could I get her back on track now I didn't live with her?

***

Afterwards, I spent a while in my former bedroom, retrieving some books I'd stored there. While doing so, I pondered the matter of Mum's medication. There had to be something I could do. But what?

On my way downstairs once I'd finished, I caught voices coming from the kitchen. I stopped to listen.

'Is this for real, Mum? You're not making this up?'

'I shouldn't have said anything. Far better to have kept quiet. Please don't repeat any of this.' Mum's tone held anguish.

So Chloe had managed to prise the gossip out of our mother. Even by her standards, it hadn't taken long.

'I won't tell anyone. You can trust me.' *Yeah, right*, I thought as I continued down the stairs and into the kitchen.

'Tell anyone what?' I kept my tone light. Both Chloe and Mum started, Mum's face guilty. As for Chloe, hers was smug. I didn't like what that might mean.

'Just some office banter,' Mum said, her face switching from guilt to panic. 'Nothing for you to worry about.'

***

She was lying again, of that I was sure, I decided as I drove home. Had Mum been passing on office gossip about Charlotte? Something Chloe could twist to her advantage?

Her cruel words about my friend came into my head. *She's like an animal that needs to be put down.*

***

17
Better Off Dead

I visited Mum again the next day, having phoned first to ensure Chloe wouldn't be there. Our conversation after I arrived did nothing to reassure me.

When she pulled open the door, her face was pale, with dark shadows smudged under her eyes. Her hair framed her face in an unbrushed mess. Love and fear squeezed my heart at the same time. She began talking the instant I walked into the hallway, her words firing out at a rapid pace. Unease prickled in my brain. As she prattled on about what her neighbour had said to her earlier, I waited, seeking an opportunity to cut in. When it didn't come, I placed my hands on her shoulders, forcing her onto one of the kitchen chairs. *Let me take care of you*, I thought. *Please.*

'I'll make some tea,' I said, urging myself to stay calm. Behind me, as I filled the kettle, spooned sugar into mugs, my mother carried on talking. This time she switched to James Matthews: what a great boss he was, how handsome, how kind. To my alarm, her words took a more sinister bent.

'We'd be so good together. Chloe's right; James needs a divorce. Once he's free…'

From the torrent of words coming from my mother's mouth, I gleaned her crush went much deeper than I'd realised. Frightened for the woman I loved so much, I abandoned all pretence of making us tea. I knew better than to challenge her delusions about her boss.

Instead, I tried a different tack. 'You look unwell, Mum. How are you sleeping?'

'Not great. I have such a headache, like you wouldn't believe. Honestly, I swear someone's using my skull as a concrete mixer…' Her words fell over themselves, so rapid was her speech, some more worrying than others. Among them, I detected ones that filled my soul with dread: *I guess I should expect this, what with not having taken a pill either today or yesterday.*

'Mum.' When she took no notice, I reached across the table, grasping her arm. Still no response. I raised my voice, my grip on her arm intensifying. 'Mum!'

The flow of words halted. My mother stared at me. She wasn't used to her elder daughter being assertive. Maybe it was a tactic I should employ more often.

I kept my tone gentle. 'Have you been skipping your medication?'

She dropped her gaze, giving me my answer. I pressed on. 'You know that's dangerous, right?'

Mum made a dismissive gesture. 'You fuss too much. What harm can it do to miss a dose now and again? Or if I take half a tablet instead of a whole one? Some days I don't bother taking anything, and I feel fine. Which means I can wean myself off the pills.'

Panic set in. 'Not without consulting your doctor.'

'He doesn't understand.' Her tone was pleading. 'When I'm on those tablets, everything becomes fuzzy, like I'm viewing the world through distorting glasses. That's not living, is it? Not the way it should be.'

'You need to take your medication. Otherwise you'll become unstable again. Why don't we go to Dr Baker together? I'll talk to him for you.'

'No.' Mum's tone was firm, which worried me. When she got like this, it was impossible to reason with her.

'Don't you see?' she continued, before I could formulate a response. 'I have to be chemical-free for James. Ready to be what he needs, what he deserves.'

I gawped at her.

'I've been so worried, what with him getting stabbed. It should have been me who cared for him afterwards, not his wife. That's what made me realise I had to get off my medication. So we can be together. Once he's filed for divorce, it'll be so wonderful between us. He's everything I've ever wanted, Megan.' She was lost in her fantasy world again, while I worked out how to get her to the doctor as soon as possible. One possibility presented itself. The night before, I'd phoned Charlotte, suggested we should catch up; she'd agreed at once, the eagerness in her voice making me aware how lonely she was. We'd arranged I'd call in after I'd visited Mum. With that in mind, I laid plans. The doctor's surgery was on the way to Clifton; I'd go in, ask to speak with Mum's doctor, stress the urgency of the situation. Either I'd arrange for him to do a house visit while I was there or I'd set up an emergency appointment and get her to the surgery by whatever means possible, even if it meant lying. Before the end of the day, or at the latest the next day, I was determined Mum would get the help she needed.

I let her talk on.

At the first opportunity, I stood up. 'I have to go,' I said, bending to kiss her cheek. 'I'll be back soon. Maybe later.' I smiled, so she'd have no idea of what I was planning. I loathed the thought of leaving her, but what choice did I have? She might go into a total meltdown if I called her doctor in front of her. I needed to be more subtle.

***

Back in my car, I placed the call, arranging to visit the surgery later that afternoon. The receptionist informed me that Mum's doctor could spare some time in between appointments if I went in after four pm and was able to wait. I agreed at once. That gave me a couple of hours with Charlotte, time I'd use to wind down, prepare myself for what might happen with Mum. Chances were she needed another spell in hospital. Emotion, hot and thick, welled up inside me at the thought, but I couldn't see any other option. At least in a psychiatric ward she'd get the help she so desperately needed. And I'd be there with her, every step of the way.

I love you, Mum. In my head, I spoke the words I rarely found the courage to say to her face.

Satisfied I'd done all I could, I drove over to the Matthews's flat in Clifton.

***

Charlotte looked better than last time, thank God. Still too pale, but she'd made an effort with her hair, and I detected a touch of eye makeup, a little lip gloss. 'You look lovely, Charlie,' I said.

'Come in. It's good to see you.'

'Likewise. How's James? I take it he's out of hospital?'

'He came home yesterday. Right now, he's back at the hospital, getting the wound cleaned and dressed, then he's running some errands.'

'Have there been any developments? With catching whoever stabbed him?'

She shook her head. 'I doubt the police will find who's responsible. Probably some druggie, intent on breaking in, not expecting to encounter James with Senna. I can't think of any other explanation as to why someone would stab him.'

'That sounds the most likely reason,' I said, taking care to keep my voice neutral.

We chatted, my eye straying frequently to the clock on the wall behind Charlotte. We talked about art, how work was going for me, the latest sci-fi series on television. Worry nagged at the back of my mind all the while, concern for my mother never far from my thoughts.

***

Before long, the clock showed three thirty. Time I got going. As the thought went through my head, a noise alerted me. Charlotte heard it too, her head swivelling in its direction. It was the sound of the back door to the flat opening, followed by footsteps in the kitchen. A frown creased Charlotte's forehead.

'I didn't expect James home so soon,' she said.

I was puzzled too. Those footsteps weren't those of a heavy masculine tread. Instead, they were barely discernible, as though made by a female. The handle to the living room door turned downward. The thick slab of wood edged open.

My mother appeared in the gap.

Shock drained the saliva from my mouth. At first I was unable to comprehend what I was seeing. Neither, it seemed, could Charlotte, her eyes wide and questioning. She'd never met Mum, could have no idea of who this intruder was. As for me, I was confused. Why hadn't Mum rung the doorbell? How had she come by a key to the back door? More to the point, why was she here?

I stood up, edging closer to Mum. Her eyes blanked me, their gaze focused only on my friend.

'Who…' Charlotte drew in a deep breath. 'Who are you? What do you want?'

Mum's reply was immediate. 'My name is Tilly Copeland. I'm your husband's fiancée.'

Astonishment washed over Charlotte's face. 'This is your *mother*, Megan? I don't understand.'

'Mum, please.' I walked over to her, took her arm, but she shrugged off my hand. Her appearance was even wilder, her hair more unruly, her eyes more manic. Love twisted my heart as I threw Charlotte a pleading glance. 'I'm so sorry, Charlie. She's not well, you see. Mum, you shouldn't be here. Let's go. I'll take you to–'

'No.' The word came out with brute force, the determination in her eyes stunning me. 'Don't think I don't know what game you're playing, Megan. You think I'm crazy. But I'm not.' She stepped closer to Charlotte. 'James and I are in love. We're going to get married.'

Charlotte's eyes raked Mum's face, her expression unreadable. 'Your daughter is right. Why don't you let her take you home?'

Behind Mum, I mouthed words at Charlotte: *Thank you. I'll explain later.*

Mum's eyes flashed with anger. 'James and I have history. We want to be together. He's worried about asking you for a divorce.'

'A divorce?' Charlotte spat the word out as if she'd found a cockroach in her mouth.

'I've told him there's no point in waiting any longer. We want to get married as soon as possible.'

Charlotte was silent. I didn't blame her, not after being accosted by a mentally unstable woman who'd broken into her home. Then she spoke, realisation in her voice. 'You're the one. You've been making those weird phone calls.'

'Mum, please,' I begged. 'Let's go home.'

She ignored me. 'I love him. We belong together. He'll go ahead with a divorce whether you agree or not.'

Charlotte's reply was calm, although her tone belied a hint of nerves. 'Why don't you sit down and we can talk?'

'He loves me. Not you, not anymore. We're going to be married.'

'You're wrong. He's my husband. He doesn't love you.'

I flinched. Unwise to attempt to reason with Mum in one of her manic phases. Before I could intervene however, she was talking again, as well as edging closer to Charlotte.

'You'd be better off dead.'

I recoiled. No way was that my mother speaking.

At that, I stepped in front of Mum, taking her by the arms. 'That's enough. Let's go.'

'Chloe understood,' Mum continued, as though I didn't exist, her gaze fixed on Charlotte. 'She's been looking out for me. Always so smart, my darling girl.'

Before I could stop her, Mum shoved me out of the way, her hand snaking out to grab a cushion from a nearby armchair. A second later, she'd thrown herself towards Charlotte, pressing the cushion over her face.

Charlotte reacted with a scream muffled by the thick foam, her upper body jerking upwards with the force of her struggle to drag air into her lungs. Mum, possessed by her mania, exhibited an unexpected strength of her own; I found myself hit by a flailing fist as I attempted to drag her away. My pleas for her to stop went unheard as I struggled to gain control; panic swept over me as to whether I could subdue her. Then Charlotte scored a fierce jab under Mum's ribs, causing her to ease her pressure on the cushion. As she did, the combined effort of Charlotte's and my struggles caused the wheelchair to become unbalanced, and the weight of my friend's body pulled it over. Charlotte toppled onto the floor.

The crash sounded throughout the room. Raw anguish tore from Mum's throat, coupled with Charlotte's agonised gasps for breath that sounded in my ears.

Before Mum could get to her feet, I threw myself on her, pinning her body to the ground. I felt the fight drain from my mother, as though she held nothing in reserve; what she'd done so far must have exhausted her energy. Her eyes were glassy, unfocused. She leaned over and vomited onto the carpet, causing a sour stench to waft into my nostrils. Then she curled into a foetal huddle, her body rocking from side to side. Harsh guttural moans issued from her mouth. A line of spittle hung from her lips. For now anyway, the fight was gone from her.

I pulled myself off my mother. My friend needed assistance. I dragged her wheelchair upright again, the effort causing sweat to break out around my neck. I stared into her pale face. 'Charlie, are you all right?'

She nodded, although she looked as if she too might vomit. 'You should call an ambulance. Your mother needs a doctor.'

I couldn't help but agree. Memories of past psychotic episodes on Mum's part, in which the police had sometimes proved necessary, haunted my head. I pulled out my mobile, placed the call, explained the situation.

'Is she still violent?' the male paramedic on the end of the line asked.

I glanced at my mother. Her eyes were tightly shut and she continued to rock, back and forth, an endless flow of words, all undecipherable, issuing from her mouth. 'Not right now. But I can't guarantee she'll stay that way.'

After that, things moved swiftly. Not long after my call, the ambulance arrived, and with it two police officers, one male, one female. I stayed silent, paralysed with worry as the man spoke to Charlotte, got her version of events. The female officer, meanwhile, concentrated on Mum, her voice soft, understanding, asking her all sorts of questions, some of which my mother could answer and some she couldn't. Mum gave her name as Tilly Matthews. When asked why she'd come to the flat, she floundered, saying she'd had a reason, a compelling one, but what it was, she couldn't remember. The police officer spoke to her reassuringly all the while.

The male officer sat beside me. 'You're Tilly's daughter, right?'

'Yes. And her surname's not Matthews, it's—'

Mum interrupted, her voice high and clear. 'I remember!' The words spoken in triumph. 'Why I came here tonight.'

'Why was that, Tilly?' the female officer asked.

Mum pointed at Charlotte. 'To set James free. From *her*. She'd be better off dead, don't you see?'

***

18

Two Victims

My mother, my meek, gentle mother, had attempted to murder someone. The facts simply didn't compute in my head, despite the knock on my door the night before. Two female police officers had stood outside, their intention to follow up on Mum's attack on Charlotte that afternoon.

'You'd better come in,' I said. What else could I do?

I listened to what they had to say. My mentally fragile mother was being detained in a psychiatric facility. Although she remained somewhat incoherent, she'd told the police she entered the Matthews's flat using the spare key hidden under a plant pot in the back yard. She'd repeated how James was keen to divorce Charlotte and marry her instead. She had reiterated her belief that his wife would be better off dead.

My responses to the police probably weren't much use, shocked as I was. One question particularly riled me.

'Of course I didn't know she was planning something like this! If I had, don't you think I'd have got her some help?' I was aware my tone sounded acidic, but why was I being asked such idiotic questions?

The police officer made some patronising response and ploughed on. How long had Mum been on her current medication? Was she generally stable? Had I been aware of her fixation on James Matthews?

I admitted I had.

'I thought she just had some harmless menopausal crush. At first, anyway.' My words were laced with guilt.

The next question floored me. Did I know where my mother was the night Mr Matthews was stabbed, between eleven pm and midnight?

Once I'd established the date, I was forced to admit I couldn't say for sure, my despair reaching new depths. Then I remembered what I'd discovered about Chloe's movements that night. 'My sister can confirm my mother was at home, in bed. Chloe went out that evening. She spoke briefly to Mum when she got back around twelve o'clock.'

* * *

Later, I tried to call Chloe, without success; all I got was her voicemail. In a way, I was relieved not to have to deal with my sister when my emotions were so raw. From what the police had said, I knew they intended to speak with her as well about Mum, so one way or another my sister would hear what had happened. And Chloe could corroborate what I'd said about our mother's whereabouts.

I didn't sleep that night. I lay in bed, trying to make sense of everything and failing completely. The scene played itself over and over in my head: Mum grabbing the cushion, her attempt to stifle the woman she viewed as her rival, the stench of Mum's vomit. My head hurt; if I'd not witnessed the attack with my own eyes, I'd find it impossible to believe.

* * *

The next morning my eyes were gritty and my skin was chalky with exhaustion. I felt like shit, but somehow I had to shove all that aside. My mother needed me.

I went as early as possible to visit her.

Before her doctor allowed me onto the ward, he warned me she wasn't in good shape. He murmured platitudes about how they were working hard to stabilise her, sort out her medication, get her on an even keel. As if my mother were a sinking ship. In a way, she was.

He explained something else as well. My mother's obsession with James: erotomania, the doctor called it. No menopausal crush, this, but her schizophrenia reasserting itself. Sufferers persuaded themselves the loved one returned their feelings, despite all evidence to the contrary. Her fixation on James made more sense. My mother had become a victim of her own brain chemistry.

Shock was my first reaction when they eventually let me see her. Her skin rivalled mine in its pallor. Her hair hadn't been brushed. Strangely, she seemed aware of it, her hands repeatedly moving over the grey strands in a futile attempt to stroke them into place. Her fingers moved as though pushing themselves through treacle. She was slow, lethargic, a clockwork toy winding down.

'Mum?' I reached out to take her hand, ease it away from the ceaseless smoothing of her hair. 'It's me, Megan. It's okay. Everything is going to be fine.' Platitudes I didn't dare to believe.

She didn't say a word all the time I was there, despite my efforts at conversation. I sat with her, holding one of her hands, while the other continued to fuss with her hair. Perhaps, in her broken mind, it was James's hand.

* * *

Two hours later, I left, promising I'd be back soon.

I tried calling Chloe again, but she still wasn't answering her phone. I left several messages, each one increasingly irate, and after the fourth attempt, I drove over to the house. Her car was gone. She was probably out spending Mum's money, I reflected sourly.

Back home, work seemed impossible, despite my backlog. Getting some sleep would have been the sensible thing but I gave up trying after a pointless hour in bed. I couldn't shut off my brain. Round and round, it looped through the events of the day before. My mobile lay on the bedside table, awaiting Chloe's call, which never came. Mum's blank expression tormented my mind for the rest of the afternoon.

* * *

My phone rang just after six pm. Chloe, at last, surely. But it wasn't her number coming up on my phone, but an unknown one.

'Hello?' How breathless, how distracted, I sounded. The police, I decided, wanting to interview me further, or else news from Mum's doctors.

I was wrong on both counts.

'Megan? James Matthews.'

A brief silence, while I tried to shift my brain into gear.

'I got your number from Charlotte's phone. I hope you don't mind me calling.'

Polite as ever. Not a social call though, obviously.

'No, of course I don't mind. I'm so sorry about what Mum did. How are you?'

'Me? I'm okay, although I still can't remember much about the stabbing other than what I've already told the police.' So he'd not said anything to them about Chloe. I didn't know whether to be relieved or dismayed.

'How's Charlie?'

'She's not great. The reason I'm calling, Megan…'

'You want me to visit her. See if I can help.' I'd been intending to go anyway.

'Yes. If you could spare the time. She's asked me to move out.'

His words floored me. 'She doesn't want you there? Not after what happened. Why not?'

'She says she doesn't feel safe, not after me getting stabbed, followed by what happened with your mother. She's moving out as well, as soon as she can find somewhere that's disabled friendly. She blames me, you see.'

'What for?'

'We've been having marital problems for a long time.'

'But why ask you to leave? I don't understand.'

'She's reacted badly to Tilly's attack on her. She insists I must have encouraged your mother, done or said something to make her think I loved her. I didn't, believe me.'

'I know.'

'There's more. Charlotte says she needs space to reconsider our relationship. She knows I've met someone else, you see.'

So he'd told her about Toby. Poor Charlotte.

'That's when she demanded I leave. Hardly surprising, I guess.'

'You've moved out already?'

'This morning. I'll be staying in a hotel tonight, but I've found a rental flat down at the Harbourside. For now, anyway.'

'What about Charlotte? Will she be able to cope alone?'

'She's always had carers to help with certain tasks: showering, getting dressed. If she gets a flat that she can adapt to her needs, she can manage most other things on her own.'

'And Senna? Who's walking him?'

'Local pet service, twice a day. He'll be fine. About Charlotte…'

'I'll go round this evening.'

I heard him exhale. 'Thanks. I knew I could rely on you.'

'Anytime.'

'How is your mother?'

The abrupt change in the conversation threw me off balance. I sucked in air in an effort to get a grip on myself. 'Okay, I guess. She's where she needs to be, in a psychiatric hospital. I'm so sorry about what happened. I was aware she had a thing for you–'

'You knew?' He sounded surprised, although he shouldn't have been. To me, my mother's interest in him had been blatant, but I'd bet money on James not realising the effect he had on women.

'I saw the way she looked at you that night at the wine bar.' I considered what to say next. 'I didn't think too much of it. I was more bothered about what Chloe intended where you're concerned.' Why not be honest? It seemed to me having a mother with murderous intentions swept away the norms for polite conversation.

'Your sister. Yes, I had quite a problem shaking her off.'

'I'll bet you did.'

James laughed, a hollow sound, clearly trying to make a joke of it. 'Like mother, like daughter, they say. You're not going to follow suit and develop a thing for me, are you?'

I laughed in return, a similarly empty one. Rarely did I find anything about my sister amusing. 'Erotomania, Mum's doctor calls it. She fancied herself in love with you, decided to come off her pills alone, with no doctor, no help.'

'She was on medication prior to the attack?' Mum had been stable at the time when James hired her. He probably hadn't been aware of her mental history.

'Do you mind me asking, Megan, what for?'

I outlined Mum's problems briefly. 'She believed she'd be able to marry you if she weaned herself off her pills,' I finished.

'Without medical supervision? That's never going to end well.'

'No. As your wife can testify. Mum coming off her medication without supervision must have triggered the violence.'

'The attack on Charlotte seems so out of character. In the office, your mother came across as very quiet, reserved. Not violent in any way.'

'She never has been. Oh, she'd get her highs, when she'd spend money she didn't have, go without sleeping, talk incessantly, but nowhere near as bad as some sufferers.' Had I been lulled into a false sense of security by the seeming mild nature of Mum's illness? By the long period of stability on her medication?

'Chloe didn't try to do anything? Get help for her?'

'Not a thing. You can't tell me she didn't notice something was wrong.' Bitterness oozed from my voice. 'Charlotte's going to be all right, isn't she, James? I'll do what I can to help, but won't she struggle living alone, given her depression?'

'I'll speak with her carers; get them to go in more often. But if you could check she's okay, Megan, visit as often as you can…'

'I will.'

'There's more than just the attack, you see, bothering her. Charlotte's been receiving these weird silent phone calls, getting her all spooked. She reckons your mother was responsible. The police say Tilly claims she can't recall ever phoning Charlotte, but I imagine that's because her brain's shot to pieces. Could be she really doesn't remember. But in case we're all wrong and the calls continue...'

'I'll be there for her, don't worry.' My initial reaction to the matter of the calls remained firm. Chloe was the culprit, not Mum, no matter what Charlotte and James believed.

***

19

Growing Suspicions

The next time I visited Mum at the psychiatric unit, her appearance, although no longer a shock, still saddened me. Her hair was neat, but her skin was dry, sallow, its tone unhealthy, and dark smudges of exhaustion sat under her eyes. Medicated out of her manic phase, she seemed bewildered, tired, lost. Her eyes were vacant, her hands restless. Pity tugged at me. Perhaps her doctors didn't have her dosage right yet. I wondered whether she remembered what she'd done. What on earth had made her believe she could get the man she wanted by killing his wife? Even taking into account her schizophrenic delusions of love, something didn't fit. To me, her actions spoke of fervour, obsession, and my mother had always been more passive than passionate.

'Mum?' I sat beside her. 'It's me. Your daughter,' I added, although if I had to remind her of our relationship there was little point in visiting her. She made no response.

I decided to risk asking her about the attack on Charlotte. If she got upset, I'd back off and leave it for another day.

'Mum, please talk to me. What happened? Why did you do it? Okay, so you thought you loved the man, but this? Attacking his wife?' I sounded judgemental, I realised, and did my best to rein it in. 'I just want to understand.'

She glanced at me then, and her vacant expression cleared a little. 'Megan,' she said, a note of... what was it, surprise, regret? in her voice. 'What are you doing here?'

'I've come to visit you, Mum. I've been before but you probably don't remember.' I winced at my little-girl-lost tone. If I'd been Chloe, she wouldn't have forgotten.

'Your sister's not been to visit me. Have you seen her?'

Resentment clawed at me again. 'No. I've spoken to her on the phone though.' I didn't need to lie about that, at least. When we'd finally connected, Chloe's comments were mostly about how Mum had always been batshit crazy. It didn't surprise me that my sister hadn't put in an appearance. She'd never be able to deal with the other patients on Mum's ward. Some of them were seriously damaged. Take the girl, fresh out of her teens, who banged her forehead repeatedly against the wall, never speaking. The man who rocked back and forth all day, shouting endless obscenities. Compared to them, my mother seemed almost normal, whatever normal was, and yet, I wondered, how many of Mum's fellow patients had taken a cushion and tried to murder someone with it?

'I expect she's found work at last,' Mum continued. 'Probably putting in long hours, poor baby. She'll come soon, I'm sure.'

'Don't be upset if she doesn't. She doesn't like hospitals, remember.'

'Such a sensitive girl.' Mum seemed quite articulate, as she'd snapped out of whatever world she'd been in when I'd arrived. Time to steer the conversation back to the attack.

'You'd not been taking your medication,' I said carefully. 'You got confused, thinking things you never would normally.'

'I wanted to be with James.' The words came out in a whisper. Her fingers plucked at the wool of her sweater. 'I thought if I went there, made her see reason... I simply intended to talk to her. Nothing else. At first, anyway.'

I decided to probe deeper. 'What about?'

She stared at me as though I were being deliberately obtuse. 'A divorce, Megan. To make her understand it would be best for everyone.' She shook her head. 'I thought she'd agree, but she didn't.'

I waited, unsure what to say.

'She called the police. Or someone did. I've no idea why.'

I took her hands, squeezing them gently. Her skin felt dry and rough under my own.

'Because you attacked her, Mum. Remember?'

'She told me James didn't love me.' She swallowed, tears in her eyes.

Those must have been hard words to hear. Had they been the catalyst that snapped my mother's fragile mind, driving her to attack Charlotte? The truth might have represented one straw too many for someone so confused.

'She told me she'd be better off dead.'

Charlotte's words, etched on my mind from the time I visited her when she was drunk. Had she repeated them the afternoon Mum attacked her? I didn't think so, but the events were a blur in my head.

'She didn't mean it, Mum. She's depressed and hates being in a wheelchair, but–'

She shot me that look again, the one telling me I was being dense. 'Not Charlotte Matthews. Chloe.'

She had to surely be mistaken. 'Chloe said Charlotte would be better off dead?'

'Yes. The evening before… before it happened. Chloe seemed so interested in my love for James. After you left, she said again how his wife had no kind of life anymore, what with her being crippled. How James should be free, how the marriage must be a sham. Told me the woman would be better off dead.'

I recalled Chloe's cruelty from that night: *she's like an animal that needs to be put down.* It seemed my sister had expanded on the theme when I wasn't around to stop her.

Mum looked exhausted. I wondered whether I should leave her be, give myself time to digest what she'd said. Her next words thrust all such thoughts from my head.

'It was Chloe's idea, don't you see?'

Dread coiled in the pit of my stomach. 'What was?'

'What I did to that woman. Chloe was right. James's wife dying would have been for the best, only I couldn't manage it.'

Denial clamoured in my brain at what I was hearing. I didn't speak, afraid if I pressed too hard, my mother would shrink back into herself.

'I'd been so stupid, Megan. When Chloe said James's wife would be better off dead, I thought she was just being a bit… you know how your sister gets at times. Then that woman said James didn't love me. So hurtful. I remembered then what Chloe had said. That's when I knew.'

I prepared myself. This wouldn't be good. 'What?'

'What Chloe had meant. For me to kill Charlotte Matthews, because it would be for the best. Oh, I was stupid, didn't realise what she'd been suggesting. But when that woman said those horrible things, it all made sense.'

Dear God. Yes, it did, but for all the wrong reasons. I stood up, unable to deal with any more.

'I understand, Mum. Why don't you try to sleep?' She did look exhausted. I kissed her cheek. 'I'll be in again soon, I promise.'

***

Once I got back to my car, I sat behind the steering wheel, my head trying to process what I'd heard. Chloe had said Charlotte Matthews would be better off dead. Knowing our mother hadn't been keeping up with her medication, that Mum fancied herself in love with James, how wild her fantasies got when she became unstable. Had Chloe played on Mum's blind love for her? How hard had she needed to push to turn my mother into a potential killer? What else might she have said that Mum wasn't telling me?

I had the advantage of being very familiar with my sister's devious ways, my knowledge honed over twenty-five years. It bore all the hallmarks of the way she operated; manipulation was her middle name. After all, living with Mum as she did, she knew better than anyone how my mother wasn't coping with coming off her medication. She stood to gain by Charlotte Matthews being dead and out of the way. A messy and expensive divorce neatly avoided. Not wanting to risk doing the deed herself, she'd primed a mentally unstable woman to murder on her behalf.

It explained why my mother's instability had taken a violent twist. All part of Chloe's continuing obsession with bagging James for herself.

Another suspicion was growing in my mind. If Mum were declared mentally incompetent, someone would need to administer her finances. Had Chloe also set her sights on Mum's inheritance from our grandmother?

I was convinced Chloe had been involved in the attack on Charlotte. To what extent, I couldn't be sure. I only knew my sister oozed poison and my mother had drunk deeply of her.

My suspicions that Chloe had engineered Alicia's death returned full force, causing my fists to ball in my lap. Tears stabbed the backs of my eyes. I broke down, sobs wrenching themselves from my throat, rivers of anguish pouring down my cheeks as I rocked to and fro. I didn't care if any passer-by saw or heard me. Sunk in my grief, I lost track of time, steeped in memories of my baby.

***

When I eventually sobbed myself dry, I tried to marshal my thoughts. What could I do about any of this? I had no proof, nothing to take to the police.

Another thought occurred to me. Hard to predict what twist Chloe's behaviour might take next, but Charlotte was vulnerable living alone. If my sister had tried to kill her once, she'd surely try again. No way could I voice my suspicions however. Charlotte was depressed enough already. I heard her voice in my head, telling me not to be so melodramatic, just as Toby would if I talked to him about my concerns. The blade of 'Not a tad over sensitive, are you?' stabbed me once more.

Toby. Oh, God. Another cause for worry shot through me. With James separated from Charlotte, chances were he'd move in with Toby before long. If he did, and Chloe found out, the consequences wouldn't be pretty. Nobody could ever accuse my sister of being open minded; to be dumped in favour of a faggot – her usual term for gay men – would ignite every one of her prejudices. The fireworks that particular flame might set off didn't bear thinking about. Toby would end up in danger. Or even dead.

I pulled out my phone. Time to arrange another meal with him.

***

20

Pasta And Wine

Lunchtime the next day saw me at an Italian restaurant I'd not been to before with Toby. I waited for him in my new dress, pricey and bought with Mum's inheritance money, nerves causing me to sweat a little. My fingers strayed to my French-pleated hair, styled by Amy that morning. Once he arrived, his eyes lingered on me a fraction longer than necessary, although he didn't say anything. Nevertheless, a flicker of hope sparked within me, despite the fact he and James had become an item.

After our starters arrived, Toby speared a salami-filled olive with a cocktail stick. 'I'm glad you called. I've been meaning to get in touch. How's your mother?' His tone held concern. I'd told him on the phone about Mum's detention in the psychiatric ward, along with the reason.

I took a sip of wine. 'She's doing okay. Getting better every time I visit. She wasn't off her medication for long, so they've been quite successful in stabilising her. Still some way to go yet.'

'She'll be in for a while, then?'

'God, yes. Don't forget Charlotte. There's the small matter of attempted murder to consider.'

'Shit. Of course. I'm sorry I've not been in touch, but I've been busy.'

'It's okay.' Over the years, I'd grown accustomed to people assuming I could cope, that I didn't need their support. I decided to pump Toby about what was making him light up like the Blackpool Tower. As if I couldn't guess. 'How are things going with James?'

He grinned. 'It's early days yet, but so far everything's great.'

The tiny nugget of hope inside me withered. I did my best to mask my disappointment. 'Sounds great. I'm happy for you.'

'Although…' His expression sobered. 'You've heard he's split from his wife?'

'I've spoken to him, yes. He told me he'd moved into a flat at the Harbourside. Things haven't been good with Charlotte, apparently. He asked me to keep an eye on her, which I've been doing.'

'She okay?'

'Not great. Being attacked like that in her own home… She's been better, that's for sure.' I took a sip of wine. 'What about James? How's he coping with the split?'

'He's okay. He seems glad of the chance to get his head around a few things. Like I said, I don't want to put any pressure on him. Not if I want what we share to go anywhere.'

So what they had wasn't simply a one-off, obviously. 'All this is a departure from the norm for you, isn't it? Being with just one person?'

'I've got tired of all the bed hopping. Time for something different.'

'He's a lot older than you. That's not an issue?'

'Told you before. I prefer the more mature man.'

My fears about Chloe and her likely reaction surfaced. Time to broach the issue. 'Chloe won't react well if you two move in together.'

Toby shrugged. 'Yeah, she had quite a thing for him, didn't she?'

'Has she contacted him, do you know?'

'He says not. Seems he told her pretty bluntly to back off, how he wasn't interested and it appears to have done the trick. He's not seen her for a while. No more hanging around at the office. Or stalking him when he takes Senna to the park.'

The latter was news to me, although not a surprise. 'You don't think she might be lying low for a while, biding her time?'

'Too subtle for Chloe. She's probably moved on to pastures new.'

I hesitated, not sure how to respond. No way could I raise my worries about Toby being in physical danger from Chloe, or her priming Mum to attack Charlotte. Toby would only dismiss my concerns. Besides, he'd never been the sort to worry about ifs and maybes. If it wasn't tangible and happening there and then, it wasn't real for him.

His next words proved my point. 'I'm not going to lose any sleep over Chloe.'

I decided to let the matter drop. For now, anyway.

Toby talked more about James, how well things were going, and I tried to appear happy for him. He mentioned he'd been out for a drink with Steve Hopkins, an old school friend of ours, living in Germany but in Bristol for a visit. Happy reminiscences followed.

Our time together flew by, and I savoured every minute, all the while reminding myself how Toby was off limits now he was with James.

* * *

Later, when I was back home working, the intercom to my flat buzzed. My sister's high-pitched voice sounded when I answered.

'Decided I'd come round for a chat.' A warning pinged in my head. Since when did Chloe ever choose to talk with me?

I pressed the buzzer. 'Come on in.'

Chloe breezed through the door, a bottle of wine in hand. 'I thought we could treat ourselves to a drink while we're at it.' She thrust the wine, an expensive Bordeaux, towards me. Some ulterior motive had prompted her visit, of that I was sure. What it was remained to be seen. Perhaps my sister was on the hunt for money, having drained what Mum had given her.

I poured two glasses of wine. 'Have you been to visit Mum yet?' She wouldn't have, but my question might have induced a twinge of guilt in her.

'Don't be stupid. No way would I visit a psychiatric ward. Too many crazy people. Have you seen Charlotte again?'

So it was information she wanted. Proving Toby wrong. She hadn't moved on to pastures new.

'I went there last night.' I didn't tell her how Charlotte had mentioned another malicious phone call. 'I'll visit again soon, check on how she's doing.'

'James hasn't moved back in, then?'

Dear God. How had my sister found out about their split? My surprise must have shown on my face, because her next comment answered my question.

'Oh, I know about his new flat down at the Harbourside.' Malice sparked in her eyes. 'One of the girls from his office told me. Got pally with her a while back, in case I needed some information.'

'The fact he's split up with Charlotte isn't your business, Chloe. You need to back off where James is concerned.' I decided to change the subject. 'Mum's doing well, in case you intended to ask.' I took a sip of my wine, savouring its undoubted quality. 'They're hoping she won't take long to stabilise. We had a good chat when I last went in.' No point in mentioning how Chloe wishing Charlotte dead was the driving force behind what Mum did. I'd be wasting my breath. Chloe would make everything sound innocent, and brand me as the bad guy for suspecting such things.

She didn't appear to be listening anyway. 'What about Toby?' Spite lurked in the falseness of her smile, causing my protective instincts to zoom into overdrive.

Fear gripped me. Her fling with him had finished years earlier. She'd hardly seen him since then, only twice that I knew of: the evening at O'Malley's and the photography exhibition. Chloe had to have some other reason to ask about him other than making small talk. Perhaps she was simply trying to needle me, being well aware of my feelings for him. Time to raise my shields and act as if I didn't care. Provoking Chloe wouldn't prove a clever plan of action.

'We had lunch today. He's fine. Been busy.'

Her expression turned feral, as if she were holding in some barely leashed secret. 'I'm guessing with his new boyfriend.'

In that moment, I regretted ever telling her about Toby and James. I'd been right. From the anger in her eyes, I deduced that every one of her homophobic buttons had been pressed. Chloe hadn't taken James's rejection well, and she was out for blood.

I schooled my face into a suitably dismissive expression. 'It's none of your business. You've hardly seen Toby over the last few years.'

'I'd never have pegged him as gay, that's for sure.' Another sneer. Distaste sat squarely on her face. 'He was all man with me. Maybe he's going through a phase, needs reminding he prefers women.' I braced myself, knowing what was coming next. 'Perhaps I'll give him a call, find out if he wants to relight an old flame.' She didn't take her eyes off me for a second, watching for my reaction.

'You don't have his number.'

'Oh, but I do. Right here.' She tapped her mobile. How she'd got hold of it I had no idea, although I wouldn't put it past her to have snooped through my phone at an opportune moment.

'Think I'll give him a call. Soon. Ask if he wants to hook up.' The feral grin had grown positively ferocious. 'We can chat about old times. Talk about how you two didn't last longer than a quickie in the back of his car. Amongst other things. Such as how you had his baby and didn't tell him.' She aimed her verbal knife straight at my heart, the pain stabbing me even though I'd been anticipating the blow. Trust her to threaten me with that. Not that I had any intention of revealing I'd already told Toby about Alicia.

I stood up. I'd had a bellyful of her. She'd wreaked enough havoc for one evening.

'It's late, Chloe. I need to crack on with work.'

She didn't move. 'That would be an interesting talk, wouldn't it? Not the only productive chat I've had recently, either.' She watched closely for my reaction. My lack of response provoked a smirk from her, aware as she must have been of my struggle to ignore her. 'Like the conversation Mum and I had the other night.'

I'll bet, I thought. When you provoked an unstable woman into attacking Charlotte Matthews. Even for a brazen bitch like Chloe, being so upfront about her manipulations must have taken some nerve.

'Very interesting, it was.' She grinned. 'You're right, I'd better be off. We must do this again sometime. It's been fun.'

My hand itched to slap her, but I decided to let it go. Keeping Chloe from targeting Toby remained my prime concern, along with Mum's wellbeing.

I took my sister's half-full glass off her. 'Goodbye, Chloe.'

***

21

No Longer Unknown

The hum and buzz of the psychiatric ward surrounded us. Opposite me, Mum's face held a wealth of hurt, which pierced me as if it were my own. Her delusions of a life with James, despite the effect of her medication, were clearly taking their time to fade.

'I know it was all a fantasy, Megan,' she said. 'I can't help feeling sad though. Sad for the loss of him, our life together, the one I truly believed we'd have. Everything appeared so shiny and bright. Now all that's gone.'

I understood. How could I not? Of course she was grieving for what had been snatched from her, even it was all make believe. A sterile room in a psychiatric hospital was all she could expect for the foreseeable future, poor compensation for her dreams of a happier life.

'The police have been here again,' Mum continued. 'They needed to interview me, now I'm on more of an even keel.'

'That must have been hard for you.'

'There's not much I can tell them. What happened that day… it's all a blur in my head. I'm not sure if I'll ever really find out why I did it.'

'Chloe told you Charlotte Matthews would be better off dead. That's why.' Try as I might, I couldn't prevent the vitriol from seeping into my voice.

'Oh, dear, you mustn't think… She didn't mean it literally. I realise that now. Chloe can be a bit… you know how she is.'

'Yeah. I do.' My tone remained waspish. Best for me not to comment further. I patted her arm. 'You want some herbal tea, Mum?'

'Please, love.' Surprise registered within me at the unexpected endearment. I smiled at my mother, despite the familiar stab of sadness at her inability to care about me the way she did Chloe.

I headed towards the drinks machine. On the way, I wondered how to bring up the subject of whatever Chloe had discussed with Mum, to get a handle on whether my suspicions were correct. Hard to do, given Mum had said the attack on Charlotte was a blur in her head. I took chamomile tea for myself and Mum from the dispenser and headed back towards my mother.

'Here's your tea, Mum.'

She took a gulp from her plastic cup. 'Have you seen your sister recently?'

'She came round the other night. She seems fine.' I knew this was a sensitive area. Reaching over, I squeezed her hand. 'I'm sure she'll visit you soon.'

Mum paused, almost as if she was gathering strength. 'Megan...'

'Yes?'

'I understand what I did was wrong. Coming off my medication so suddenly – it wasn't a good idea. I didn't want to kill that woman, honestly I didn't.'

'I know.'

'I've been wondering...' Mum bit her lip, dropping her gaze. 'If she's all right. I wish I could tell her how sorry I am.'

She watched my face carefully. Mixed emotions must have been passing through my expression. I was editing what to tell her. What I could safely say about Charlotte.

'I visited her not long ago.' I kept my tone measured, careful. 'She's badly shaken up. But she'll be okay.'

'And what about...' Mum hesitated. 'James? Is he all right?' The distorting prism of the medication hadn't affected her feelings for him, that much was clear. He remained the man she loved, even if out of reach.

'I've not seen him. I've spoken to him on the phone though.'

'He wasn't there when you visited his wife?'

'No. He's moved out. Charlotte needs some space.' We were venturing into difficult territory. I drew my chair in closer. 'Don't read anything into that, Mum. Please. Whatever is going on between James and Charlotte, it doesn't involve you.'

'I understand.' Hurt crept into her face. For a moment, the old blankness returned to her eyes, causing alarm to spark within me. Was her mind swimming back into the past, to her imagined future with James, one in which Charlotte no longer existed? Right when I began to consider whether I should call a nurse, she spoke again.

'I was so happy when James offered me the job at his office.'

'Mum, please. Can we not talk about James?'

'I couldn't believe it when I saw him again at the interview.' Her smile was wistful. 'He's so good looking. He always was, especially as a young man.'

At first what she'd said didn't register. Then it did. Alarm shot through me. 'What on earth do you mean?'

She didn't reply.

'Talk to me. How can you possibly know what James looked like when young?'

'Because I knew him back then.'

Disbelief shot through me. Why had she never mentioned this? My doubts must have shown in my face, because she continued. 'A long time ago. He'd recently graduated from university. So handsome, he was.'

'You never said you'd met him before. Why ever not?' Her eyes slid away from mine, and she didn't reply.

I wasn't sure how far I could, or should, press her. The last thing I wanted was to agitate my mother, but her words signalled a piece of the puzzle I needed to uncover. I reached over and clasped her hands. To my relief, she didn't pull away. Instead, she raised her eyes to mine, and in them I glimpsed a myriad of emotions: nostalgia, regret, sadness. Along with fear. Confusion hit me. What reason would Mum have to be afraid?

I smiled at her, an attempt at reassurance. 'You know you can talk to me, right?'

'Can I?' Her voice held a tremble, which tore at my heart. I gave her hands a quick squeeze.

'Whatever the reason, it'll be okay, Mum.'

'You won't get mad?'

I shook my head. 'I promise.'

'I thought it was for the best, I really did.'

'What, Mum?' I kept my voice steady, patient, despite my growing curiosity.

Still she didn't reply.

'Tell me. Please.'

'You're James's daughter, Megan.'

The breath stopped in my chest. All I could do was gawp at her. Stunned, I let go of her hands. A million emotions swirled through my brain: shock, denial, bewilderment.

'Oh, God. I didn't mean that to come out the way it did.' Mum edged closer, concern on her face. I continued to stare at her.

'You can't be serious.' My voice, thick with incredulity, challenged her. 'You're telling me James Matthews is my father?'

'Yes.'

'You're not making this up?'

'No. I swear I'm not.'

'This isn't the bipolar or the schizophrenia talking, is it?'

She shook her head, her fingers twisting in her lap.

'Talk to me. Please.'

A flush stole over her face. 'It's difficult,' she said eventually.

I didn't doubt that. 'Tell me,' I pleaded, my tone insistent.

Mum took a deep breath, her hands still twisting in her lap. 'I met him when we were both in our early twenties. We had a one-night stand.'

'When? How?'

'We were both at a party. He suggested we go for a walk to escape the noise and drunkenness; I suspect he loathed the party circuit as much as I did. Natural introverts, both of us.' Mum smiled, the memory clearly a fond one. 'We went back to his place.'

'That's when you slept with him?'

'Yes. Only the one time though. So long ago, but I've never forgotten it. I recognised him straight away when we met again. I only knew him as James before, you see. I called myself Tilda back then. No surnames, not for a one-night stand. So I thought nothing of it when I saw his name on the letter offering me a job interview, although I couldn't be sure it was the same James Matthews.'

I watched as tears misted her eyes. 'He didn't recognise me, but I knew him straight away. All the old feelings flooded over me once more. Back then, I'd hoped... but he offered me a lift home afterwards without mentioning meeting up again. He hasn't changed. A bit greyer now, a few laughter lines, but he's still the man I fell in love with all those years ago.'

Had she? After one night together? Perhaps her mental health issues had started earlier than I'd realised. 'And you thought... you hoped?'

Mum shook her head. 'I'm not sure exactly what went on in my brain. He's been married twice since our night together; nearly thirty years have gone by and I've grown old and foolish. I hoped he might remember me, but he didn't. He's not changed, but I have. Years of medication and psychiatric wards have that effect. What's more, I've put on weight, let myself go. Small wonder he never twigged who he had working for him.'

'Why didn't you tell me before?' Disbelief had been replaced by anger, my earlier promise not to get mad forgotten. Mum had become a prisoner in the dock, me her prosecutor. Guilty as charged. She should have told me. Didn't I have the right to know?

She stared at the floor, seemingly unable to meet my eyes. 'I always meant to. The time never seemed right though. Besides, I didn't have a clue what to say. Not an easy thing to tell a child she's the product of a one-night stand.'

My expression didn't soften. 'You've never told him either? I presume not, otherwise he'd have said something.'

'No. Like I said, he doesn't remember me. He's forgotten our time together.' Sadness crept across her face.

Stunned as I was, I couldn't bear to see her distress. My anger melted away. Who was I to judge her? I'd had my own one-night stand with Toby after all. Didn't I write the book on unrequited passion? I smiled, in an effort to show that my rancour was forgotten.

Mum returned my smile, in a moment of mutual understanding. Love for her surged through me.

'I asked Chloe not to mention anything to you, not until…' She broke off, panic in her face. I stared at her in shock as her words torpedoed into my brain.

'Chloe? What the hell does she have to do with this? Are you saying she already knows?' My finger jabbed the air in front of her face. 'You told her before telling me?'

Shame crept into her expression. 'Yes. I shouldn't have. It was wrong of me.'

'Not just wrong. Grossly unfair too, I'd say.'

'That as well. Please try to understand, Megan.' Mum's face wore a silent plea for forgiveness. 'It was the night you shared that chicken casserole with us. By then, I'd started to come off the pills, confident I'd be okay. Whereas, in reality, I was becoming unstable. She wormed it out of me. I'm sorry.'

It appeared I'd discovered the sword Chloe had brandished above my head the other night. Not that I could deal with it. I got up from my chair, grabbing my jacket. 'Time I went.'

'Don't go.' Mum stood up too, moving to block my exit. 'Stay.' She saw me hesitate. 'Please. I have more to tell you.'

My eyes slid away from hers; my initial reaction was to push past her, get the hell out of there. Instead, I sat down again, defeat hunching my shoulders. Mum also returned to her chair. Anger burned fiercely within me once more, but she was still my mother. Whom I loved. Mindful of the need not to upset her, I decided to hear her out.

'What else do you want to say?'

Her fingers began their restless twisting again. 'To apologise. I don't want to make excuses, my love, but life wasn't easy, raising two girls alone, battling all the bad stuff in my head. The post-natal depression after your birth – it was awful. I struggled to be a mother to you. I did my best but it hasn't been good enough, has it?'

'No.' My eyes shot forth daggers. 'You should have told me before about James. How can I be sure this isn't another one of your fantasies?'

'I can prove he's your father.'

I snorted. 'How?'

'The night I spent at his flat…' Mum hesitated. 'I grasped he wasn't interested in me, not the way I wanted. It hurt, but I told myself I'd take something away from our time together. I didn't realise I'd already got myself pregnant.'

'What are you talking about, Mum? Take something? What, exactly?'

'He'd not long left university, as I said. I spotted his graduation photo in his bedroom, with him looking so handsome in his cap and gown.'

'And?'

'I stole it.'

Stunned, I remained silent.

'He didn't notice, not when he seemed so keen to drive me home. Afterwards, I'd gaze at it often, hoping I'd meet him again at some party or other.' She smiled sadly. 'I keep it hidden in the chest of drawers in my bedroom.'

'Why are you telling me this?'

'Because it's proof of what I'm saying. The photo's still in the bottom drawer. Even Chloe doesn't know I've got it.' That scored points with me, as Mum must have known. 'Look in my bedroom and you'll realise I'm telling you the truth. Even if it's way too late.'

***

22

Jumping To Conclusions

James pounded his fist against a wall in Toby's flat. Pain flared through his knuckles; they smarted like hell but the hurt helped to channel his anger. How could he have been such an idiot? Toby had never harboured any intention of a serious relationship.

Sure, he'd been saying and doing all the right things. They were spending more and more time together, and James rarely returned to his rented flat except to collect his mail. He'd started to feel alive, truly alive, for the first time ever. Life no longer consisted of merely going through the motions. Toby made him laugh more than he'd ever done before. The man was exhilarating to be with and the sex – that had got more fantastic every time they made love.

Now their relationship had turned as sour as month-old milk and James couldn't see any way they could continue if Toby couldn't keep his trousers zipped up. Christ, it hadn't taken him long to start screwing around, had it? So much for being sick of bed hopping, his hollow promises of being ready for something different.

How gullible he'd been. A mere fifteen minutes earlier, after Toby had gone to buy steaks for them to grill, James had congratulated himself on his luck. After years in the sexual wilderness, he'd finally met a guy he could relate to, build a future with, but then James heard the ping from his phone. He grinned as he picked up his mobile, expecting the text to be from Toby.

But it wasn't.

The message came from an unknown number. 'Check the texts on your boyfriend's mobile. He's cheating on you.'

James had stared at the phone in his hand, stunned. He knew he should ignore the text. His gut told him Toby wouldn't fuck around. Besides, when would he have done so? They'd been together almost every non-working hour since James had moved into his rented flat.

No. Not every hour, James remembered. Last week they'd spent a night apart. Toby had told him a friend who he'd not seen for years, a guy who lived in Germany, was visiting Bristol and wanted to catch up. Steve something or other. Hopkins, that was it. Toby had said he thought the evening would prove too dull for James, what with all the likely reminiscences from schooldays. James had laughed, telling him to go and have fun. Afterwards though, it had felt weird spending the night alone in his flat. The place seemed cold, sterile, a bolthole that had served its purpose. That evening, he'd contemplated talking to Toby about the two of them moving in together. He'd lain on his bed, making plans, and life had never seemed so good. He'd never once considered Toby might be screwing around with the guy from Germany.

How naive he'd been. Telling Toby he wouldn't come round that night so Toby could spend time with his friend. He'd assumed he'd been giving him space, cutting him some slack after they'd spent so many hours together, even though Toby had never hinted he needed time apart.

The urge to check Toby's mobile grew stronger. *Don't invade his privacy*, his gut urged. *Do the right thing. Delete that text, before it sours what you're building.*

He couldn't though. Despite his efforts, James knew himself too well. Before long, he'd end up checking his boyfriend's mobile.

The phone would probably be where Toby often put it when he got in from work, on the table beside the bed. James walked towards the bedroom door, his head a mess, the warning from his gut sounding again. He pushed it aside, choosing to pick up the phone and jab his finger against the new message notification.

'*Srry nt txted b4, bn busy. Rlly gd time last wk. Fckng gr8 fck u r, m8! Will txt nxt time in Bris.*'

Sent about five minutes earlier. No name listed, just a number. Proof of Toby's infidelity.

His rage boiling, James slammed his fist into the wall. How stupid he'd been to get in so deep with Toby when he hardly knew anything about him. Once a player, always a player, it seemed. Perhaps the age gap had proved too great. James had clearly not been enough; he couldn't have been, not if his boyfriend screwed around with the first warm body he found.

Toby's step sounded on the stairs, his key turning in the lock. He came in with a bag of groceries, carrying it into the kitchen.

'Want a beer?' Toby's voice sounded so normal, but then he had no idea his escapade with the friend from Germany – if that's who the guy was, James couldn't trust anything Toby told him anymore – had been uncovered.

Toby walked into the living room. 'Did you hear me? I brought you one anyway.'

James's rage cracked through its wafer-thin barrier.

'I do not want a fucking beer.' His arm smacked the can out of Toby's hand, sending it flying across the room. Toby stared at him, shock on his face. In the short time they'd been together they'd never rowed, never raised their voices to each other.

'What's the matter with you? You were fine when I went out.' Toby looked lost, uncertain how to react, not that James intended cutting him any slack. Around them, the atmosphere tightened with tension.

'You bastard. You goddamn prick.' He moved closer to Toby, getting into his space, wanting to gauge his reactions. 'You didn't waste any time, did you? You must have been laughing your socks off at how stupid I've been, but I don't intend being gullible any longer. We're through.'

Toby was a good actor, James had to give him that. What appeared to be genuine astonishment flooded his face.

'What are you talking about?' He shook his head. 'I don't get it. We agreed this was what we both wanted. I thought we'd been doing great – more than great – the last few weeks.' Toby's voice shook slightly and he had gone very pale. 'Talk to me, James. Are you having some sort of panic attack here? What's brought all this on?'

'You did. By screwing around behind my back last week.' No way existed to seal his words back up in the bottle or lessen the damage they inflicted. Their stench hung in the air and if Toby had appeared dumbfounded before, it was nothing compared with his countenance now. *Yep, he really is a good actor*, thought James.

'What the...' Toby backed away, sitting down. He stared at the floor, a stunned expression on his face. 'I never... you can't suppose... I went for a few drinks with Steve, nothing more. I told you who he was, how I knew him, where we were going. We had a couple of beers and then I came back here. Alone. No way would I ever go to bed with him. He's married, for one thing.'

'A wedding ring didn't prevent you from coming on to me when we met.'

'Oh, for God's sake, that was different. You weren't happy with your wife and you're gay, damn it, whereas Steve is blissfully content with Louise. They've got two kids and he's as straight as the proverbial poker.'

'And I'm supposed to believe you?'

'Yes. You are.' Anger in Toby's voice. 'That was the deal. You, me, together, nobody else. I told you, James. My days of playing the field are behind me and I don't miss them.'

'So how do you explain last week?'

'I already have. Why the hell are you acting like this?'

'He texted you. He was very complimentary about your sexual prowess.' It sounded bad, admitting that he'd breached Toby's privacy but he was the one who'd been wronged. Besides, a bit of snooping hardly compared to full-blown infidelity.

'You read my phone messages? Why?' Disbelief, censure, in Toby's voice. 'I have no idea what you're talking about. I've never had any such text. I didn't sleep with him, okay? Are you getting this? I didn't have sex with Steve.'

'Check your mobile.' James's voice was curt. Toby could deny it all he wanted but the evidence said otherwise. He recalled the message. *Rlly gd time last wk. Fckng gr8 fck u r!* Rage surged through him again.

Toby went into the bedroom, returning with his phone, pressing the screen to find his messages. His silence as he read the text that had irritated James. He wanted to goad Toby, provoke him into something other than controlled calm.

'Well? You can see what's pissed me off, can't you? You goddamned lousy, faithless bastard. He's right about you being a great lay but that's not enough for me; I wanted you to keep your dick in your trousers. Too bad you couldn't manage that.'

'I did. No matter what you believe. I've no idea who's behind this text but Steve certainly isn't. Did you ever consider, you stupid idiot, that someone might have sent this message by mistake? Punched the wrong number into their phone?'

'No, I didn't.'

'Screw you! You accuse me of being unfaithful, acting as judge and jury without even bothering to talk to me first? I had no idea you were so damned paranoid.'

'Yeah. Like I'm the guilty one here.'

'At least I'm not as insecure as a fucking teenager.' Toby jabbed his finger against his phone then thrust it towards James. 'Look. There's Steve's number in my contacts list. This text didn't come from him.'

'Doesn't mean a thing. Like people don't change their numbers? Or have more than one mobile?'

'Call him. He'll tell you nothing happened between us.'

'What would be the point? He'd deny it, same as you're doing. You've probably both had a good laugh at me for being so goddamn gullible.'

'Jeez! No talking to you, is there? I'll ask you again and perhaps this time I'll get a straight answer. What made you look at my phone?'

James pulled his mobile from his pocket and brought up his messages. 'This.' He handed the phone to Toby.

Silence hung, thick and heavy, between the two men. When Toby spoke, his voice shook. 'I don't know what this means. Or why anyone would send you a text like this. Either someone wants to cause trouble – and has succeeded – or else this is some vile practical joke. I swear to God I've not been screwing around.'

'Why would somebody play a joke like that?' A thought occurred to him. 'What makes more sense is your new boyfriend wants me off the scene, so he did this. First he got my number from your phone, then sent the text to get me out of the way. I wouldn't want to disappoint him.' James stood up. Time to go home and lick his wounds.

Toby placed himself in front of James, blocking him from leaving. 'This is a windup. Someone's out to cause trouble. There's no way Steve's behind either of those messages. Look at them. Totally different styles of writing. Sent by two separate people.'

'So what's your theory on that? Got some glib explanation?'

'No. I can't explain this. I haven't slept with anyone else, not Steve, not anybody. I've no idea who's trying to cause trouble here but they mustn't win. Don't let them, James.'

James didn't answer. He recalled the shock, the anger, he'd felt when reading the text on Toby's phone. The urge to protect himself proved greater than his desire to trust Toby.

'You'd take the word of some cowardly anonymous texter over me? Is that how you operate?' Bitterness had replaced the anger in Toby's voice. 'You really have so little faith in me you choose to believe shit like this?' He shook his mobile in James's face. 'If that's the case, then I agree with you. We're through.'

James jerked his head up. He hadn't expected that. Wasn't he the wronged one here? Looking at Toby, he detected no anger in his face, just weary resignation, an expression James had no idea how to interpret.

'For some reason, you're hell-bent on believing I've been unfaithful. I don't like what that says about you. About us.'

Toby pushed James aside in order to hold the door open. 'You need to leave. Now.'

Too stunned to reply, James walked past him, down the stairs, and out of the building, into the cold night air. A mixture of sadness, anger and jealousy gnawed at his core.

He sat in his car, drained, for a long time before driving off.

***

Once home, he poured himself a whisky before throwing himself on his bed, unplugging the phone and switching off his mobile. After what had happened, his rented flat seemed a welcome refuge.

Anger, hot and molten, seared his brain at the idea of Toby – his Toby – touching another man. James thrust it aside. Time to pull himself together, think objectively about what had happened. In his head, he heard Toby's cold words: *You need to leave.* The suspicion he may have acted too hastily nagged at him wouldn't let go.

He sipped his whisky, allowing its liquid fire to soothe him. As he drank, his anger drained away, to be replaced by doubt. Guilt too. He had no solid evidence of Toby screwing around apart from the two texts. What did they actually prove? Nothing. Had he found the message on Toby's mobile without the prompting text, it might have seemed conclusive proof of infidelity. The first text, the one to his own phone, was the one causing him doubt.

For a start, it was anonymous and not from anyone in his phone contacts. Had some past lover of Toby's sent the text out of jealousy to break them up? But who? Toby had already said his previous relationships had all been casual. Not the sort to invoke the dark malice the texts indicated. Moreover, hadn't Toby mentioned he'd had a dry spell sexually before they hooked up?

Or perhaps the sender harboured a grudge against him, James.

If so, only one person came to mind. Along with the dark fury in her eyes when he'd rebuffed her.

From what he'd seen, Chloe Copeland was a cold-hearted bitch, every bit malicious enough to pull a stunt like this. The style of the texts suggested two different people had sent them, but, he realised, that would be simplicity itself to fake. She could have sent them from two separate phones, bought for the purpose, the texts five minutes or so apart. Hell, she'd spent long enough hanging around outside his work each day, the hallmark of an obsessed stalker. Odds on, she'd done the same outside Toby's flat, thereby discovering the evening with his old school friend.

James's suspicion that she'd been responsible for the texts resurfaced. As did his inkling she'd been the one who stabbed him. A frisson of fear shot through him.

His gut feeling told him he'd stumbled on the right track. Leading to the conclusion that, if Chloe had sent the texts to stir up trouble, Toby hadn't been unfaithful. Ergo, he'd behaved like an idiot. He'd not even given Toby the chance to tell his side of the story before throwing accusations around, which posed a dilemma. Had he screwed things up for good?

Only one way to find out. He'd have to tell Toby he believed him, beg him to put the whole sorry mess behind them. Go on to forge something so strong that a thousand gold-digging bitches like Chloe Copeland couldn't break them apart. Time to man up. He'd talk with Toby the next day, the sooner the better. Perhaps the police as well, about the stabbing.

In the end, the waiting became intolerable. It was past midnight, but he needed to resolve the matter straightaway. He'd drive over to Redland, ask for another chance and do whatever proved necessary to get it.

***

Once outside Toby's door, he sat in the stairwell, the cold steps chilling the backs of his legs through his trousers. *You can do this*, he told himself. Then he rang the bell.

After what seemed like forever, the door opened. Toby stood there, still dressed; clearly he hadn't made it to bed yet.

'We need to talk.' Too late, James realised his words sounded bald, presumptuous even.

Toby shook his head. Icy detachment was all James could discern in his face. 'Haven't we said everything there is to say?'

James's gut clenched at hearing the flat, emotionless tone of earlier. He resisted the urge to grab Toby, pull him towards him, kiss him senseless, anything to rekindle their passion. He'd been a fool before; once was enough. 'Please, just hear me out.'

For a moment, he thought Toby might refuse. Then he stood aside. 'You'd better come in.'

James followed him inside.

Then Toby turned towards him, his expression blank. 'Well?' was all he said.

Not a great start. 'I've been an idiot,' James said.

'Yes. You have.'

'And I'm sorry, Toby. Really sorry.'

'And?'

'It won't happen again, I swear. If you'll just give me another chance…'

'Not the answer I was looking for.'

Shit. He had to get this right. He mustn't fuck up and lose Toby forever. He wouldn't, he couldn't, allow him to slip away so easily.

Realisation hit him. He'd been incredibly dense yet again, but no more.

He moved closer to Toby, putting his hand on his arm, grateful Toby didn't pull away. James took that as encouragement.

'I know you didn't cheat. I've been a fool and I realise that now.'

'I didn't and yes, you are. One hell of a fool. How could you believe I'd mess around?'

'I don't. Honest to God I don't. I screwed up, got everything arse backwards.'

Toby gave him a slight nod and they were so close, James couldn't resist even though he'd promised himself he'd stay in control. He hauled Toby towards him, kissing him, Toby pulled away initially, then responded. When they did break apart, both men were breathing heavily.

James leaned in and rested his forehead against Toby's. 'I'm sorry. I'll say it however many times you need me to. You didn't fuck around. Somebody is out to make trouble between us.'

'Any idea who'd pull such a stunt? I've thought of little else but I can't come up with anyone who'd do something so vicious.'

'I can. Chloe Copeland.'

'Chloe?' Toby looked puzzled before giving a brief nod. 'Yeah, maybe. You really think it was her?'

'Probably, although I don't know exactly how she managed it. Let's not waste time on her. I just want to make things right between us. Can we get back to what we had before I turned into such an idiot?'

Toby stepped back, his tone leaving no room for doubt. 'I have to be sure this won't happen again. I want to be able to meet a mate without getting a boatload of accusations afterwards. What happened earlier has to be a one-off. A repeat performance will spell the end for us. I mean it, James.'

***

23
Something To Tell You

I went to Mum's house in St George the next day.

'Picking up some of her clothes,' I told Chloe once I arrived.

She shrugged on hearing my fib. 'Whatever. I'm on my way out anyway.'

I found the evidence Mum had mentioned easily enough, right where she said it would be; under some clothes, wrapped in tissue paper, in the bottom drawer of her bedroom cabinet. A soft waft of perfume reached me as I took it from its hiding place. I had no intention of taking Mum the photograph. Her obsession with James, not yet quenched as far as I could see, didn't need any encouragement. I drew out the photograph, my fingers shaky, and stared at the face of my father, seeing my own mirrored there. The man I'd always yearned to meet and about whom my mother had told me nothing. Until the day before.

Chloe's comments from the other night, about having had a chat with Mum, made sense. *Very productive*, she'd said. I recalled the gloating, the triumph in her tone, the pleasure she obviously gained from withholding something from me. She'd have relished every second when Mum was telling her. How she must have loved having something else with which to torment me. If Mum hadn't let slip the truth, I didn't doubt Chloe would have waited until the most opportune, the most painful, moment to throw the shit at the fan.

My father and I. Parent and daughter. Plain to see, if you knew what you were looking for. He'd given me my height, my blue eyes, my dark hair. My own graduation photo came into my mind. Set the two next to each other, and the resemblance, accentuated by our caps and gowns, would be obvious.

As my mother had done all those years earlier, I put the photograph in my bag. It didn't belong to me and it wasn't hers either. I grabbed my coat and car keys and went back to my flat, unwilling to face Chloe should she return early. I couldn't deal with her wise-ass comments in my current mood.

***

Once home, I set the photograph face down on my coffee table and pulled out my mobile. I'd waited twenty-nine years to meet my father. I didn't intend to delay any longer.

James answered on the first ring. My voice shook with nerves when I spoke.

'I need to see you,' I said. 'As soon as possible.'

'Is Charlotte all right?' His concern for my friend touched me. He may not have been the husband she had hoped for, but the man who had fathered me still cared about his wife. Hope rose within me that someday he'd feel as much for me.

'She's fine. I'm not calling about Charlotte. There's another matter I'd like to discuss, but I'd prefer to tell you face to face. It's not something I want to go into over the phone.'

In the end, he agreed to come to my flat after he finished work.

The time dragged throughout the afternoon, work failing to distract me from my fears. Would he believe me? How would he react to having a daughter? Perhaps my news wouldn't be welcome. How would I deal with rejection from the man I'd been searching for my whole life?

The doubts swirled through my head, causing me to second-guess the wisdom of phoning him. More than once I almost called to cancel, before I administered a mental head slap. *This has to happen*, I told myself. *He deserves the truth, and you need a father*.

He arrived just after six. I opened the door, the photograph still lying face down on the coffee table behind me. Blue irises met my own, my height meaning our eyes were almost on a level. For a moment, a prayer drummed through my brain: *please don't reject me.*

'Megan.' He smiled politely but his mouth held tension.

'Come in. Have a seat.' I gestured towards the sofa next to the coffee table. 'Can I get you something to drink? Tea?'

'Yes, please. Strong, no sugar. What's this about?'

I went into the kitchenette, busied myself with mugs, water, tea bags. No way could I tell him just yet. So I prevaricated. 'Let me fill you in about Charlotte first. I've been round to see her, as I promised, and I've spoken to her on the phone a few times. She's not great but she's getting there.'

He came in and stood behind me, leaning against the doorframe. 'You're sure?'

'Yes. She's strong, despite everything that's happened. She's dealing with things okay. I'll keep an eye on her, don't worry.' I poured boiling water into the mugs. 'Like I said, it's not her I need to talk to you about.'

'What then? Sorry, I don't have a great deal of time. I'm meeting someone at half seven.'

'You mean Toby.' I smiled to reassure him I was okay with it, even though I wasn't.

'You know about me and him?' He nodded thoughtfully. 'Of course you do. You've been friends since school. He was bound to have told you.'

I picked up the mugs of tea and led the way into the living room. 'I need to talk to you about Mum.' We both sat down, with the photograph a smouldering fuse on the coffee table. 'And about me too. I've got something to tell you.'

My father didn't speak, giving me the space I needed to get my head together. I had no idea how to do this.

In the end, I simply turned over the photograph and let it do the talking for me.

He stared at the picture of himself, so young and yet not so different, picking it up. 'My graduation ceremony.' Lines of confusion puckered his forehead. 'What the hell? I don't understand, Megan. How did you get this?'

'Mum had it. The two of you have met before. A long time ago.'

James frowned. 'What are you saying? I don't recall meeting your mother before her job interview. I don't... I can't get my head around this, sorry.'

'She said she met you at a party. How you spent the night together, just the once. Afterwards she took the photo. As a keepsake, I suppose. Seems she held a torch for you even then.'

James frowned again. 'One of my graduation photos did go missing from my bedroom. At the time, I blamed my flatmate. Thought he'd smashed the glass and didn't want to admit it. I never thought it could be anyone else. Certainly not...' He broke off, shaking his head.

'You don't remember Mum at all?' Sadness for my mother washed over me.

'Not really. I mean, yes, I vaguely recollect a girl, a party, about the time I accused my flatmate about the photo. It was all so long ago though. I've no memory of her name or what she looked like. I suppose it explains why your mother developed such an obsession with me when we met up again, given her mental history.' His fingers tapped the glass. 'Thanks for returning this.' His tone made it clear he considered our business settled.

'There's something else I need to tell you.' I twisted my hands around my mug, groping for the right words, nerves nipping at me.

'Out with it then.' He glanced at his watch. I detected his impatience, mindful as he must be of getting back for Toby.

Worry constricted my throat; I could barely squeeze out the words. 'When I last went to see Mum, she said...' Out it came. 'The night the two of you spent together. She told me you're my father.'

'What…?' Shock washed over his face. 'She said that?' He'd gone pale, glancing from the photograph to me, and I saw the moment when he registered what I was saying as true. The veracity of my words was evident in our similar features and colouring. James now knew he'd fathered a child on that night of forgettable sex with my mother. What he did with the information was up to him, but I prayed he'd be okay with it. Would it be so bad to have me for a daughter?

'I thought…' He sounded hoarse. 'I didn't ask… I assumed. Obviously I shouldn't have done. That she was on the pill.'

Perversely, as he believed me, I felt compelled to offer him further proof. 'We can do a DNA test. Get it confirmed beyond all doubt.' I picked up the photograph. 'It seems pretty obvious, however, from the resemblance between us. Besides, Mum's bipolar, sure, as well as mildly schizophrenic, but she's never been a liar. I can't see her making up something like this, not now she's back on her medication.'

I tried to lighten the tension lying thick between us. 'Weird, isn't it? For years, you've been Charlotte's husband to me, nothing more. Now it turns out you're my father.'

He shook his head. 'Weird doesn't begin to describe it. I never thought I'd be a parent. And yet here you are.' I couldn't detect how he really felt, what with his customary reserve masking his emotions.

'Same here. Mum wouldn't tell me anything about you when I was a kid. I'd always wondered, always needed to find out.' Something compelled me to mention the other thing on my mind. 'And now you're Toby's partner. The guy I've been friends with for years.'

Maybe something in my tone gave me away; I remembered his suspicion of me when we'd met in O'Malley's. The inkling I'd had of his jealous streak. He frowned. 'You've always been just friends though, right?'

'No.' His expression darkened; I hastened to reassure him. 'What we had ended long ago though. Like you and Mum, it was just for one night.' I went over to the wall and took down a photograph. Toby and me, both eighteen, cropped from a group photo, smiling at the camera, me unaware of already being pregnant by him.

Definitely not the time to let slip that James had once been a grandfather either. I'd found what we'd said already tough enough. My father was bound to ask where my child was, if I'd been expecting, and I couldn't go there. Revealing his paternity had drained dry my emotions, and I couldn't deal with more angst. Instead, I thrust away the memory, shoved it into the box in my head where it lived, and turned the key.

I handed James the photo. He probably harboured the same reservations I'd done, how it was all a bit incestuous for his partner to have slept with his daughter. However long ago it might have been.

'Toby and I were just school kids messing around.' James still looked bothered. 'Now we're friends, good ones too. I'm pleased he's found you.' There seemed no point in a dog-in-the-manger approach.

He glanced at his watch again. 'I have to go, Megan. This has come as a huge shock, as you'll appreciate. I need time to take it all in.' He swallowed. 'I agree a paternity test might be a good idea. Don't get me wrong; I believe you, but even so, it would be sensible.'

'I agree. And I understand you need time.'

'I'll call you.' He stood up and made for the door, with me close behind. There was a moment of awkwardness as he turned the doorknob, and then it happened. He leaned towards me and gave me a quick peck on the cheek, nothing earth shattering in itself, but for me it meant everything.

I'd found my father at last.

***

24

Dark Jealousy

Back at his flat, James poured himself a whisky and downed it in one. Space, along with time to reflect, was necessary before he drove over to Toby's.

He didn't doubt the truth of what Megan had said. His gut told him she wasn't trying to con him, that she wasn't a gold-digger like her younger sister. Besides, a paternity test would scotch any such attempt. There was also the undeniable resemblance between them, prejudging the results of any DNA analysis.

Vague memories of the night with Tilly Copeland filtered down through the years. Young, reckless and in a hurry to disprove his homosexuality, he'd not scrupled about sex with her. With hindsight, he realised she'd probably been too shy, too modest, to mention contraception. Carelessness that had resulted in a female copy of himself.

He was a father. Although Megan's revelation had come as a huge shock, he couldn't help being delighted. Part of the battle he'd waged with himself about his homosexuality was the fact he'd always thought he'd make a good father, the sort his own had never been. James had come to accept he'd never have children, but despite that, he was a parent anyway. Too late for Megan's first steps, her earliest words, but nonetheless he had a daughter, a woman who he'd always liked. Elation flared deep within him at the thought.

Yet despite his joy, a worry, ugly and unwelcome, kept intruding into his head. His daughter had once slept with his partner and still maintained a close friendship with him. Sexual chemistry had once existed between Megan and Toby; what if it flared into life again, fuelled by alcohol or the urge to take a trip down Memory Lane?

Insecurity rose thick and fast within James. He'd never felt or looked his age and hadn't given the issue much consideration. He and Toby had always seemed so in tune, what with their mutual love of cars and motorsport. Toby and Megan were the same age however. Even if Toby had meant what he said about liking older men, perhaps the difference in years might prove too great.

James shook his head. Hadn't he promised his boyfriend such suspicions were a thing of the past? No way could he afford such thoughts, not if they were to make a go of their relationship. A fresh start was needed, unsullied by demons from the past.

How to break the news to Toby was James's main concern. Without letting his fears about Megan surface, without picturing the two of them together.

Concentrate on having found your daughter, he told himself. *Make that your focus, not petty insecurities.*

Besides which, he needed to leave, and soon. It was already quarter to eight, and they'd arranged James would go over to Toby's at half seven. He pulled out his mobile.

'Hey, you.' Guilt hit James at the warmth in Toby's voice, a contrast with the darkness of James's recent thoughts. 'I was about to ring you. Beginning to worry you'd forgotten me. We did say half seven, didn't we?'

'Yeah. Sorry, something came up. I'm just leaving.'

'Get yourself over here. I'll have the drinks waiting.'

* * *

Toby made good on his promise. His boyfriend handed him his second single malt of the evening as soon as James arrived, his expression growing quizzical as James downed it in one. 'Something on your mind?'

'Let's just say I had one hell of a surprise earlier.'

'Care to share?'

James set his empty glass down on the coffee table. 'Megan called, asked me to go to her flat.'

'Really? What did she want? Is Charlotte okay?'

'It wasn't about Charlie. Megan had some news.' He sucked in a deep breath. 'She told me something her mother said the last time she visited.'

'Which was?'

A pause. There seemed no easy way to say it apart from simply getting the words out. 'Tilly Copeland says I'm Megan's father.'

'What?' Shock flooded Toby's face. He frowned, his expression puzzled. 'Maybe she doesn't realise what she's saying. That sounds like her mental illness speaking.' He stared at James. 'You didn't know her before she came for her job interview, isn't that right?'

'No. We'd met before. I just didn't remember.' Another shot of whisky would go down a treat. The effects of the last two were becoming evident, however, and if he'd ever needed a clear head, now was the time. 'We had a one-night stand, something I'd long forgotten. We didn't use contraception and Tilly ended up pregnant.'

'How can you be sure you're the father?'

'Megan showed me a photograph, taken at my graduation, one that went missing. Apparently Tilly stole it as a keepsake.'

'Even so…' Toby shook his head. 'Although I suppose it explains why she had such a thing for you, if she wound up pregnant, had your photograph, etc. Are you going to get a paternity test done?'

'Yes. Megan suggested we should, and I agree. I'm convinced she's my daughter though. There's the undeniable resemblance. She's got my height, my colouring, my features. I've never noticed before, but it's obvious to me now.'

'Shit.' Toby sounded bemused. 'Megan's been a friend of mine for years. Finding out she's your daughter… You've got to admit, it's a bit weird.'

'She hasn't always been just a friend though, has she?' James winced at the jealousy in his voice. *Go carefully, for God's sake,* he reminded himself. It was not the time to alienate Toby, and yet the image of his boyfriend in bed with Megan strode into his mind. He didn't think she'd sleep with Toby now she knew he was her father's partner however. She struck him as too principled. So was Toby the one he still didn't trust?

'She told you that? Okay, I admit we slept together. Only the once. I didn't see her for years afterwards.' He drained his drink. 'Does it bother you?'

'Like you said, the whole thing's a bit weird.'

'And long in the past.' A warning note in Toby's voice.

Before he could stop them, the words came. 'I can't help wondering whether it might happen again.'

Toby blew out an irritated huff. 'I told you, she's just a friend. Besides, I'm with you now. I'm done with screwing around. I thought we'd got that clear.'

'We did.'

'Then why bring it up? What happened was a one-off. Like you with Tilly. I'm not even sure why Megan mentioned it to you.'

'It came up in conversation.' James paused. 'It struck me as strange, seeing how you dated her sister for a while, fancied yourself in love with her.'

Toby shook his head. 'I can see that might be weird for Megan and Chloe – God knows they've never got on – but not for you. I've learned my lesson with Chloe, following her behaviour after the meal at Greens.'

The sharpness in Toby's tone set off alarm bells for James. *Back off*, he warned himself, but the words came out anyway. 'What do you mean? I didn't think you'd been in contact with her since then.'

'Let's not discuss Chloe. She's not important.'

'Someone as twisted as Chloe is always important. You did see her after Greens, then?'

Toby's face signalled his anger. 'Why do I get the impression this is becoming an interrogation? Do I have to account for all my movements, who I speak to?'

'No. Not if it's all above board.'

'The last time I saw Chloe, you and I weren't an item. So I don't owe you an explanation.'

'If it's all so innocent, why not tell me?'

'Look. I bumped into her in the street, up in Clifton, after work. She'd been waiting for me. Creepy, now I think of it.'

'That's it? She didn't have some angle, something she wanted?'

Toby didn't reply and the certainty hit James of Toby holding something back. With Chloe Copeland involved, things were starting to smell bad. Really bad.

Toby stood up abruptly, frustration seeping from every pore. 'I told you, Chloe is in my past. Do you really think I'd cheat?'

So the bitch had turned her attentions to Toby. She must had twigged their mutual interest, and set out to cause trouble. When it hadn't worked, she'd resorted to sending those texts. Malevolent didn't begin to describe her. Given James's suspicion that she'd been the one who stabbed him, she bordered on the psychopathic.

Too late, James registered the fact he'd not replied to Toby. And how his silence might be interpreted. It was his lack of response, he later realised, which sealed how it ended between them.

'You do. With Chloe Copeland, of all people. Here we go again. Like when you accused me of banging my mate Steve.' The anger had gone, the flat unemotional tone James had heard before replacing it.

'No. No, I don't.' He edged closer but Toby backed off. 'It's just that Chloe... you know what she's like.'

'You obviously have no idea what I'm like.'

'Toby–'

'I told you I wouldn't fuck around. I also made it clear I wouldn't stand being with someone who didn't trust me. What'll it be next? Am I supposed to ask permission before I go out, before I meet anyone?'

'Of course not. I'm sorry–'

'That makes two of us. Seems whatever I say or do, you'll question my every move. I can't take it. I shouldn't have to either.'

'Don't let Chloe Copeland come between us, Toby. That's exactly what she wants.'

'Don't you get it? Chloe's not the one breaking us up. You are.'

'Toby, I've screwed up, I know, but—'

'Yeah. You have.' Toby thrust James's jacket towards him. 'I made myself very clear. I warned you this possessive crap wouldn't wash with me. First Steve, now Megan and Chloe. I've had a bellyful of your shit. Get the fuck out of here. We're through. For good.'

***

25

Pizza And Perfume

'What's up?' Ever sensitive to Toby's moods, I could tell something was wrong the moment I answered the phone. His voice sounded flat, dull, in my ear.

'Can I come over?' He sounded so sad, and my heart clenched with love.

As if I could refuse, despite it being almost midnight. 'Of course. Whenever you like. I'll open a bottle of red.'

***

Within half an hour, Toby was at my door. I hugged him tightly, inhaling his aftershave, the scent of his shampoo. Then I waved him inside, concerned by the bleakness in his expression. The contrast from the last time I'd seen him was marked.

I poured him a glass of wine after we'd gone into the living room. He sat down opposite me, his expression tired.

'Sorry to land myself on you this way,' he said. 'The thing is, I could use a friend. Someone to spill my guts to.' He took a gulp of wine.

'What's up?' I asked.

The anguish in his face when he spoke pierced me. 'James and I have split up.'

Shock replaced concern. 'I don't understand. How? Why? I thought you two were rock solid.'

'So did I.' He drained his wine, then poured himself another. 'I'd not bargained with how jealous the man is though.'

Anxiety hit me. Had Chloe sunk her claws into Toby again? I forced my voice to stay calm. 'What happened?'

So he told me. About going for a drink with Steve Hopkins, the malicious texts that followed. How Toby couldn't deal with James's jealousy, not when he'd never cheated on the man anyway. He talked, and as he did, his expression became less pinched, less hurt. It seemed telling me was a catharsis of sorts. I was certain he was holding something back though. What it might be, I wasn't sure.

It turned out I was right.

'He told me you're his daughter,' Toby said.

I wasn't certain how to respond. Surely that couldn't have been a factor in their breakup? 'It came as a shock,' I managed to say. 'I had no idea.'

'He knows something happened between us a long time ago,' Toby continued. 'I didn't tell him about Alicia though.'

I exhaled a sigh of relief. 'Thank you.'

'It bothered him.' Toby shook his head. 'When he grilled me about Chloe too, that was the final straw. I told him we were through.'

My sister's name struck a warning in my head. 'Chloe? How is she involved?'

'She's not.'

Was he lying? I couldn't be sure. Then he continued. 'She probably sent those texts, trying to break James and me up. A ploy that succeeded.' He gulped down more wine. I glimpsed the hurt in his eyes, and wanted nothing more than to sweep him into my arms, soothe away his pain.

'You really think she was behind them?'

He nodded. 'Who else could it have been? James agreed. Before he went off on his jealous rant, that is.'

'It's the kind of thing she'd do. I know you think I'm too hard on her. But she's warped, Toby. Capable of anything.'

'You're right. I should have listened to you before.'

'James's wife was getting weird phone calls a while back, silent ones that freaked her out. She blames Mum, but stuff like that's more Chloe's style.'

'I agree.'

'There's more, Toby.'

'Such as?'

'Like her manipulating Mum into attacking Charlotte.'

'What?' Toby's face signalled his shock. 'You really think…'

'Yes. Hear me out. Chloe met James, pegged him as a meal ticket, and decided she wanted him. His wife was in the way though, and Chloe hates anything obstructing what she wants. My mother isn't capable of plotting to kill anyone. Chloe must have manipulated her into attacking Charlotte by playing on her crush on James, along with her shaky mental health. You've got to admit, if Mum planned to murder Charlotte she made a piss-poor job of carrying it out.'

'You can't be serious.'

'I've no proof, but Chloe told Mum, who she knew to be unstable, how Charlotte Matthews would be better off dead.'

Toby whistled. 'Who's to say that wasn't just Chloe being Chloe, saying spiteful things the way she does? I'm well aware she's no angel. I've found out how cruel she can be, on more than one occasion. It's a hell of a step from catty remarks, spiteful texts and freaky phone calls to murder though.'

Frustration swept over me, not that I blamed him for his scepticism. I realised how bizarre my words sounded. I'd always been able to detect Chloe's manipulations better than anyone however, and I didn't need proof of her psychopathic nature. Whether I could convince Toby was another matter.

Before I could continue, he was speaking again. 'I realise this is a sensitive subject, but we've been here before, haven't we? When you told me you thought she'd killed Alicia.'

'She did. I just can't prove it.'

'Exactly. Sorry, I just don't buy it. The texts and phone calls, yes. Not the rest though.'

So Toby still refused to see how evil Chloe was. Did it matter? Now he and James were no longer together, weren't Toby and Charlotte both okay? Could I relax, knowing they were safe from Chloe's scheming?

Except that didn't include my father. I decided to try one more time to convince Toby.

'What about James getting stabbed?' I saw shock fly into his face again. 'James himself said he thought his attacker was a woman. At the time it happened, he'd just rejected her. She didn't take that well, from what I saw. Not to mention what she told me too.'

He nodded slowly, giving me hope I might eventually convince him. 'It's possible, I guess.'

'Believe me, Chloe stabbed James. Like everything else though, I can't prove it.'

He didn't reply, and I sensed we were through talking. My earlier urge to hold him returned full force, and I set down my glass of wine before moving to sit beside him. Hell, I needed a spot of comfort too.

He seemed to sense my intention. Our arms wound round each other, his head resting on my shoulder.

We stayed that way for a long time, until at last he spoke. 'I've been a fool. About Chloe. I see that now, what with those texts. Those phone calls to James's wife.'

Hope stirred within me. *At last*, I thought. Without stopping to consider what I was doing, my hand rose to stroke his hair, my arms pulling him closer.

'It hurts,' he said. 'The breakup with James, I mean.'

'I understand,' I whispered against his cheek. I breathed him in once more while squeezing him tighter. A sweet memory, to be relived later in my head.

'I've made such a balls up of everything.' His voice held a wealth of pain.

'Not everything,' I replied as I pulled back to look at him. His eyes met mine, and understanding flared in them, then my mouth met his. In that moment, nothing else mattered but him, and me, and my yearning for the man I'd loved for so long. All considerations about my scheming sister vanished, as did any thoughts of my father. Yes, I shouldn't have kissed his ex-boyfriend so soon after their split, but I was beyond needy, so desperate. We both were, I think. So we kissed, and one thing led to another, and at last I got the comfort I'd been seeking.

I didn't kid myself about Toby's motives. Like me, he'd needed comfort sex, being as emotionally bruised as I was. I didn't dare hope he harboured any great depth of feeling for me beyond our friendship. I didn't have a pretty face or good body to offer him, no matter what Amy said. Yet suddenly he seemed keen for us to make love.

Me, I'd wanted the man for years. A little thing like pride wasn't going to get in the way.

At one point, he reached into his wallet for a condom, but I stopped him.

'I'm on the pill. Helps my skin.' I was clean and didn't doubt he realised that fact, what with the lack of men in my life. As for him, while he may have played the field, Toby had always been the careful sort, from what he'd told me. Apart from when we'd conceived Alicia. He was a mere boy then though. We'd both been careless that night. Now was different.

Comfort sex or not, what we shared turned out good. Any initial awkwardness faded under the pressure of mouths, hands, bodies. If comfort was the order of the day, I supplied it and took a large measure for myself.

We didn't say much afterwards, but he left me the next morning with the hope it wouldn't be a one-off, unlike before. Perhaps I'd managed to catch a break for once.

***

Conflicting emotions warred within me later as I attempted to work. One part of me was still raw with the certainty Chloe had murdered our baby, had manipulated our mother into attempted murder. The other part painted a smile on my lips as I remembered the previous night's lovemaking.

As the morning wore on, an unpalatable thought slapped me round the face. How would my father react on discovering his daughter was sleeping with his ex-boyfriend? Not well, I suspected. If things did develop between Toby and me, then we'd do well to lay low for a while, until I'd established a relationship with my father and he'd had time to get over their break-up. I didn't want to sour matters between us.

In the meantime, I had Chloe, my psychopathic half-sister, to consider. She wouldn't have found out yet about Toby having broken up with James. I came to a decision; I'd tell her about the split to head off any plans she had to harm him, the way she'd done with Charlotte. Revealing I'd slept with him wouldn't be on the agenda. Then I'd work out how to keep my father safe.

My plan meant having to see her again. The idea didn't sit well with me, but I'd use Mum as an excuse. Besides, I had another reason for visiting the house.

Do it today, I thought. *Get it over with.*

***

That afternoon I drove to St George, parked up, and rang the bell.

Chloe had her coat on when she answered the door, a sulky expression on her face when she saw me. 'Back again? No getting rid of you, is there?'

'I'm picking up some stuff for Mum. Clothes, books, those sorts of things.'

'You'll have to get on with it yourself. I'm off out.' She made to move past me but I blocked her.

'Hang on a minute, Chloe.'

'Can't. I'm late as it is.'

'Will you be back soon?'

'I'm dropping the car off at the garage, getting the back light fixed. Won't be long.' She didn't seem bothered about why I needed to know and it would have been futile trying to stop her. Chloe never heeded anything I said. She'd probably be back within half an hour; her garage wasn't far and letting her go seemed easier than dredging up some reason she should stay. Before I could reply, she pushed past me and banged the front door shut.

I glanced around. Empty pizza boxes littered the dining room table, grease smears staining the wood. Plates with smudges of jam and butter were strewn over the floor, half-full coffee mugs beside them. The place had a rank smell. Chloe wouldn't have even thought of cleaning it. I shut my eyes to the chaos and went upstairs, into her bedroom.

It had occurred to me I might uncover some clue as to what Chloe was planning if I looked through her things. I had no idea what to search for, or whether there was even anything to find. To hell with the fact I'd be snooping. By then I was past caring, and besides, prying paled into insignificance next to Chloe's behaviour.

The mess was worse in her room, clothes and makeup strewn on every available surface, but at least it stank of perfume rather than pizza. The bed was unmade, the bedside cabinet drawer open. I peeked inside. Used tissues, a trashy magazine, a half-eaten bar of chocolate. I reached in a hand to check what lay underneath. My fingers connected with a thick pile of envelopes.

I pulled out a bundle of letters and rifled through them.

Shit. I'd known Chloe was a high spender, aware she lived her life in a permanent state of debt but I'd no idea things were this bad. Demand after demand, pressing for payment, threatening court action. She'd plainly used the inheritance cheque from Mum to pay off some of it, but that money had been nowhere like enough, and nothing had been paid off since. Interest and penalties were piling on thick and fast. Her car, the fancy clothes – all shored up by a sea of debt. No income to repay any of it.

Then I spotted her laptop. Time to check it out.

Her password was her birth date, thanks to my sister's lack of imagination. I clicked on her browser to scroll through her favourites: social media sites, plenty of celebrity blogs, several fashion and beauty websites. Typical Chloe. I checked her browsing history. Not much there either. The garage where she'd taken her car, her doctor's surgery. I had no idea why she'd need his number and I didn't care.

Perhaps there might be something of interest in her emails. I clicked the icon. I'd only been perusing what I found for a few minutes before I heard her key in the door. What I read in that short space of time horrified me.

I switched off her laptop, moving swiftly into Mum's room, opening drawers, cupboards, pulling out anything I found to validate my reason for being in the house. Chloe was clomping around downstairs, not caring what I was doing. I stomped down the stairs, my arms full, heading for the cupboard in the kitchen where Mum kept used carrier bags. I stuffed her clothes into them, my mind on Toby. As well as the other thing I needed to tell Chloe.

My sister came up behind me. I turned to look at her, wanting to gauge her reaction.

'Mum's told me the truth at last,' I said. 'About James Matthews being my father.'

Surprise blinked over Chloe's face. I saw she wasn't best pleased; one of her weapons against me had suddenly been rendered useless. 'So you know at last. She told me ages ago.'

'Yeah, whatever. I've told him I'm his daughter. We've talked about it, him and me. Broken the ice.'

The inevitable dig came. 'Bully for both of you.' Her tone was sour.

I was on a roll. 'And I've got some gossip for you.'

'What?'

'Toby told me he's split up from James. For good, it seems.'

She looked smug and again I fought the urge to slap her. 'You don't say. Doesn't come as any surprise. After all, Toby can't be queer or else he'd never have slept with me.'

Her arrogance nauseated me, but I nodded. 'You're right. He texted me last night to tell me he'd met some woman, and that he'd ditched James.' A distortion of the truth, but too petty to worry about. Anything to stop my sister finding out about Toby and me. If I had to pretend he was with someone else, so be it. Chloe would believe me; she had no reason not to.

She laughed. 'So James is a free man. Almost, apart from his crippled wife, but he'll be divorcing her before long. What's the betting I end up as your stepmother?'

I reminded myself to stay calm. 'Not funny.'

'And Toby's found himself a new squeeze. Didn't come running to your door after the breakup, did he?'

I stayed silent, savouring the unusual moment of triumph. The memory of the previous night in all its glory rendered me immune to my sister's spite.

'I wonder who his new woman is. Whoever she is, I bet she looks like me. Not scrawny and scruffy like you. He never did get me out of his system.'

Not trusting myself to answer, I headed for the door.

'Maybe I'll do what I said. Text him, snap my fingers. He'll come running.'

Time to get out of here. I'd listened to enough of Chloe's manipulations. Besides, it was a case of mission accomplished. I'd been worried for Toby's safety with Chloe thinking he and my father were still an item. I didn't have to concern myself about that anymore. I'd visit Mum, give her the things I'd taken, and then seek refuge in Toby's arms, allowing his kisses to soothe away my sister's malice.

'So long, Chloe.' I opened the door. Her only response was to slam it behind me with a laugh.

***

That evening, in Toby's flat, I stared at him as he ate. He'd cooked Chinese food for us, a simple chicken stir-fry, and it tasted wonderful. I tried to analyse why he held me in such thrall, the way he did most women. Men too, apparently. His blond hair flopped over his eyes as he shovelled meat and noodles into his mouth, his concentration intense. An ordinary man, nothing remarkable, but he meant the world to me.

My scrutiny must have alerted him. He glanced at me. 'What's up?'

'I went to see Chloe today.' I wouldn't tell him why I'd gone. He was safe; I couldn't risk him dismissing my concerns as more sibling rivalry. 'I told her you'd split up with James.' Another small lie seemed in order. 'I didn't mean to. It just slipped out.'

'Doesn't matter.' Beansprouts and carrots disappeared into his mouth. 'Both James and Chloe are ancient history as far as I'm concerned. Time to move on.'

To me, I thought. Hadn't I waited long enough? 'She told me she might end up my stepmother. Can you believe the nerve of her?'

He laughed. 'Honestly, Megan, you've got to credit her with enough brass for an entire band. You didn't let her get to you, I hope?'

'A bit.'

He laid down his chopsticks, reaching for my hand. 'Ignore her. You've had enough practice.'

'Can we go to bed? Now?' My need for him overwhelmed me. And if I was honest, I wanted him to prove wrong the voice of insecurity telling me this couldn't be real, not for me with my flat chest and pitted skin.

He looked surprised, but grinned. 'Your wish is my command.'

The sex turned out even better than the previous night. My fears ebbed. What with all that time Toby had spent playing the field, he certainly knew his way around a woman's body. I became a harp in the hands of a master tuner.

My worries returned later, however, as Toby lay beside me. Was it my imagination or did he seem distant, the post-coital glow muted? I didn't say anything, not wanting to push him further away. I huffed out a sigh of frustration, my yearning fierce to fuse us into a couple strong enough to withstand whatever difficulties life threw at us. Problems like Chloe, or my father once he found out I was with Toby. I clamped down on both thoughts. I'd find a way of dealing with my sister, and I'd make sure a fair bit of time went by before my father heard about Toby and me.

I wouldn't wait too long before seeing James again though. I made a promise to myself. If he'd not been in touch again within a week or so, I'd contact him, suggest we meet up. I'd waited too many years for my father.

Decision made.

In my head, I hovered over the box marked 'Chloe', unsure whether to tick the option marked 'never see the bitch again'. The memory of what I'd found in her emails stabbed me once more. At some point, I needed to decide what to do about my sister, but dealing with her required more energy than I possessed.

Decision deferred. For now, anyway.

* * *

26
Girls' Night Out

I sighed. I wasn't looking forward to spending an evening with Chloe.

At least she'd not been her usual rude self on the phone when I'd called. No jibes, no hints about trying to seduce Toby, no catty remarks about my appearance. Not like Chloe, but I wasn't complaining. Either I'd caught her at a good moment or else she'd decided to keep me sweet for some reason.

'Good luck. You're going to need it,' had been Toby's response when I'd told him I'd invited Chloe to an evening at Greens. A week had passed since our Chinese meal, and he and I had seen each other every day since. Every night, too. 'She'll try to tap you up for cash, you do realise that?'

'Of course.'

'Can I ask the obvious question?'

'Go ahead. I can guess what it'll be.'

'Why?' Puzzlement laced his voice. 'Given that you give every impression of thoroughly disliking your sister, why have you invited her out for a meal?'

'I guessed right.'

'Not to mention the fact the other night you accused her of killing our baby and manipulating your mother into attacking Charlotte Matthews. Stabbing James too. Help me out here, Megan. I'm struggling to understand this.'

I didn't blame him. Given the choice, I wouldn't have spent one minute with Chloe, let alone buy her a meal at a pricey restaurant. Not that I'd be footing the bill.

I'd last visited Mum two days earlier. She seemed more stable, almost back to her usual self, medicated of course, but functional. She appeared pleased to see me, although I noticed her eyes searching behind me as I entered, as if she'd hoped Chloe might have tagged along. As ever, she wanted my sister, not me. Her marked preference still hurt, even after all these years.

We talked. She expressed concern about dealing with an in-depth police investigation of the assault on Charlotte Matthews, now her doctors were pleased with her progress. Her fears over whether she might face a trial if judged fit to do so. The possibility of a custodial sentence. Prison would break my fragile mother. I prayed it wouldn't come to that, hoping she'd be assessed as being of unsound mind when she carried out the attack. Surely to God she would be.

'I'll be there for you,' I reassured her. 'Whatever happens.'

'You're a good daughter, Megan.'

'I mean it. It's not just words.'

'I'd like you to do something for me.'

I took her hand. 'Anything.'

'Remember the drawer where you found the photograph of James? In the one above there's an envelope containing some cash. I always like to keep money in the house for emergencies. It's of no use to me in here. Take it, why don't you? No, seriously,' she continued, as I started to protest. 'Treat yourself and Chloe to a night out. I'd like to think of my two girls enjoying themselves, having fun. And it might give both of you a chance to get on better.'

I felt uncertain how to respond.

'Please, Megan. Do it for me. It would make me happy.'

I didn't have it in me to say no. Her smile when I agreed made everything worthwhile, despite my reluctance to spend time with Chloe. I reminded myself I was making Mum happy and a decent meal would dilute my sister's bitchiness. Besides, I'd get to sample the fillet of beefsteak I'd denied myself when we last went to Greens.

I called Chloe that evening to make the arrangements. We settled for going on Thursday, in a couple of days' time.

***

On the night, I arrived at seven to pick her up. I'd elected to drive, what with her being more of a drinker than I was. She looked stunning, as usual. A shift dress in pale buttermilk, opal stud earrings, and a simple clutch bag, finished off by her trademark high heels, wedges this time. Jealousy clawed at me; even if my skin hadn't been pitted, I'd never be able to compete with Chloe looks-wise.

She didn't have Toby though. I did, a thought so glorious it didn't matter that I faded into nothing beside my sister's Hispanic sexiness.

'Megan.' She stood back to let me in. 'I must say, I didn't expect you to buy me a meal. Have you landed a big commission or something?'

'No. I decided it would be a good idea to have a night out, just the two of us. There's been too much cat-fighting going on lately. It's time we had some fun instead.' Not my suggestion, but I didn't intend to tell her who had proposed it.

Chloe definitely planned to ask me for money later, I concluded. Otherwise, she'd have picked up on my comment about having fun, saying how I never did, or suchlike. Instead, she smiled, sweet and entirely false. 'I'll grab my jacket.'

'Fine. I need to use the loo.' I headed upstairs, not into the toilet, but into Mum's bedroom.

The envelope of cash was where she'd said it would be. I jammed the thick wad into my purse and went downstairs.

***

The drive from St George didn't take long. I parked in the NCP in Trenchard Street, a short walk from Greens, and we made our way to the restaurant.

Men's heads swivelled to slide lustful eyes over Chloe's body as she walked past their tables. The waitress showed us to a quiet table towards the back, on a raised part under the cathedral-style windows.

We ordered: scallops for Chloe to start, with the baked Camembert for me, followed by two fillets of beefsteak, both rare, with chunky chips. To hell with my usual frugality. Tonight was different. I ordered salad as well, and a pricey bottle of Spanish red, pouring Chloe a large glassful and a tiny measure for myself.

'Got to take it easy on the wine, what with driving. Need to make sure you get home safely.' We chinked our glasses. 'Mum sends her love, by the way. I went to see her a couple of days ago.'

Chloe feigned interest. 'How is she?'

'Better. For now, anyway.'

'She still got her crush on James?'

'Hard to tell. She's not said much about him since telling me he was my father.'

'That had to have been pretty weird for you.' She was halfway through her glass of wine already. 'I'm sorry Mum told me first instead of you. She wasn't thinking straight, you know. She spilled the beans shortly before she attacked Charlotte Matthews, so she must have already been a bit flaky.'

An apology. From Chloe. An unprecedented occurrence. 'It's okay. Doesn't matter.'

'Have you been in touch with James?'

Was she fishing for information about him? Probably, but I saw no harm in being honest. 'We've spoken on the phone a few times, and we're having lunch together next week. Me being his daughter came as a shock to him, of course. Said he needed time to take it in. He'll be okay with it eventually.'

'He's that sort of man.'

'What's that supposed to mean?'

'The sort who always does the right thing. Mr Morality, I reckon. Now he knows you're his daughter, he'll want to make up for lost time, once the surprise has worn off.'

It was rare for Chloe to say anything that made me hope it was true. 'You look so alike.' She drained her glass, which I topped up. 'I never noticed it before but now it's out in the open, it's obvious. The height. The blue eyes.'

At least she didn't make a jibe about his skin not being pitted like mine. Chloe seemed on her best behaviour, which probably meant a request for cash wouldn't be long in coming.

'I'm not really planning to sleep with Toby again.' She gazed at me over a raised forkful of scallops. 'I just said I would to piss you off. You know how I get at times.'

Yeah, I did. If I had my way, he'd be too busy with me to spare any time for her. Although he remained obstinately blind to her worst faults, my sister represented a road he wouldn't be walking down again. I no longer feared for his safety now Chloe knew he'd broken up with James. Charlotte seemed safe as well. Chloe's taunt about my father getting divorced and her becoming my stepmother indicated she expected Charlotte to disappear through legal means rather than violent ones.

I shrugged. 'I haven't seen much of Toby recently.' A lie, but a necessary one.

'I don't suppose I will, either.' She took a mouthful of wine. 'Have you told him yet about having his baby?'

Time for more dishonesty. I didn't intend to discuss Alicia with Chloe. 'No.'

She drank more wine. I noticed the bottle was three-quarters gone already and I'd only had an inch or so in my glass.

'What happened with Alicia was an accident, Megan. I'm sorry Mum and I lied, but we thought it for the best. You were in such a state. Things like my whereabouts seemed trivial.'

Another apology. She even sounded sincere.

'It's all a long time ago.' Not much, but the most I could manage. My daughter's death would always be an open wound. 'More wine?' I positioned the bottle over Chloe's glass.

'Go on, then. Fill me up. I've got a doctor's appointment first thing tomorrow, but it looks like I'll be turning up with a hangover.' She laughed, the sound turning into a hiccup.

We finished our starters and set to work on the main course. I was almost enjoying myself, replete with good food and apologies from my sister. The Camembert had been sublime, the steak was as tender as they came, and I wasn't about to complain about a respite from Chloe's taunts. I poured myself a smidgen more wine and raised my glass. 'To Mum. And new beginnings.'

Chloe shot me a strange look, no doubt unsure about the last part of my toast, but she clinked her glass against mine. 'To Mum. And whatever else.' Her words were slurred, the bottle empty. I ordered her another glass of red and a mineral water for me, along with two blueberry cheesecakes.

The attempt to get money out of me came as our desserts arrived.

'It's a bit difficult for me, what with Mum no longer being around,' she slurred. 'No jobs to be had either. I hate to ask, but could you lend me some money?'

For an instant, the memory of the baby sister I'd loved so much hovered before my mind's eye. Rendered magnanimous by a full stomach, mindful of her debts, I smiled at her. 'Of course.' She blinked, not expecting such an easy victory. Mum would have been proud of me. 'We'll sort something out later.'

Chloe declined coffee when the time came. 'Why spoil the effects of a good wine?' She could barely get her words out, her eyes glazed, her movements clumsy. I suspected she might have already downed some alcohol before I picked her up, beside what she'd drunk with her food.

I laughed. 'Good job it's me driving. Come on, let's get you home.'

We'd taken a long time over the meal. Darkness had arrived by the time we left, with me having to put Chloe's jacket, her arms flailing uselessly at the sleeves. Christ, she seemed barely able to stand. She'd always been able to pack away a lot of booze but I'd never seen her so drunk. I grabbed her arm as we made our way down the steps to the street; she'd definitely have fallen if I hadn't. The combination of drink and her four-inch wedges didn't make for steady walking. She shrugged me off once we reached the pavement however. We proceeded slowly down Park Row towards Trenchard Street,

Chloe tottering helplessly but bravado forcing her to decline my offers of help.

'S'been really nice, Megan.' A loud burp. 'Must do it again sometime.'

I thought of the soft Camembert, the bloody juices running from my steak, the rich dessert, and I smiled. Not such a bad evening after all.

'I'd like that,' I replied, with a quick squeeze of her arm.

She swayed heavily against me, her wine-soaked breath wafting into my face. 'Careful, Chloe,' I warned. 'Look, we're almost where we need to cross. Not far.'

We had about ten yards to go before the lights, which showed red for pedestrians. Traffic was sparse at that time of night. Beside me, Chloe belched again. 'Think I'm going to be sick.' She tottered towards the gutter.

The sheer force with which the lorry struck her seemed huge even though Chloe was so petite. My head thudded with the noise of the impact as her blood, warm and smelling of copper, sprayed into my face. One minute she'd been heading for the gutter to puke and the next her bloody mangled body lay crumpled in the road. The brakes shrieked as the driver skidded to a halt, seconds too late to save my sister. He never stood a chance of avoiding her at the speed he'd been doing, not with her being so drunk, barely able to stand in those heels.

Later, I'd have difficulty remembering exactly the order it all happened; did the brakes sound before I saw her body, or afterwards, and what did it matter anyway?

I screamed, just the once, a high-pitched futile wail carrying into the night air.

Two passers-by, both male, crossed the road, running, one of them pulling out his mobile, calling 999 I assumed, doing his good citizen bit. Chloe's body lay inert in the gutter, some distance away, thrown there by the force of the impact. I looked up and saw the lorry driver walking towards me. In shock, no doubt, poor bastard, and he wasn't the only one.

I leaned over and puked my guts. Half-digested cheese, steak and chips flooded out as I retched until my stomach was sore.

Once I'd finished, I gazed up at one of the men who'd run over, clutching frantically at his arm.

'I was supposed to make sure she got home safely,' I managed. Right then, it seemed important I told him that. 'She's my baby sister. I promised her.' Then I vomited again.

* * *

27

For How Much Longer?

The screech of the ambulance siren sliced through my head. The paramedics had been quick to arrive, although I had no idea how much time had passed since hearing the sickening crunch of the lorry smashing into Chloe. The man who'd called 999 kept his arm wrapped round me, helping to stop me shaking. Two paramedics – one male, one female – jumped out, gear at the ready, although from the state of Chloe I reckoned they'd arrived too late. So much blood; she had to be dead. Too numb to cry, I looped through an endless replay of Chloe tottering towards the gutter, the impact, the screech of the lorry's brakes.

From somewhere, I dredged up the wherewithal to give them Chloe's name and age, as well as tell them I was her sister. The woman sat up sharply after bending over Chloe's prostrate body. As she spoke, I realised what she was going to ask, the memory of Chloe's booze-soaked breath coming back to me. She must have smelled like a grapevine.

'Has she been drinking?'

'Yes.' I suppressed another urge to puke. 'She had a bottle of red wine with her food. We'd been for a meal at Greens, you see...' The paramedic, not interested in our social plans, turned back to my sister. I stared, helpless and silent, as the two of them got to work. An immobilisation board, blocks, neck collar, oxygen mask. Calls were made, the Bristol Royal Infirmary being only a few hundred yards down the road. I registered them saying something about three on the Glasgow scale, although I had no idea what they meant. My brain wouldn't function properly, but through the fog came the thought: *They've not said she's dead. She must still be alive.*

Followed by: *For how much longer?*

I'd thought I had nothing left in my stomach, but I still managed to heave up some more, my mouth rank and sour.

The man's arm tightened around my shoulder. Embarrassment led me to push him away, even though he'd remained with me throughout. From somewhere, a phrase came to me: *the kindness of strangers.*

'They'll take good care of her, love.' We both knew his words were hollow. He'd seen the state of my sister after all. He must have questioned, as I'd done, whether she could still be alive.

Boarded, blocked and masked, her clothes soaked with blood, Chloe's body was loaded into the ambulance.

'Can I ride with her?'

When the male paramedic nodded, I climbed in the back to sit opposite my sister. I didn't speak, not until we arrived at the Bristol Royal Infirmary, where she was rushed to Accident & Emergency, the doors swinging shut behind her.

I had no idea whether I'd ever see her alive again.

***

A while later, I spoke to a doctor, gave him answers to his questions, clocking his frown when I mentioned the bottle of wine Chloe had drunk. I had no idea how much time passed before I was informed the police needed to speak with me. Routine, I was told, when there'd been a traffic accident. Every nerve in my body protested, desperate to find out how Chloe was, despite it being too early to get any information. I'd have to go along with it however. A young female police officer guided me into a side room.

We went through the standard preamble in such situations: how she realised how concerned I had to be, how she wouldn't keep me long.

'Was the driver of the lorry speeding, in your opinion?' she asked. The memory of the man walking towards Chloe's body, hands cupped over his mouth as though he were about to vomit, came back to me.

'No, I don't think so. He had a green light, you see, and we'd not yet pressed the button for the crossing. If only she'd not drunk so much…' Chloe's face as she knocked back the Spanish red, the unexpected apologies, her words as we left the restaurant, flooded into my head. *S'been really nice, Megan. Must do it again sometime.* In that moment, I doubted we ever would.

'How much did she have to drink?'

'Almost a bottle of red. Plus an extra glass. She likes her drink, you see.'

'And you, Ms Copeland? Did you have any alcohol?'

I shook my head. 'Just a finger or two of wine, then mineral water. I was driving tonight. I said…' Those ironic words again. 'I told her I'd make sure she got home safely.' I couldn't meet the police officer's eyes.

Her tone held empathy. 'Can you tell me exactly what happened?'

Thank God, my shaking had ceased. *You can do this*, I told myself. 'She was pretty drunk. As I said, she likes her drink. She couldn't stand up by the time we left the restaurant.'

'Did you hold her arm, assist her, anything like that?'

'On the steps down from the restaurant, yes. She'd never have managed them otherwise. Once on the pavement though, she wouldn't let me. She can be very determined, my sister. Her shoes didn't help. Wedges, they were. Chloe always wears heels because she's so petite. She was awfully wobbly on her feet. And then when we were nearly at the crossing…' The coppery smell of Chloe's blood hit me again, so real I could almost taste it. Bile rose in my throat at the memory. 'She must have fallen over or something, because one minute she was there beside me and the next – that's when it happened.' My voice rose high and thin, as though I were running out of air.

More questions, notes being taken, my signature required. I stumbled through the motions, all the while thinking: *What the hell is happening in A and E?*

The police officer eventually left and I went back into the reception area, staring at the patients. A couple of drunks, bruised and bloody from God knew what, a screaming baby with its parents, a lad who looked like he'd been glassed. Nothing seemed real. I stared at the clock. An hour and a half had passed since we'd arrived; the time was just before midnight. Then one of the doctors approached me.

'Ms Copeland?'

The start I gave betrayed my frayed nerves. I grabbed his arm. 'How is she? When can I see her?'

His voice cut through my babbling. 'We've stabilised your sister, done what we can for her.'

'Will she live?'

'I can't tell you right now. Her most serious injuries were sustained to her head. An MRI scan has shown a depressed fracture of the skull. We also suspect a clot on her brain. She's being transferred to Southmead Hospital.'

'Why? Can't she get the treatment she needs here?'

'Southmead is the main centre in the west of England for neurosurgery. They can help her better there. We're getting her prepped for the transfer.' His tone sounded sympathetic. Did he, this man who must have seen so many accident victims, believe she wouldn't make it? I didn't risk such a loaded question. The one I did ask, on reflection, seemed a stupid one.

'Has she regained consciousness? Is she able to speak?'

He shook his head. 'She's in a coma. When we brought her in, she wasn't responding to any stimuli. How she progresses at Southmead will be crucial for your sister.'

'How long before…'

'I won't lie to you. The MRI scan results weren't good. Her exact prognosis will become clearer once the doctors at Southmead have had a chance to examine her. She'll need the operating theatre there as soon as possible.' He laid his hand on my arm. 'Like I said, they're specialists at the neuroscience unit. She'll get the best attention, I assure you.'

His words confused me, my brain being in no state to absorb anything. I didn't, I wouldn't, let myself contemplate what state she'd be in if she lived. The doctor had mentioned brain damage. What exactly did that mean? Permanent, or was damage to the brain like a bruise, something that got better, given time and the right treatment? If the damage proved to be lasting, how badly would it affect her? Would she be able to function; speak, for example? Walk, feed herself?

Shortly afterwards, I rode in an ambulance for the second time that night. Chloe was unrecognisable, bandaged, splinted, the mist of her breath on the mask the only sign of life. God only knew how she'd survived this far. She'd need every ounce of strength she possessed to get through this. If she ever did.

Chloe was whisked from my sight as soon as we reached Southmead. I grabbed myself a coffee but my stomach rebelled, forcing me into the nearest toilets to vomit again. Shaking, I paced around, stared at the notices on the wall. Flyers advertising fundraising galas, helpline numbers, stern warnings about not abusing the staff, either physically or verbally. Speech wasn't a possibility for me, let alone verbal abuse. The events of the night had drained me, exhaustion overwhelming my body and mind. One question hammered through my brain. Would Chloe make it?

* * *

The night ticked slowly by. Two o'clock came, then three o'clock. I dozed off a couple of times, the hard chairs not conducive to sleep; I ended up jerking awake, cramp preventing any rest, no matter how much my body, taut with tension, screamed out for it. I longed to call Toby but I didn't, what with it being so late. Besides, what would it accomplish? Nothing of any real value. His being here with me wouldn't help Chloe, wherever she was. I'd call him in the morning.

I glanced at the clock once more. Half past three.

Minutes later, a doctor strode through the swing doors to approach where I was sitting. 'Ms Copeland?' she enquired.

'Where's my sister? Can I see her?'

'I'm afraid not. She's still in surgery.'

'Will she be okay? What are they doing to her?'

'Come with me, please.' She placed her hand on my arm, guiding me into a room off the main lobby. 'Can I get you anything? Tea, coffee?'

I shook my head violently. 'No. Just tell me how she is. How bad is it?' I wondered how often she had to do this and how much it drained her each time.

'It's not good, I'm afraid. Your sister has sustained substantial head injuries. She's undergoing a procedure to relieve the pressure on her brain from the swelling and she'll be in surgery a good while longer. She also has several cracked ribs, a fractured jaw, collarbone and pelvis. In addition, both legs have been broken. The fact she had such a high blood alcohol level complicated matters.'

A strangled sound came from my throat.

'I won't gloss over how serious your sister's condition is. What happens now depends on how the surgery goes. She's young and appears in good health, but I can't give any indication at this stage of what her outlook will be.'

* * *

What seemed like an eternity later – light was dawning through the windows – a different doctor approached me. He introduced himself as one of the team who had operated on her. She'd survived the surgery, from what he told me.

I grabbed his arm. 'How is she? Can I see her?'

'She's in intensive care. I believe Dr Walker has already informed you that Chloe has suffered severe injuries, in particular to her head. Her skull was badly fractured, with bleeding and swelling of the tissue underneath. We needed to operate to relieve the resulting pressure. She's sustained extensive damage to the front temporal lobe of her brain, which isn't good, I'm afraid. What happens next and how Chloe responds to the surgery will determine her long-term outlook and the extent of her recovery.'

'Can I see her?'

'Yes. She's unconscious, but you can sit with her.'

I made to move, but he stopped me. 'I should warn you she may remain in a coma for some considerable time. The longer it is before she regains consciousness, the more likely it is she will have serious and permanent disabilities arising from the accident. We'll do everything we can, but you should prepare yourself for the possibility that, if she survives, your sister may face significant challenges.'

What the hell did he mean, I wondered. What was the front temporal lobe, what did it control, how badly was Chloe's damaged? I was being unfair, I decided. Chloe was too badly injured; he couldn't give me an exact prognosis, not so soon.

'You should be prepared for what you're going to see. She has suffered life-threatening injuries, which is reflected in how she looks.'

I would never have recognised her. So many bandages and dressings covering most of her head and face; tubes everywhere, in her arms and down her throat. I sat beside her, remembering the baby sister I had adored as a child. Chloe as a toddler, throwing tantrums when unable to get her own way and Mum laughing it off as the terrible twos. It all seemed a very long time ago. So much had happened throughout the years to bring us to this point.

Serious and permanent disabilities. Brain damage. The words spiralled in my head, along with visions of Chloe in a coma for months, needing a wheelchair, unable to speak ever again. Endless possibilities. What was the phrase people used? Something about a vegetable? Permanent vegetative state, that was it. I'd heard of the condition but had no real concept of what it meant, other than it sounded like a living death. My sister might well end up that way, alive in her body but dead in her brain.

I'd never seen her so still, so silent. She'd always had so much to say. The chances were she'd never talk again. Never remember anything either, our night of steak and wine swept away in a split second, leading to this room, this bed, those tubes.

Chloe, Chloe, I thought. *How did it ever come to this?*

'One more thing, Ms Copeland.'

I'd all but forgotten the doctor was still beside me.

'Were you aware your sister was pregnant?'

***

28

Bedside Revelations

Christ, hospitals were grim places, James decided. He wouldn't have wished this on Chloe Copeland, however much of a first-class bitch or borderline psychopath she'd been.

He'd been at work when Megan had phoned him. Afterwards, his first thought had been how glad he was she'd called, despite their contact since the revelation of his paternity being limited to phone conversations. Along with the promise of lunch together the following week. No matter. A crisis had occurred in her life, and she'd turned to him. Megan was his daughter, and he wouldn't let her down.

She'd sounded calm, although evidently keeping her emotions under tight control. The same way he'd have done. He suspected her sangfroid masked a wealth of turmoil. She'd not said much on the phone. How Chloe had been seriously injured the night before, had been taken to Southmead with extensive head trauma, was in a deep coma.

'She might not recover,' Megan had said, and the quaver in her voice told James she needed him, without her having to say the words.

'I'll come straight away. Is that okay? Does that fit in with the visiting hours there?'

'Yes.' She gave him directions to the intensive care unit. 'One thing I should mention…'

'What's that?' He expected a warning about Chloe's condition, how she looked, but what Megan said next was very different.

'Toby's here. I asked him to come.'

Toby. Even hearing the name hurt. Not that he would let on. Time to man up, pretend seeing his ex wouldn't be as painful as he knew it would. Hell, Megan deserved that at least. The two of them were friends. It was only natural she'd asked Toby to support her.

On the drive over, James wondered how bad it would be with Chloe. Deep coma, extensive head injuries; might mean anything from death to a full recovery or somewhere in between. What the latter might result in, he hadn't a clue. Would Chloe be disabled, either mentally or physically? Both perhaps? He pictured Charlotte in her wheelchair, her depression, and remembered Chloe, all sass and flirtation outside his office. Her brash stranglehold on life reduced to nursing care, supported living, dependency on others. All wrong somehow. *Get a grip*, he told himself. *Find out what the doctors have to say first.*

He located the intensive care unit, spotting Toby as he strode in, buying coffee. Damn, but the man looked good, tall and craggy, stirring something deep and primeval within James. A faint waft of Toby's aftershave dredged up sweet memories. Had James been able to keep his jealousy under control… but he hadn't, and there they were, standing beside a coffee machine, in a hospital. They'd be polite with each other; such dire circumstances demanded nothing less.

'James.' Toby's tone was cool, measured. 'You came, then. Megan said she'd call you.' He extracted his coffee from the machine. 'I should warn you before you go in. Chloe looks bad. Really bad. It's pretty serious, from what I can make out.'

'Christ. How did it happen? Megan didn't go into details on the phone; she'd simply said Chloe had been in a traffic accident.'

'They'd been on a night out. Greens, of all places.' He ran his hand through his rumpled hair. 'Megan said they'd had a good time, put aside their differences for once. Chloe had drunk a lot, however, was incapable of even standing properly. Seems she strayed into the path of an oncoming lorry before Megan could stop her.' Toby gestured in the direction of the ward. 'She blames herself. Hasn't left Chloe's side, apart from when the surgery was going on.'

James's daughter needed him. He started towards the double swing doors, but Toby grabbed his arm.

'Before we go in, there's something I should tell you. I'm with Megan now. We're an item.'

His suspicions hadn't been so far out of line, then. Still, the break-up with Toby had been his fault; he'd ruined something good. *Suck it up and move on*, he told himself.

'We have history, the two of us. More than I'd realised, it seems.'

'Meaning?'

Toby sipped his coffee. 'We had a night together, years ago, as I told you. It didn't mean anything to me at the time. I was young and shagging pretty much every girl around. Afterwards I lost touch with Megan for a few years. More or less forgot it ever happened.'

'So what changed? You said you were friends, nothing more.'

'She had my baby.'

'What? Toby…'

'A girl. Alicia, her name was.'

'You never mentioned it.'

'Megan didn't tell me at the time. I only found out recently.'

'But where's the baby?'

'She died. A tragic accident.'

Christ. He'd had a granddaughter once. Poor Megan. 'How old was she?'

'Nine weeks.' Toby shook his head. 'I should have been there for Megan, but like I said, I didn't know. Once everything was out in the open, it brought us together. She was hurting, still is, about our baby's death. I was sore after what happened between us at the Cornucopia. One thing led to another.'

'I hope you're happy together.' He forced the words out, but then realised he meant them. Discovering about his granddaughter, about Toby and Megan, had sounded the death knell for his lingering hopes. Too much bad blood had passed between them. Megan was Toby's peer, his school friend, the mother of his child. Besides, this was the first fatherly thing James could do for her, other than stay at the hospital with her. However painful he found it, he'd allow her the man with whom she was obviously in love.

And he'd make damn sure he crushed any remaining torch he carried for Toby. Time to man up again. He'd do the right thing by Megan the way he'd never managed with either of his wives. If it hurt, he'd just have to ride out the pain. Megan was blood, family, his daughter. She had to take precedence over Toby if it came to a choice.

That settled in his mind, James motioned towards the swing doors. 'We should go in.'

Megan's head jerked up as the two men entered. *God, she looks rough*, James thought. What had happened followed by a night of no sleep would have that effect though. He noted how pale she was, the smoky circles etched under her eyes. She smiled faintly at him. 'You came. Thank you.'

'How is she?' James gestured towards the bed. Chloe looked every bit as bad as Toby had warned she would. James had no idea where the bandages ended and Chloe Copeland began.

'The doctor said they'd be taking her for more tests, another scan, but they don't think…' Megan's voice cracked. 'They don't hold out much hope.'

James dragged a chair over to sit beside his daughter. Toby stood behind her, his hands on her shoulders.

'She's taken too much in the way of injuries to her brain.' Megan twisted in her seat. 'There's still a lot of swelling, which they're fighting to get under control, but the damage is extensive. Something about her front temporal lobe being affected.'

'What does that mean? In practical terms?'

'I'm not sure, but they say there's the likelihood she may never come out of the coma, and she might end up in a…'

James squeezed her arm. 'A what, Megan?'

'Persistent vegetative state. She might wind up conscious, but unable to speak, communicate, feed herself, ever again.'

Christ. He had no words to offer his daughter, no response to such devastating news. Despite the fact the two sisters didn't get on, Megan had to be hurting, and badly. Especially if Toby had been right and they'd put their issues aside for once. Perhaps Tilly being in a psychiatric institution had drawn the two of them together at last.

A tear slid down Megan's cheek. 'I'd hoped things could change between us, you see. We'd got on so well during the meal, and I thought…' She swallowed. 'That we might be able to grow closer. Set aside our differences.'

'You've been a good sister to her, from what I can tell.'

'No. No, I haven't.' Her voice rose dangerously high. Another tear slid down her face. 'I let her drink too much wine, didn't try to stop her. I should have held her arm, kept her from falling, but I didn't. She wouldn't let me, you see.'

'She can be very determined at times.'

'Everything's my fault. I blame myself, don't you see? I'm responsible for…' Megan's hand waved wildly towards the bed. '…this.'

James grasped her shoulders, forcing her to look at him. Hidden behind her exhaustion lay something he couldn't identify, something dark twisting her from inside; from what she'd said, he deduced it to be guilt. His daughter was taking on the burden of culpability for her sister possibly being declared a vegetable – what a vile term – and he had to stop her.

'Listen to me. This isn't your fault. Chloe wouldn't let you help her. It was an accident, sweetheart, pure and simple.'

'Her heels. She could hardly walk. We were so close to the car park. Another minute or so, and we'd have been there.'

'You couldn't have done anything to prevent what happened.'

'I said I'd make sure she got home safely. I failed, didn't I?'

Toby walked over. 'She keeps saying that. Can I get either one of you a coffee?'

'Black for me.' James needed the caffeine jolt. 'Megan, you should have something. Have you eaten today?'

She shook her head. 'The thought of food makes me want to throw up.'

'I'll bring you a sandwich. In case you change your mind.' Toby disappeared through the swing doors.

Megan's face was still unnaturally pale, her eyes fixed on her sister.

James had no idea what caused the next words to come forth from him, words he knew would only remind her of another pain, long ago. Maybe they'd started to forge bonds, the two of them, here in this sterile hospital ward. The words were out before he realised what he'd said. 'Toby told me about your baby.'

Megan's eyes grew wide with alarm, her gaze firmly on him. 'What did he say?'

'That you'd had a child by him and how he'd not known until recently. How she died when she was very young.'

She remained silent at first. Then: 'I called her Alicia. After my grandmother.' Megan blew her nose. 'Sorry. I've never really talked about it until I told Toby. Kept it all buried deep inside. The only way I knew how to deal with the pain.'

'I understand.'

'Do you?' She smiled faintly. 'I should have told you as well, but somehow it didn't seem the right time. Not when I'd just landed you with the news about being your daughter.'

'I get it, I really do.' He did too. 'Seems strange, to have been a grandfather when I only found out recently I was a father. You were so young, Megan. It must have been hell, going through something so awful, when you'd only just become a mother.'

'Mum was a rock to me. She helped, but it all got too much. I dropped out of college, lost the plot for a bit.'

'I want to be here for you.' His words surprised him, but hadn't they been brewing ever since the moment he'd kissed her cheek? A gesture signalling his acceptance of her as his daughter. He meant what he'd said. Judging by the bandaged body in the bed, they'd have some tough times ahead.

Her face glowed with pleasure. 'You do? Really?'

'Yes. Whatever it takes. I'd like to be more involved in your life, get to know you properly.'

She didn't reply, but her smile told him what he'd said wasn't unwelcome.

'And there's something else. I'm glad about you and Toby, really I am.'

'Thank God.' Her voice was back to somewhere near normal. 'He's told you. I've been dreading you finding out, wondering how you'd take the news. We didn't mean to hurt you, honestly we didn't. Neither of us planned it; it just happened. Sounds clichéd, I know, but it's the truth.'

'It's okay. Really. I'm too old for Toby. He'll be better off with you. I want you to be happy, Megan.'

'You've no idea how much that means.'

Toby swung back into the room. 'One black coffee.' He thrust a plastic cup James's way. 'One sandwich.' He offered a wrapped triangle to Megan.

'I need some air.' She grabbed her jacket. 'I won't be long.' She strode rapidly towards the double doors and pushed them open, heading in the direction of the car park.

Toby pulled up a chair beside James. 'There's something else I should tell you. Not sure if Megan mentioned it when I was getting the coffee, but Chloe was pregnant.'

'What? She was having a baby?'

'Yes. Not very far along though. She's lost it.'

Something about Toby's tone, the way his gaze slid to the floor, ignited suspicion in James's brain. 'Was the baby yours?'

'Yes. At least, I think so. Chloe hadn't said anything to me however.'

'But... you and her.' Jealousy twisted James's gut. 'You told me you'd learned your lesson with Chloe. How...?'

'Yeah, I did say that, didn't I? That was after she dumped me. We had a one-night stand a short while ago. Before you and I got together, in case you intend freaking out. It was after you told me you were straight, that nothing could happen between us. I was hurt, James. Pissed off, angry, needing a revenge fuck. Like I told you, Chloe waited for me outside work one day. She'd already texted me, not long before, about how she'd never got over me. I thought she was messing around at the time.'

'What changed your mind?'

Toby grimaced. 'You've had first-hand experience of how persuasive she can be.'

'You fell for her line about never getting over you? Really?'

Toby exhaled slowly. 'Like I said, I was raw, bruised. She found out you'd given me the brushoff and poured on the sympathy. I lapped it up. She said she'd realised what she'd thrown away with me. Begged me to give her a second chance.'

'So you ended up in bed.'

'Yes. Megan's always told me I'm blind where Chloe's concerned, how I make excuses for her. She's right, I do. Or rather, I did. Not anymore though. Anyway, what with her coming on to me so strongly, being so damn hot, I couldn't resist. We went back to my flat, ended up sleeping together.'

'Without using contraception, obviously.'

'We got carried away. I only remembered afterwards we'd not used a condom.'

'But you're with Megan now? How did that come about? After the thing with Chloe?'

Toby grimaced again. 'Chloe dumped me the morning after. The night we were together she was all sweetness and light, making out she was so happy we were an item again. I fell for it, believing she'd really changed her tune. She hadn't though. She waited until breakfast the next day. Then she ditched me.'

'So why did she—'

'To piss off Megan, pure and simple. It was all a game to Chloe. She told me I was pathetic, a loser, how she'd done it to prove she could snap her fingers and I'd come running. Said she'd bide her time, wait until it would hurt Megan the most, and then tell her. Spiteful, and so incredibly petty. Seems Megan's always liked me, and Chloe played on that.'

'Shit, Toby.'

'I reckon that's why she didn't insist on a condom. Chanced her luck and ended up pregnant. She didn't tell me until after we'd had sex about not being on the pill.'

'You didn't check?'

'No. I assumed – wrongly – she would be.'

'What about Megan? Christ, do you care anything about her? Or is she just another revenge fuck?' James saw Toby wince at the censure in his words.

'It's not like that, I swear.'

Anger shoved aside James's former jealousy. 'You bastard. You're using her.'

Toby sighed. 'I accept I reverted briefly to type, what with Chloe and then Megan. Not anymore though. We share so much history, after all. Things are shaping up nicely between us. It's early days so far, but we'll see.'

'Don't hurt her, for God's sake. She deserves better. Megan's a good person.'

'Yes. She is. I'm well aware I've behaved like a complete prick. Believe me, I'm not proud of the fact. She has no idea about my recent fling with Chloe. I'd rather it stayed that way.'

'So would I. Megan has enough to deal with. Has she said who she thinks might be the baby's father?'

Toby shook his head. 'All she said was how Chloe's always been promiscuous. Megan's probably got some faceless, unknown man pegged.'

'She doesn't suspect it might be you?'

'No. The timing fits in with me being the one who got her pregnant however. Of course, I'll never be sure.'

The double doors swung open, Megan appearing through them. 'The doctor's on his way.'

***

29
The Longer She Takes

After a couple of days, I knew I'd go stir crazy if I spent any more time at the hospital. I'd gone home briefly to grab some sleep and change my clothes, but nothing else. Toby practically had to force me out of the door. My concern was Chloe regaining consciousness when I wasn't there beside her. She'd need her family when she did, and with Mum in hospital, I was all Chloe had.

Toby, as ever, was pragmatic.

'She won't come round, not yet. In the unlikely event she does, the hospital will call you.'

The image of Chloe opening her eyes, moving her lips, starting to speak, stirred in my brain again, but Toby was right. I couldn't sit at my sister's bedside indefinitely; there had been no change in the two days she'd been at Southmead. She was still deep in the coma, unresponsive, and the longer she took to regain consciousness, the worse the prognosis for her long-term outlook. It was a miracle she'd even survived. The words 'extensive damage to the front temporal lobe' echoed in my head again. Chances were, even if Chloe regained consciousness, she wouldn't be doing much of anything.

'Go home, Megan.' Toby gave me a quick kiss. 'Get some kip.'

So I did. The break did me good; after a long sleep, a hot shower and some food, the exhaustion that had overwhelmed me since the accident receded. I made my way back to the hospital refreshed, better able to deal with the situation.

***

After that, it became easier to allow myself time off from my bedside vigil, as well as being there if Chloe ever woke up. Being a freelancer helped. Okay, so I wasn't earning money while I sat by her bedside but I didn't have to drag myself in to a regular job. I still spent several hours a day with her, at least during the first week. What was going on in her head as she lay there, I wondered? Only the occasional twitch of a finger or facial muscle betrayed the fact she was still alive. The doctors did more tests, more scans, and I noticed how the tone of their voices wilted as the week went on. Clearly, they weren't optimistic for my sister's chances.

'I've been too hard on her,' I told Toby on one occasion, his hand holding mine as we sat beside Chloe's bed.

He squeezed my palm. 'What do you mean?'

I looked away, unable to bear his gaze. 'I've said terrible things about her.'

'You mean about…' he hesitated. 'Our baby.'

'Yes. And Chloe pushing Mum into attacking Charlotte, stabbing James.'

He placed an arm around me. I sank against him, pillowing my head on his shoulder. 'You didn't mean those things,' he said. 'You were hurt, confused.'

'I know that now. Chloe can be spiteful but she's not a killer. Alicia's death was a tragic accident.'

He nodded. 'Same with Charlotte Matthews. Your mother was ill, didn't realise what she was doing. As for James, some druggie probably stabbed him.'

'You're right. But I blamed Chloe. You know what's really eating me up?' I swallowed a sob. 'The fact I might not get a second chance. That Chloe will die, or stay in a coma, and I'll never get to tell her I love her. To be a better sister. I can't bear it, I just can't.'

His arm squeezed me closer, and his lips pressed against my hair, a gesture that cheered me more than words. Besides, what could he say? So I drank deeply of his comfort, my gaze never leaving the inert body in the bed.

***

Every evening I'd either go to Toby's flat or he'd come to mine. I'd update him on Chloe's progress, which was zero, and he'd do his best to reassure me, usually with sex. I ate very little that week. 'My stomach can't take it,' I told a concerned Toby, also mentioning how my guts hadn't been right ever since I'd puked after seeing Chloe's body crumpled in the gutter. He muttered something about how stress could affect people that way. Lying in bed with Toby, a hollow in my belly where food should be, we'd make love and my shattered nerves would knit back together a little.

'I just want another chance with her,' I told him often.

During the second week, when Chloe still showed no sign of coming out of her coma, I started to spend less time at the hospital. Or rather, I went to a different sort of hospital. Mum still needed my support, despite what had happened to my sister. I'd left it too long since I'd last seen her. On the eighth day, I took the afternoon off and drove over to see Mum, relieved to be out of the claustrophobic atmosphere surrounding Chloe's bedside.

Once at the psychiatric unit, I broached the subject of Chloe's accident with Mum's doctors. I didn't think she'd deal well with hearing the full extent of her daughter's injuries and they agreed. The outlook on Chloe's long-term future still seemed so bleak, so uncertain. *A bridge to cross later*, I told myself. With one of her doctors beside me, I went to sit with Mum, praying her medically induced calm would prevail through what I had to say. I told her Chloe had been in an accident and was in hospital. I played it as low-key as possible. Anyone listening would get the impression Chloe merely had a few bumps and grazes.

Mum still became agitated. 'She'll be all right, won't she? Please tell me my precious girl is okay.' Her voice shook with emotion.

'She's in good hands. Getting the best possible care.' Not a lie, of course, and it seemed to be enough. After I reassured her a few more times, Mum appeared to accept what I said. She commented on how Chloe had always been strong and healthy, and would be discharged from hospital in no time.

'Make sure she doesn't feel obliged to come here when she does get out,' Mum said. 'She's not comfortable about visiting somewhere like this. Tell her I understand.'

I reached over and took Mum's hand in mine, squeezing it gently, my reward a smile from her. She'd been through so much, I thought: her mental health issues, her struggles as a single parent, the trauma of Alicia's death. Time for me to support her. I'd never abandon my beloved mother. Her doctors were still assessing her mental state, the better to decide her future. Her whereabouts, whether prison or a secure psychiatric facility, made no difference to me. I'd still visit her regularly.

Before I left, I leaned over and kissed her cheek.

'I love you, Mum,' I said. 'I'll always be here for you. Everything will be all right, I promise.'

***

On the ninth day, I went to visit someone else. James. My father.

He'd been to the hospital several times and he'd phoned me on numerous occasions, but I needed more. Even with all the upheaval surrounding Chloe's accident and with Mum still in hospital, I'd never forgotten I'd found my father, a man whom I yearned to get to know better. The lunch we'd arranged had been cancelled, of course, following what had happened. The memories of him kissing me, telling me he wanted to be more involved in my life, had seared themselves into my brain, filling me with a slow-burning joy.

That evening, after yet another day without any progress from Chloe, I needed someone else besides Toby. So I called my father.

His response was exactly what I'd hoped.

'Come over right away,' he said. 'I wanted to talk to you before, about us getting together, but what with Chloe being so ill… I wasn't sure if you could spare the time.'

Always for you, I said to myself.

I drove straight to his flat.

His first question, after giving me a hug, was about Chloe, of course. 'No change,' was my answer. There didn't seem to be much else to say other than that. He knew as well as I did how serious my sister's condition was.

'I don't suppose you've visited Charlotte recently?' he asked.

I shook my head. 'I will, as and when things calm down a bit. What about you?'

'No. We've spoken on the phone, arranged to meet up next week.'

'Is that good or bad?'

'We're talking divorce.'

I wasn't surprised. Saddened though. 'I'm sorry. Really I am.'

He shrugged. 'It's for the best. I can't give Charlotte what she needs.'

The rest of the evening went better than I'd dare hope. Any initial awkwardness soon melted away, James kissing my cheek again as I left. Happiness sparked in my belly.

***

Life settled into a pattern of visits over the next few weeks. Chloe, Mum, James, in a regular cycle. My father and I slipped into a routine of me cooking Sunday lunch for him every weekend at my flat. We'd chat, with James's reserve melting under the influence of my roast lamb with garlic. We were making progress; the DNA test we'd taken had proved I was his daughter, as expected. Soon, I promised myself, there'd be three of us sitting down to eat. After all, Toby and I were talking about moving in together.

I visited Chloe every day. Never missed going in once, despite the lack of any progress in her condition. Hour after hour, I sat beside her bed, my sister still deep in her coma. The only signs of life were the flickers across her eyelids, the occasional twitch of her fingers. The doctors at the Bristol Brain Centre at Southmead were superb, so caring and professional, but as time slipped by, Chloe's chances seemed ever bleaker. A fact underscored by the regular discussions I had with the medical team.

One Sunday, James and I were talking following one of our roast lunches.

'Still no change with Chloe?' he enquired.

I shook my head. 'None. It's been two months.'

'She was lucky to survive the accident.'

'I'm not sure she'll ever regain consciousness. Not now.'

'You can't be sure of that.'

'Some people stay in comas for years.'

'She'll wake up when she's ready, not before. Two months seems a long time but given her horrific injuries, it's not surprising.'

'I guess you're right. I just want my sister back.'

'I know you do, sweetheart.' He drew me into a fierce hug.

We chatted for the rest of the afternoon, both of us enjoying the easy familiarity we'd managed to forge.

Not long before the time when James usually left, my mobile rang in my bag.

The ensuing conversation was short. I jabbed the off button on my phone.

'That was the hospital. Chloe's regained consciousness.' My voice shook with the plethora of emotions overwhelming me.

James stood up, pulling me into another hug. For a long moment, we stood, father and daughter, with me luxuriating in the comfort he gave. Then he drew back. 'I'll drive you there.'

Despite me trying not to think too hard, a thousand questions crowded into my brain during the journey. How Chloe would appear, whether she'd be able to speak, what her chances for recovery might be. Would she remember what had happened? The sight of the unresponsive figure in the bed had become so familiar I couldn't imagine her sitting up, talking, eating.

When we got there, the reality of Chloe being conscious wasn't much different to the comatose version. She had her eyes half-open, sure, but no life flickered in them. Something vital was missing. Her gaze rested briefly on me before wandering off without any recognition. Her hands plucked restlessly at her bed coverings, the movements unfocused. The person in the bed didn't seem like my sister, not Chloe, not all dash and brash, her quick tongue ever ready to deliver some barbed comment. Looking at her, I doubted whether she ever would again.

'Will she be able to talk? Walk again? I mean, not right now, but eventually. If she does get better?' I directed my question at Dr Hussein, the most approachable member of the team looking after Chloe.

He shook his head. 'We can't say at present. We'll run more tests tomorrow. They'll give us a clearer picture of where we go from here. And what Chloe's prospects might be.'

'Does she remember anything? Will her memory be affected?' My chest grew tight with worry. 'What I mean is, could she be reliving the accident in her head? Be in distress?'

Dr Hussein shook his head again.

'She's just come out of a long coma. She won't be thinking anything much.'

He was right. Chloe's vacant gaze didn't hold much indication of brain activity.

That night, in bed, Toby held me tight after we'd made love. Recently, I'd clung to sex as the only life raft I had available, a way of blotting out hospital beds and bleeping machines, lengths of tubing and twitching hands, pushing Chloe and her battered body far away, leaving only Toby and the solace he provided.

'We'll know more soon.' His fingers stroked my hair.

I swallowed hard. 'I just want my sister back the way she was. So I can make things right between us.'

He nodded. 'I'll be there for you, whatever happens. I promise.'

I burrowed further into his arms. 'James said much the same thing.' Had it been a mistake to mention my father? Maybe not. I'd observed them earlier at Chloe's bedside, and I reckoned it would be all right between them. Eventually.

The relaxed tone of Toby's next words confirmed my thoughts. 'He'll be a good guy to have as a father.'

'You don't miss him?' I was straying into dangerous territory, fuelled by my deep insecurity where Toby was concerned.

He shook his head. 'He had too many issues. Too possessive, for one.'

'Is it weird seeing him at the hospital? Knowing he's my father?'

Toby shrugged. 'A little, I guess, but that'll wear off in time.'

In time. I savoured the words. They held the promise of continuity for Toby and me, and I needed stability, craved the safety it offered.

A growl from deep within me ruined the moment.

Toby laughed. 'Someone sounds hungry. Your stomach better now?'

'Mostly.'

'Good. Been ages since I've seen you tuck into a decent meal.'

Another gurgle from my stomach. Toby laughed again. 'I'll make you a sandwich.' He pulled away from me, swinging his legs out of bed. 'I'm here for you. We'll get through this, Megan. Together.'

Lying there, in the half-light, I decided he was right. We would come through the other side of the nightmare at some point. He'd stick to his word too. He'd be there for me when the doctors did their tests, in the coming days when Chloe's prognosis grew clearer, when the shrinks and the police decided how to proceed with Mum.

The next day and over the coming few weeks would be when I'd need Toby the most. My father too. We'd find out exactly what the outlook was for Chloe. How persistent, how vegetative, she'd end up being. I recalled her vacant stare, the restless hands. Right then, I didn't hold out much hope for my sister's future and neither, I felt certain, did Dr Hussein.

***

30
Finally Balanced

At the hospital the next day, Toby and James at my side, I prepared myself for whatever Dr Hussein might throw at me. When they came, his words held no surprise. No hope, either.

Chloe had regained consciousness, but nothing else. No awareness. No recognition. She couldn't speak or get out of bed, feed or toilet herself; she remained dependent on the nurses for her every need. She was indeed in a persistent vegetative state. She'd require twenty-four hour nursing attention until she died, with no real prospect of any further recovery. The damage to her brain had been too severe. She'd need to stay in hospital a while longer to allow her battered body to continue to heal, but Dr Hussein advised us to look for a suitable care facility for when he deemed her ready to leave.

I didn't have any money for the fees. Mum had her inheritance, but I'd rather she kept every penny for her own future, uncertain as it was. At first, I thought Chloe would end up in government care, but my father insisted on funding a private nursing home. I protested – it didn't seem right – until Toby pointed out James probably wanted some way to do the fatherly thing and help me. It wasn't as though he lacked the means to do so.

James pulled me close. 'We'll find the best place for her, sweetheart. Somewhere she'll get the support she needs. We'll sort it together, don't worry.'

My sobs were choking me up too badly to allow any reply.

***

Back at my flat later, when finally alone, I didn't cry, not at all.

Instead, I laughed.

Neither Toby nor my father had sussed my tears weren't motivated by sadness about Chloe.

I'd wept from sheer relief instead. At last, I'd received the reassurance I'd been craving. The ability to remember or speak about the accident had been wiped from my sister's brain. Seemingly permanently.

The irony of the situation was what caused me to laugh. Chloe had worked so hard to get her hands on James's money and she'd accomplished precisely that. Although not in the way she'd envisaged.

Chloe. My bitch of a sister. How things had changed. From the sassy, brassy female who'd caught my father in her sights at O'Malley's, to the vacant-eyed cabbage I relished the sight of every time I visited. Dependent for every shit, every piss, every sponge bath, on the goodwill of her nursing team.

The best part? How I'd been the one to make her the empty shell she now was.

Yes, I, Megan Copeland, the sister she'd loved to mock, to taunt, to despise. I didn't think I'd ever forget the strength in my hands as they pushed, firmly and decisively, against her drunken body, shoving it into the path of the oncoming lorry. It seemed I'd got away with it too. The police had spoken with the two men who rushed to help, but neither of them had seen anything; the few people who had been around had been oblivious to us. Once the investigating officers accepted the driver hadn't been speeding, they wrote the whole thing off as a tragic accident. Case closed. Throughout the past weeks, I'd relived the moment repeatedly, savouring it, and I'd smile every time.

I'd planned it, of course. After Mum planted the idea in my head, albeit unknowingly, when she suggested I should take Chloe out for a meal. I'd already arrived at the conclusion I needed to kill my sister. Our evening together provided the perfect opportunity.

I'd been fair, I thought, in following the tradition of giving a condemned prisoner whatever they requested as their last meal. Chloe had enjoyed every mouthful of her scallops, steak and cheesecake before facing the justice she'd deserved for so long.

As for what, I'd never truly know. Perhaps Alicia's death had been a tragic accident, perhaps not. The demise of her ex's former girlfriend might have been a coincidence, nothing more. Same with the attack on Charlotte. Chloe might have manipulated Mum, sown the seeds of murder in an unstable mind, or maybe she was simply being her normal spiteful self. My sister was shallow, selfish, cruel, of that I had no doubt. Capable of killing a rabbit, making creepy phone calls to a vulnerable woman – they were pure Chloe, nothing to do with me – but whether she was capable of murder, I'd never be certain.

On balance though, I believed her guilty of all charges.

One thing I did know for sure. My baby's death had twisted my soul, changed me forever. The discovery it may have been deliberate had warped me beyond repair, turned me into someone dark and dangerous, prepared to do bad things. I could almost weep for the naive girl I once was. And at times I hardly recognised the woman I'd become.

Chloe, me. Sister, psychopath. Who was who in our relationship?

I shrugged. I was past caring. Her recent fling with Toby was what lay behind my decision to kill the bitch.

Oh, yes. I'd been painfully aware she'd bedded my man before he turned to me. I'd read on her laptop Toby's angry email after she ditched him, as well as her reply. So cruel, making it plain she'd only slept with him to hurt me. How long would it have been before she'd have twisted the knife? Torturing me with her conquest of him?

Then came the news at the hospital of her pregnancy, how she'd lost the baby. Everything clicked into place. The internet search for her GP's surgery I'd found on her laptop. Her mention of a doctor's appointment. The bitch must have done a test, found she was pregnant and planned to have an abortion. She'd got her wish, after a fashion.

I'd suspected Toby had to be the father. Something confirmed by the deer-in-headlights expression on his face when I relayed the news. As well as the timing, revealed by the email. His child, no doubt about it. I'd have to keep a careful eye on Toby in the future, given his former penchant for playing the field. He'd need to toe the line, or suffer the consequences. I was very sure about that.

He'd never admit to me he'd got Chloe pregnant, of course. Just as I'd never tell him I was the one who trashed his flat.

I'd been so mad at him the night I told him about Alicia. Whatever I'd hoped for, I didn't get it, just his cutting remark about sibling rivalry. My anger had festered after I left his flat, expending itself in an orgy of fury when I returned to smash crockery, slash furniture. I'd felt bad afterwards, but cleansed. Besides, he'd deserved it.

I'd come out well in the end however. No complaints from me; I was happy, something I'd not been for a very long time.

'You're looking great, babe. Seems you were right about Toby being up for grabs with a little effort,' was Amy's comment when we met for lunch.

Yes, life was good. For one thing, I was rebuilding my relationship with Mum now my sister was off the scene. My mother would have to be told the full extent of Chloe's injuries, but only when strong enough to deal with the shock. By then I'd have re-established myself in her affections, my love a constant source of support. My scruffy rented flat would soon be behind me as well; I intended to move back into our family home in St George. I'd paint new pictures to hang on the walls, in the art classes I'd decided to resume, perhaps with Charlotte. Toby would move in with me; we'd already discussed the idea. One day perhaps, Mum would be able to come home and when she did, I'd care for her, bond myself to her, so she'd never want us to be apart again.

She'd be a grandmother by then as well.

My stomach was starting to curve gently, proof of the new life inside me. Toby's baby, one that would live, grow and thrive, healing the raw wound of Alicia's death. I didn't kid myself he loved me as much as I did him. No matter. That would come, given time and the birth of our baby.

I'd needed to trick him. I'd told him I was on the pill as it helped my skin. True in itself. What he didn't realise was I stopped taking it after we started sleeping together, spotting my chance to get both him and the baby I so desperately wanted. The sickness after the accident helped. I'd pretended it went on longer than it did, feigning an intermittently upset stomach for weeks. I'd apologised, telling him I'd forgotten being sick might render the pill ineffective.

I told myself my minor deception was payback for him fucking Chloe. He took the news about the baby well, despite the shock.

So did my father. He appeared stunned, but delighted, when I told him he'd be a granddad, and I knew he'd be a help financially once I was a mother and my paltry earnings from freelance work dwindled.

I'd not always been honest with James either. Take those texts I sent, the idea planted in my head after Toby told me about his evening with Steve Hopkins. Or the way I deliberately mentioned my past with Toby, realising James possessed a jealous streak, aware it might lead to an argument. Toby was better off with me though, and my father was perceptive enough to acknowledge the fact.

I didn't feel guilty about stabbing him. Thanks to Senna's intervention, I'd only managed to inflict a flesh wound, and besides, I hadn't known he was my father back then. He had posed a real threat to my hopes of getting back with Toby, and I'd acted accordingly. James had healed, however, and we could all move on.

***

Over the next month or so, I visited various nursing homes with James and Toby, playing the concerned sister all the while, fussing over staff-to-patient ratios and window views. My stomach continued its gentle swell. My breasts joined it, my chest no longer pancake flat, another smack in the face for Chloe after her cruel comments.

Eventually we found a suitable nursing facility not far from Bristol. Once we got her settled in, I carried on going in each day. At first, I'd thought I might not bother, but I found I enjoyed my visits. I'd worked so hard to portray myself as the devoted sister and it would have seemed odd if I'd stopped going. Besides, I got a thrill every time one of the staff told me how caring I was, how Chloe was lucky to have me for a sister. I'd smile, thank them, and carry on the charade. Really, I should have been an actress, not a proofreader.

* * *

One day on the drive there, I felt the baby move inside me for the first time. Proof of the positive direction my life had taken.

Once in her room, I pulled up a chair beside my sister's bed and smiled at her. 'Hello, Chloe. How are you doing today?'

A stupid question. Chloe was doing what she always did, drooling and looking vacant. I stared at the girl who had once been so stunning, who had believed she possessed a God-given right to anything she wanted, at whatever cost. How much better it was that she'd lived. At first I'd been disappointed when I'd realised my sister would survive the accident. Now though, I wouldn't change a thing. This way was better. I could visit Chloe regularly and enjoy seeing the drool, the vacant stare, in the knowledge I'd made her the cabbage she now was.

People might find it odd, but I considered myself a good person, despite what I'd done. Take my love for others; Alicia, Mum, Toby, my father. Not to mention the baby who had so recently kicked inside me. I intended to be a wonderful daughter for James, a loving wife to Toby – we'd get married after our child was born, I'd decided – and the best mother ever. Inside me, my baby stirred again, a gentle, almost imperceptible fluttering, the sensation stroking its way out of my womb and across my heart.

Things finally felt right in my world. At last, the scales of justice in my head were on an even keel.

Almost.

One last thing was required to get them perfectly level. I remembered the promise I'd once made myself. My palm itched with the memory.

I stood up so I could exert more force. The crack of my hand as it slapped my bitch of a sister as hard as possible, once, twice, staining her cheeks red, sounded throughout the room, but not, I felt sure, through the thick door. No one would hear what I'd done.

Nor, it would seem, Chloe's thin, high-pitched wail, her startled moans, her gasps of shock as her vacant eyes met mine. For a second, I saw fear and bewilderment in them. The sight gave me sweet satisfaction.

Pathetic. She couldn't even scream properly.

Finally, the scales were balanced.

I looked down at my sister. 'Welcome, Chloe, to the rest of your life.'

Acknowledgements

Thanks to:

Karen, Mary, Jacqui and Jeanette for their invaluable help and feedback.

I've said it before and I'll say it again: thanks to X, for giving me the kick up the backside I so desperately needed.